DARK
Perfectly

No incidents on record. No signs of disobedience. The perfect submissive.

Multilingual. Fluent in current affairs. High aptitude for math.

I digested all the information as I memorized the portfolio laid out before me. After two years of searching, I'd finally found an ideal candidate, and just in time, too.

Item number seventeen, a twenty-two-year-old Caucasian female with striking features.

But her lack of rebellious instincts concerned me. Could I mold her into what I needed?

Any blood virgin I chose would require the same intense retraining. It might break a weaker mind, rendering my financial investment moot. But I had to try.

The brunette's photo glinted in the room's overhead lighting. All was revealed, including her supple breasts, slender waist, and feminine hips. Absolutely gorgeous. She would cost a small fortune.

I drew my thumb over my bottom lip. There was a fire in her near-ebony eyes that the others lacked. I'd use that to my advantage. Craft and mold her into the perfect poison.

The Blood Alliance would never anticipate it.

A hundred years of plotting, all culminating in the hands of a beautiful woman. She'd be the greatest weapon ever created and I would own her. Entirely.

Yes.

This was the one.

Hopefully, she wouldn't shatter under my command. If she did, I'd fix her. And start all over again. Until the endgame.

Which I would win.

At any cost.

Even if it meant sacrificing her life, in addition to mine. *Fuck the Blood Alliance.*

Blood Alliance Series

Chastely Bitten

CHASTELY BITTEN

LEXI C. FOSS

Editing by: Loves2ReadRomance & Delphine Noble-Fox

Proofreading by: Barb Jack, Allison Irwin & Outthink Editing, LLC

Cover Design: Covers by Julie

Published by: Ninja Newt Publishing, LLC

Print Edition

ISBN: 978-1-950694-23-5

To Julie, for inspiring me to write this world…

Chastely Bitten

Book One

A NOTE FROM THE AUTHOR

Be warned: Darius and Juliet's romance is unconventional and grounded in a very dark world. Humans hold no rights, and my lycans and vampires are not the kind you find in fairy tales.

There will be biting.

Cheers,
Lexi

Once upon a time,
humankind ruled the world while lycans and vampires
lived in secret.

This is no longer that time.

Welcome to the future where the superior bloodlines
make the rules.

PROCEED AT YOUR OWN RISK.

ᏇHE ᏴLOOD ᎯLLIANCE

International law supersedes all national governance and will be maintained by the Blood Alliance—a global council of equal parts lycan and vampire.

All resources are to be distributed evenly between lycan and vampire, including territory and blood slaves. Societal standing and wealth, however, will be at the discretion of the individual packs and houses.

To kill, harm, or provoke a superior being is punishable by immediate death. All disputes must be presented to the Blood Alliance for final judgment.

Sexual relationships between lycans and vampires are strictly prohibited. However, business partnerships, where fruitful and appropriate, are permitted.

Humans are hereby classified as property and do not carry any legal rights. Each will be tagged through a sorting system based on merit, intelligence, bloodline, ability, and beauty. Prioritization to be established at birth and finalized on Blood Day.

Twelve mortals per year will be selected to compete for immortal blood status at the discretion of the Blood Alliance. From this twelve, two will be bitten by immortality. The others will die. To create a lycan or vampire outside of this process is unlawful and punishable by immediate death.

All other laws are at the discretion of the packs and royals but must not defy the Blood Alliance.

Part One

Chastely Chosen

DARIUS

"Item seventeen is a twenty-two-year-old Caucasian female with mahogany hair and chocolate-colored eyes. Human is five foot seven, one hundred and thirty pounds, and speaks English, Spanish, Japanese, and German. Her other intellectual aptitudes are detailed on page nine of your guide."

I studied the brunette on the podium and recalled the qualities I memorized an hour earlier. Her profile suited my tastes and purpose—intelligent, multilingual, gorgeous, and innocent. Just what I needed.

The voracious gazes in the room confirmed this would be an expensive venture, but I enjoyed a challenge.

"Shall we start the bidding at one million?" The portly announcer seemed quite pleased with this amount.

I doubled it with a wave of my paddle.

Her sweet blood sang to my baser senses, which was entirely the point. She came from a rare breed of human who resembled ambrosia to my kind, and her virginity only enhanced the allure. The loss of her innocence would tamper the taste slightly, but not by much. Hence her value. I could keep her for days, months, years, or eternity, if I chose.

A beautiful pet to own and do with as I wished. And I would, just not in the way everyone anticipated.

I smiled as I raised my paddle again, tripling my neighbor's amount.

This woman would belong to me by the end of the night. To fuck. To eat. To kill. Whatever I wanted.

Poor thing. I almost felt sorry for her. But she seemed strong enough standing nude on the platform for all of us to examine her every attribute. I doubted she saw much beyond our legs, given the spotlight illuminating her gorgeous assets and face.

So pretty.

And so very much mine.

Chapter One

JULIET

Sleek black shoes.

That's all I knew about my future.

No name, no face, just a vampire who bid the highest in the room for my body and blood.

"Remember your purpose," my matron murmured as she pulled a flimsy white dress over my head. It left me feeling more exposed than I had on the altar moments ago.

"Yes, Madam." The words burned against my dry throat. Standing naked on ceremony for a room full of society's most affluent monsters had nothing on what would come next.

Twenty-two years of training taught me what to expect and how to behave.

Bow.

Do not make eye contact.

Obey.

Three rules of etiquette all blood virgins followed. If I was lucky, he might let me live afterward.

My matron draped a deep-red cloak over my shoulders and tied it at the neck, hiding my sheer gown. A false sense of propriety that served as a way to preserve my innocence for my new master.

"You are ready, my child," my matron said as she secured the hood over my brown hair. The cape and gown were the only items I was permitted to keep outside these walls. I couldn't even take a pair of shoes.

"Thank you, Madam." An automatic reply brought on by years of strict discipline. If I performed as expected, I could one day become a matron too and instruct future blood virgins on proper protocol. But I had to endure and survive my own initiation first.

My palms heated as the doors of the ceremony room whispered open. Two vampires stood waiting in the stark white hallway. They weren't escorts, but guards meant to ensure my cooperation.

Running was never an option.

Neither was fighting.

Survival meant following procedure.

I swallowed the urge to scream. That never ended well. This would happen whether I agreed or not.

"Don't keep him waiting," my matron whispered, caution in her voice.

Part of the ritual was walking down that hallway willingly. Or so it would seem, anyway. Was it really consent when I didn't have a choice?

"Good day to you," I managed. My version of a goodbye to the only woman in my life I ever considered to be family. Not that I dared to tell her. Emotion equaled weakness when displayed outwardly, and I couldn't afford for anyone to consider me pathetic. Not if I wanted to live.

"And to you," she replied.

I inclined my head in a notion of respect before starting the path toward my future—to the male vampire I would call Sire.

My legs felt heavier with each step. I'd never ventured outside this compound. What existed beyond the front door other than a starless night?

The guards followed on either side, careful not to touch me. I belonged to someone else now. They were only permitted to handle me if I chose to fight, but I knew better.

My bare feet were silent against the pristine marble while the cloak rustled softly over my legs. I could feel the guards inspecting me. They had all seen me naked on that altar—like an animal put up for auction. Which was exactly how society perceived me.

An animal without rights.

I paused at the building's primary entrance and examined my destiny—a door handle. Once I twisted it, there would be no returning. Not without my Sire's permission.

But there isn't a choice.

I never had one.

My unique bloodline placed me here at birth.

The guards beside me shifted, an indication that my hesitation had not gone unnoticed. Any longer and I would be at risk of insubordination. I didn't want to end up there again.

My heart beat unsteadily as I pulled open the door to reveal the late hour of the night. A limo waited ominously in the driveway. No external lights. Vampires preferred the dark. Only the hallway behind me illuminated the outside.

I stepped onto the porch and flinched as my feet touched the cold surface. The sensations grew with each move forward, then hurt as I found the cobblestone sidewalk that led to my fate.

The guards kept pace beside me, their gazes vigilant.

And then the back door of the limo opened.

I immediately fell to a bow, my knees touching the uneven stone as my forehead and palms met the ground. Vampires of status required complete and utter submission, especially a master. To greet him in any other manner would result in punishment, and I preferred to avoid that for my first night in his hands.

Expensive shoes appeared in my peripheral vision as a deep voice said, "I will take it from here."

"Of course," the guard to my right replied.

They disappeared on silent feet, leaving me at the mercy of my new owner.

Would he take me here? On the lawn? For all the others to see?

I trembled at the very real prospect.

He owns me.

I remained obedient, awaiting the inevitable. My matron prepared me for this moment. She taught me all the appropriate responses and platitudes to please my new master. But nothing could have equipped me for the reality.

What if I misspoke?

What if I couldn't handle the pain?

"Rise," he commanded.

Bile taunted my throat as I forced myself to comply. My eyes remained on his shoes as I stood gracefully with my hands clasped at my front.

Silence.

A test of my obedience? Vampires loved a good reason to invoke discipline, especially on the innocent.

Unfortunately for him, I excelled at these games. And I refused to break.

He circled me slowly, his steps soundless even in the still evening.

I focused on breathing steadily as he stopped right in front of me. Peppermint tickled my senses, as did a splash of something decidedly masculine. In the thickness of the night, I could barely discern his black suit, but he reeked of

4

elegance and prestige. All vampires did.

He yanked the hood off my head so quickly my balance faltered, as did my pulse. I held my breath as he traced my jaw with the tip of his finger.

A male is touching me.

Forbidden.

Until now.

I knew to expect it, but the warmth of his touch was unlike anything I anticipated. Cold, harsh movements were what my matron told me to expect. Not this gentle exploration of my face. He paused at my chin and tilted my head upward and to each side, inspecting my neck.

"Have you been harmed in any way?" he asked, his voice softer now than before.

His word choice confused me until I translated his meaning. I swallowed twice before answering, "No one has touched me before you, Sire."

Only matrons were allowed in my quarters. The vampire guards could look, but not indulge, and their temptation was diluted anyway. Matrons satisfied guards as a form of training for the blood virgins. Some of those episodes would remain in my nightmares for years to come. Assuming I survived that long.

"I said harmed, not touched," he replied as he dropped my chin. "Get in the limo."

"Yes, Sire." I curtsied before adhering to his command.

I left my hood down since he didn't fix it and moved across the bench to allow him entry. He slid in beside me and closed the door with a finality.

Alone.

With a hungry vampire.

My stomach churned as the reason for my matron denying dinner tonight became obvious. She hadn't wanted me to throw up all over my new master.

I clasped my hands in my lap as the limo started to move and strived not to dig my nails into my palms. At least he hadn't taken me on the sidewalk. That had to be a positive sign. But now we were very much secluded and shrouded in darkness.

It felt more ominous this way.

His shifting did not help. Was he moving closer to me or farther away? The sifting of material suggested he was undressing.

Should I be removing my cloak as well? No. He would do that for me.

Oh, Goddess. We would do this now. I preferred the soft leather over the concrete outside, but—

"What is your given name?" he asked, interrupting my thoughts.

I swallowed the rocks in my throat, so I could force a response. "Whatever you desire it to be, Sire." Could he hear the raspy quality of my voice? The nerves escaping what should otherwise be steadfast control?

"Emotion will get you killed," my matron said more than once.

Pull it together.

"That is not what I requested," he replied, his voice holding an edge. "What is the name you were given at birth?"

I blinked. This did not follow proper protocol. Masters chose a blood virgin's identity. Who or what I was prior to meeting him no longer applied. Only my training mattered. But his tone left no room for disobedience. I would comply because I had to.

"Juliet."

More of that rustling occurred from his side of the car, followed by a snick of silk. Him removing his tie? Some of the guards did this when they wanted to play with a matron's pain tolerance. They would bind their hands or use the fabric as a blindfold. A chill swept down my spine. *What is he planning to do to me?*

"Juliet." It sounded as if he was tasting my name and found it to his liking. "I'm Darius."

I froze. This definitely broke protocol. A blood virgin

always referred to her master as Sire. Never his name. My matron did not prepare me for such a twisted conversation. What sort of game was he playing?

No response felt appropriate, so I remained silent. His goading would not convince me to break decorum.

Light blazed around us, shocking my eyes. They shut automatically as I tried to quickly regain my composure, but he'd no doubt seen my startled reaction. His vampiric gaze wouldn't sting from the sudden brightness inside the limousine.

Something popped, but I couldn't see it.

My heart sang in my ears as I attempted to recover control of my wandering emotions. I felt sick and light-headed at the same time, and helpless.

Tears dampened my cheeks both from the abrupt brightness above and the terror building in my chest. I'd prepared for this. I knew what to expect. This should not be happening.

Stop reacting.

Focus.

Breathe.

My lungs refused as my hands fisted. All manner of punishments filled my thoughts. Not even ten minutes in and he'd managed to break right through my barriers and forced me to slip up.

By turning on the lights. Of all things to set me off...

"Here. This will help," he murmured as he nudged my hand with something cold and solid. "Drink."

I wrapped my quivering fingers around the thin stem and lifted the glass to my lips. Something sharp and fruity touched my tongue, causing my eyelids to spring open. The liquid sputtered from my mouth as I gasped.

"Well, that was graceful," he remarked as he bent to retrieve something from a cabinet near his feet.

He'd taken off his jacket and tie, leaving him clad in a black dress shirt that he'd unbuttoned at the neck to reveal a glimpse of olive skin.

My eyes moved of their own accord to catalog his handsome features.

Elegantly cropped dark hair.

Defined cheekbones.

Square jaw.

Striking green eyes framed with thick dark lashes.

Oh no.

I immediately dropped my gaze. In my moment of shock and confusion, I'd studied my master's face.

Could this go any more wrong? I knew the rules, yet it'd taken mere minutes to throw them all out the window.

"Forgive me, Sire," I whispered. "The alcohol startled me." It was expressly forbidden. Blood virgins did not imbibe. Ever. It tainted our bloodlines.

He plucked the drink from my shaking hand and draped a towel over my fingers. "Clean yourself up, Juliet."

My throat clogged with repressed emotion. To perform so poorly reflected not only on me, but also on my matron. He would seek her punishment in addition to mine.

How had I managed to mess this up so spectacularly?

I used the cloth to clean up my hand and cloak and started to kneel to wipe up the droplets on the floor, but his hand on my wrist held me in place. He said nothing for so long I wondered if he was struggling to determine how first to hurt me. Vampires were notorious in their cruelty. I'd witnessed so many executions, floggings, public rapes, and blood baths that I could too-well imagine his intentions for me.

He let go of my wrist to switch off the lights. I sat still in the shadows of the limo, waiting. My limbs shook with confusion and fear, too fierce to hide. Not that it mattered anymore. I'd more than earned my sentencing. A little emotion sprinkled on top would neither improve nor worsen my pending chastisement.

"You are forgiven, Juliet," he said quietly. "We will be traveling for some time. I recommend you sleep."

"You wish for me to sleep, Sire?" The waiver in my voice couldn't be helped. He claimed to forgive me, but vampires excelled at lying. I knew better than to let those words placate me.

"Yes. Rest."

"A-as you wish, Sire." Did he intend to wake me cruelly? Would that be my penalty for misbehaving? That seemed rather docile, but it depended on his methodology.

I closed my eyes in a false attempt to follow his command but knew my heartbeat gave me away. He would know the truth, but I had to try.

Anything to appease him.

My master.

It was my duty to obey. My duty to accept punishment. My duty to give my body and blood. Only to him. Until he no longer had use for me.

There was no escape.

Nowhere to run.

Follow the rules or die.

I didn't want to die.

Chapter Two

JULIET

"Miss." A sharp shake, followed by, "Please. You must wake up."

I blinked, startled by the unfamiliar voice. It didn't belong to my matron or any other woman in my history.

I sat upright in the foreign bed and took in my surroundings. Royal blues and golds flourished throughout the oversized room, all illuminated by candlelight. "Where am I?"

"Master Darius's home," a stout woman with graying hair informed. "He mentioned you may be drowsy from your long sleep, and also as a side effect of compulsion."

Perspiration dotted my brow and hands. The last thing I remembered was attempting to sleep, then nothing. I didn't even know how long we drove, or where he'd taken me.

"Master Darius requests you for dinner," the older woman said as she laid a revealing black gown over the bedsheets. "You are to wear this."

I studied her. "Are you my new matron?" Her age indicated her humanity, but I didn't recognize her as one of the blessed.

"Er, no, I'm one of Master Darius's housemaids. There are several of us, as well as other servants who maintain the manor." Her blue eyes crinkled. "You may call me Ida, love. Darius informed me to call you Juliet."

My brow furrowed. "He did?"

"Yes, is he wrong?"

"Oh, of course not. If he has chosen Juliet, then that is what I am to be called." How bizarre, though, that he would select my given name. Perhaps he liked it?

Ida looked me over with interest. "I've heard rumors of your kind. Master Darius is in for a treat."

I shivered at the underlying meaning of her words. My body would be his *treat* for *dinner*. I supposed that was better than the lawn outside the Coventus, or in his limousine.

"I shall prepare myself," I said quietly as I slid out of the silk sheets.

Someone had removed my cloak, leaving me in the sheer white gown from earlier. I pulled it over my head and traded it for the black dress. It was no less revealing than my previous outfit, with its sheer bodice and slitted skirt. Both my legs were exposed to the hip, and my breasts were pronounced beneath the translucent material. Typical blood virgin attire. Although, usually a woman in my position only wore darker colors after losing her virginity.

Unless…

Had he taken me while I slept?

Goose bumps filed down my arms at the very real prospect.

Perhaps that was the true purpose for knocking me out.

I spied a mirror in the corner near a door leading to tiled floors. *A bathroom.* One meant only for my use? *Not important.*

I moved on wooden legs, terrified of what I might see, but found my appearance to be normal with the exception of my sleep-nested hair. No visible marks on my neck, arms, or thighs. And I didn't feel sore anywhere. From what my matron told me, it would hurt, perhaps for days afterward. If he'd taken me, I should know.

"There is a brush and other essentials in there," Ida said, reminding me of her presence. She stood off to the side, hands folded before her, appearing curious. "Do you require any assistance?"

I cleared my throat. "No, Madam, but thank you."

She smiled. "I will wait for you by the door, then." She pointed to the large wood panel across the room and bowed her head slightly before leaving me by the bath area.

A human maid. How intriguing. I supposed vampires and lycans would employ them. My bloodline was too cherished and rare to be influenced by humanity. We were owned from birth and protected by vampire guards. Or perhaps *incarcerated* was the better word. Not that I could use it out loud.

I found a brush in the bathroom and went about fixing my brown hair into voluminous waves. My matron claimed it to be my best feature, so I would showcase it accordingly. Once finished, I brushed my teeth and added a few other feminine touches. I was already prepped and shaved from the auction, so it didn't take me long to return to Ida.

She smiled kindly, her eyes crinkling at the sides. "I wish we could all be so confident." She handed me a pair of four-inch heels with the words.

"I beg your pardon?" I asked, confused as I slid on the

stilettos.

"Nothing, darling. Master Darius is waiting. He has two guests with him as well."

My heart sped up as we walked. "Guests?"

"Yes. Master Trevor and Master Ivan."

I swallowed the tremor bubbling up my throat. "Both are here for dinner?" *To enjoy me?*

"Yes," she replied as she escorted me down a very wide staircase leading to a grand foyer below.

Three vampires at once? I nearly missed a step at the thought. Surely Darius couldn't mean for them all to have me tonight. Unless he intended for me to die, in which case, he certainly did mean for this to happen.

"This way," Ida said as we reached the bottom step. My heels clacked against the marble tile, announcing our path. It reminded me of beating drums before an execution, or perhaps that was just my heart thumping an ominous rhythm.

Most blood virgins did not return to the Coventus. Our blood was so potent and addictive that vampires could hardly contain themselves and drank us dry.

Or so my matron warned.

I could do nothing to stop him if that's what he desired. Screaming only sweetened the moment. I was the equivalent of an expensive steak meant to be devoured, or savored, whichever my master preferred.

That thought used to bring tears to my eyes, but I learned long ago that fate would never change her path for me. At least my end would be quick.

Ida knocked on a dark-wood door.

"Enter." Darius's deep voice sent a flutter to my lower abdomen. I remembered the face that paired with the tone, and his bright-green eyes. I never should have looked.

"He means for you to enter, dear, not me," Ida murmured with an encouraging nod.

Of course she would prefer me to join the feast and not her. Clear self-preservation. I couldn't fault her for that.

"You've been very kind to me," I told her. "Thank you."

Her lips curled into a bemused grin. "A treat indeed." She shook her head. "Go now before he asks again."

I nodded. "Yes, of course." Vampires did not appreciate having to wait.

I pushed open the door to peek inside and found the room lit by more candles. A long mahogany table graced the center beneath a chandelier with enough chairs around it to seat an army. Expensive cutlery and plates adorned four place settings, and before them was an array of platters with scents that tickled my nose.

Master Darius stood against the wall just inside the door, flanked by his two suit-clad counterparts.

"Sire," I greeted as I assumed my position on the floor near his feet with my forehead touching the marble ground.

Their eyes felt like brands against my exposed skin, leaving marks as they admired my submissive position. They said nothing, yet I *felt* every unspoken word. Hunger and arousal thickened the air, churning my stomach as I waited for the first one of them to pounce.

This is my purpose, I reminded myself as I steadied my breathing.

In. One, two, three.

Out. One, two, three.

Focusing on my inhales and exhales did little to still my thundering heart. I couldn't hide the harsh sound from their predatory senses. It served as a beacon, alluring me to them more.

A tremor traversed my spine.

Three on one. I'd seen it done too many times. Would I be able to handle their penetrations? Would I die swiftly?

Goddess, I prayed, evoking the highest power on Earth. *Please end it quickly...*

Their shoes whispered over the floor as they circled

me.

"She's exquisite," one of them murmured. "And there's no denying the temptation."

"Yes." The familiar masculine tone called to my training and demanded complete surrender. He owned me in every way.

"But can she be reprogrammed?" the third voice asked, his tone decidedly foreign.

"Time will tell," Master Darius replied as he crouched before me. "Are you going to do this every time you see me?" His finger found my chin as he forced me to meet his gaze. "Because I'm already annoyed by it."

"Sire?" I asked, confused as I tried to look anywhere except his face. To meet a master's stare was expressly forbidden. It suggested challenge, and I did not wish to engage him in that manner.

He pinched my chin hard, bringing tears to my eyes. "Look at me, Juliet." I swallowed and forced myself to comply. Those sharp green irises burned into mine. So hypnotically handsome, yet lethal. And so very old.

"You are not to bow in this manner unless I expressly request it. Do you understand?"

Not really... "May I seek clarification, Sire?" A bold question, one that could earn me additional punishment, but I needed more details to comply.

"You may," he replied, and I swore he sounded almost amused.

"How would you prefer me to bow?" I asked. "This is the way of my training, but as it displeases you, I will conform my methods."

"No bowing at all," he clarified.

"Shall I curtsy, then?"

"No." He dropped my chin and stood. "Rise, Juliet."

"Yes, Sire." I rose swiftly to my feet and averted my gaze once more to the floor.

Silence.

I didn't quite know what he wanted me to do with my

hands, so I left them at my sides while the three of them admired my dress.

"She's truly lovely," one of the males murmured.

"Indeed," my master replied. "Shall we eat?"

My stomach churned at the casual words. No more platitudes or demands, just *dinner*.

"I'm famished."

"Likewise."

"Excellent," my master said as he moved into my personal space. I remained still as he placed a hand at the small of my back.

This was it.

My final moments.

If I complied, it would be less painful.

I pulled my hair over one shoulder, exposing my neck, and waited.

Please let it be quick.

Chapter Three

Darius

Fuck, she smelled amazing.

My maker—Cam—had once warned me of the temptation brought on by a blood virgin, but I'd never taken him seriously. However, after several hours in the limo beside Juliet, I finally understood.

The woman was irresistible.

My incisors ached with the need to taste her—even if for a second. Trevor and Ivan would feel it too, but propriety kept them from trying anything.

And Christ, the bowing. To put herself in such a submissive position aroused all my darker needs, which was obviously the point.

It had to stop. Everything she did, every word she said, were all express signs of submission ingrained in her from years of indoctrination. It shouldn't appeal to me, but damn if I wasn't aroused right now.

Ivan's amusement rolled off him in waves. Of course he was enjoying this. He'd been all for our royal friend's ridiculous idea that I purchase a blood virgin for status. Oh, it would work, assuming I could withstand the temptation of taking her too soon.

Juliet's pulse thrummed healthily in her exposed neck, taunting my instincts. I could devour her and she would do nothing to stop me—maybe even encourage me.

But it wouldn't be real.

All trained responses meant to please the highest bidder. Not that I blamed her. She was a victim of her bloodline.

I flexed my palm on her lower back to pull her slightly closer and lifted my opposite hand to curl around her nape. She leaned into the touch and closed her eyes, but her lips trembled slightly.

Fear.

It seemed no amount of preparation could properly ready her for this moment. Not surprising.

I flicked my thumb over her pulse and her jaw clenched.

Mmm, a fighter lurked beneath the surface. She wanted to live in a world where most humans preferred death. Fascinating.

I leaned in to inhale her addictive fragrance. So sweet, and alluring. Knowing I didn't have to resist only deepened my desire to taste her. To take her.

My lips found her pulse and kissed her neck coaxingly. She seemed to melt against me, her body recognizing its purpose. But her jaw remained tense.

I'd chosen well.

Very, very well.

I nibbled her tender skin, careful not to break the surface, before placing my lips at her ear. "Bow or curtsy in my presence again, and I will bite you next time, Juliet."

I nuzzled her cheekbone as she shivered before pulling back to meet her gaze. "And I expect you to look at me when I'm talking to you."

She blinked, as if dazed. "But decorum states—"

I nipped her pulse, silencing her trained response.

"I don't care what decorum states, Juliet."

I laved the scratch created by my incisors and closed my eyes as a spec of her essence met my tongue. Fucking heaven. What I wouldn't give to sink my teeth into her vein and take my fill.

But I needed her alive, and I desired her acquiescence. It would make taking her all the sweeter. Because I would have her and her permission. Eventually.

I allowed myself one more taste as Trevor and Ivan watched with envy in their gazes. It wasn't just her blood that teased them, but this revealing dress. I'd chosen it to show them how lucrative she would be, and their expressions confirmed my every suspicion.

"I apologize for displeasing you, Sire," Juliet whispered.

I suppressed the urge to growl. My aristocratic brethren fancied this obedient behavior. Submission I understood and enjoyed, but her subservience was evoked by fear of harsh punishment. I preferred the pleasurable kind of reprimand, something Juliet would soon learn.

But I had a few walls to break down first.

And twenty-two years of ingrained etiquette.

"You are to do as I say, correct?"

"Yes, Sire."

"Then you will obey my requests not to bow or curtsy in my presence unless otherwise requested." I forced myself away from her neck and tilted her head in a way that made it impossible for her to avoid my gaze. "And you will make eye contact with me whenever we are speaking with one another. Do you understand?"

"I…" She swallowed visibly but held my stare warily. "Yes. Of course, Sire."

"Excellent." I released her nape and pulled her toward

the table. "Take a seat."

"You always were gifted with the ladies, Darius," Trevor remarked, his humor evident.

"We should take notes," Ivan agreed.

"For when we buy our own fuck dolls?" Trevor asked, a smile in his voice.

"Absolutely. I want a redhead."

"Hmm, yeah, I'm craving a brunette right about now."

"I think we all are, mate."

"Enough," I growled as I helped Juliet into her chair. She sat very still and kept her focus on the table while I took a seat beside her. It seemed the eye contact thing would take some work.

Trevor and Ivan sat across from us, their expressions matching ones of amusement.

"Why did you both drop by, again?" I demanded.

"You know why," Ivan replied. "Trevor wanted to see your new toy."

I rolled my eyes. "She's not a toy."

"She's a walking fuck doll with delectable blood," Trevor murmured. "Definitely a toy."

Juliet didn't react to the crude description and remained outwardly complacent with her hands folded in her lap. That sort of control would come in handy later.

I reached for a platter of roasted duck and slid a few slices onto Juliet's plate before serving myself.

Trevor and Ivan followed suit, taking several sides and lathering their dishes with Gladice's fine cooking. They frequently tried to buy her from me, but I always refused. I had one of the best chefs in the region and did not plan to give her up anytime soon. All my servants were my own. I protected them fiercely, just as I would the beauty beside me.

She eyed the food I placed in front of her before shyly glancing around the table.

I grinned as understanding slithered through my thoughts. Juliet expected to be the main course. A definite temptation, one I might indulge another night when we were alone. Assuming she was willing.

My friends had obviously come to the same conclusion because they both smirked at her confusion.

Poor girl. She had no idea what I'd dragged her into, but she would soon learn.

I draped my arm over the back of her chair, crowding her personal space, and pressed my lips to her ear again. "Vampires eat food too, darling."

It was more of an unnecessary indulgence since we didn't require it to survive, but my taste buds appreciated the flavor.

"I know," she whispered. "Of course I know that." That last bit seemed more for her than for me, but I replied anyway.

"Good." I nipped her pulse and thought of something else. "You'll know when I intend to bite you, Juliet. Because I'll warn you before our first time."

She startled at my words, her perception clouded by what the Coventus had drilled into her pretty head. What she didn't realize was that not all vampires were created equal. And I prided myself on being a rebel.

"Eat," I told her as I righted myself. "You'll need your strength."

Juliet required a gradual introduction to my needs. If I rushed it, she'd die, and I needed her very much alive. I also required her trust, and that would be the trickiest emotion of them all. Because no sane human trusted a vampire.

Trevor lifted his wine glass in salute. "To new endeavors."

"To the future," Ivan added.

"To change," I replied, saluting them both with my glass.

Juliet was the only one who didn't indulge because she didn't yet understand. But she would. And soon.

I smiled as she picked up her fork to oblige my

demand. That little obedient habit would come in handy over the coming months. She would do whatever I wanted, wherever I wanted.

Not a toy but an asset. With perfect breasts and the face of a goddess, no one would suspect her. And I owned every mouthwatering inch of her.

"Seems you'll have quite the training on your hands, Darius," Ivan said as he nodded to an apprehensive Juliet. She picked up a slice of meat and nibbled it gingerly before setting her fork down with a confused expression.

"Do they not allow duck in the Coventus?" I asked dryly.

She blinked big brown eyes up to mine and grimaced. "I... yes... but not quite like this."

"Like what?"

"Rich," she whispered. "It's decadent, Sire." She started to drop her gaze in submission but lifted them before I could comment on it. Yes, her obedience training would certainly suit my plans.

"You mean it's savory," I interpreted. "Let me guess; they forced you to live on the bare essentials and outlawed all foods with actual flavor?" Typical brainwashing technique. It also served to keep her figure in check, and they'd certainly accomplished that.

"My blood is pure, Sire."

"Pure." The word tasted sour on my tongue. Society meant to control her appearance to increase her worth, not strengthen her bloodline. She would taste the same no matter what she consumed, and her virginity wouldn't impact her natural flavor. "My brethren have molded you into the perfect woman, Juliet. Delectable, demure, gorgeous. I can assure you the eating habits ingrained in you only impact one of those traits, and it is not your blood."

I sampled the duck and found it cooked to perfection, as always, while Juliet frowned. Not her best look, but I preferred it to the fear radiating from her.

"Forgive me, Sire, but I do not understand your meaning. Is this a test of sorts?" She licked her lips. "I do not wish to fail you."

Trevor smirked as Ivan shook his head with a bemused smile. Both of them were enjoying this far too much. They knew my patience rarely upheld in these types of matters, but I could hardly fault the woman for what my kind had done to her.

I set my fork aside and wrapped my arm around her chair again. She stopped breathing as I traced the column of her neck with my index finger. "You denied my champagne in the limousine," I murmured. "Because alcohol is forbidden, yes?"

Her eyes—still holding mine as instructed—flared. So much for her terror level decreasing.

"Yes," she whispered. "I-I'm sorry, Sire."

It took me a moment to realize what she meant—spewing her drink all over the place after I demanded she take a sip. Most in my position would have punished the new pet for behaving impudently, but I saw her as something else entirely.

"I already forgave you," I reminded. "But I would like to teach you a lesson."

Her heart beat loudly, alluring all the vampires in the room, including me. Trevor and Ivan stopped eating, their focus shifting to the frightened blood virgin and her singing pulse.

"Of course, Sire." The words were so soft I nearly missed them.

My arm fell to her shoulders to hold her close as I said, "Give me your hand, Juliet."

She presented the one closest to me, as if her body was a puppet for me to command. I grasped her wrist with my free hand and brought it to my lips for a kiss.

Her body trembled, belying her stoic expression. I truly missed the days when human females provided at least a little bit of sass or fight. Perhaps I could instill some in this one, over time.

"You've been taught that alcohol and rich foods will tarnish your bloodline, yes?" I traced her pulse with my tongue and enjoyed the way it skipped beneath my touch. So lovely.

She nodded. "Yes, Sire."

"You've also been taught that keeping your blood pure is important to please your master?"

Another nod, this one firmer.

"Excellent, then this should be an easy lesson, darling." I nipped her tender skin, eliciting a tender blush across her hand. "I'm going to taste you now." I didn't wait for her compliance as it wasn't required. She knew her purpose.

My incisors pierced her vein with practiced ease, pulling just enough of her sweet essence to satisfy my curiosity and not excite the hunger within.

Heaven, my instincts murmured as my stomach clenched with the need for more.

It would be so easy to drag her into my lap and take everything from her. That dress left nothing to the imagination—a mere rip would remove it. And she would acquiesce to my every request.

Because she belongs to me.

Fuck. I never expected that to be so erotic. The art of owning a person was morally wrong, and yet, I couldn't bring myself to regret it.

One night and already my control threatened to slip from a single taste of her euphoric blood. I expected it to be alluring—addicting, even—but not this erotic inclination to take her completely.

She quivered as I allowed myself one more swallow, and her sweet arousal prickled the air. I had chosen unconsciously to introduce pleasure with my bite rather than pain. Her little trembles almost encouraged me to continue, but we had a lesson to finish. I released her vein—with considerable effort—and licked her wound while holding her drowsy stare.

"Try the wine," I told her with a hint of compulsion underlying my tone. "Now."

She lifted the glass with her free hand and brought it to her lips before realizing what I demanded. "Sire…"

"Now," I repeated.

Tears glistened in her gaze as she followed my command and sipped the red wine. Her throat convulsed around it as she swallowed, and her eyes closed. I didn't chastise her for the disobedience but instead laved at her wound and gently bit her again, this time a little deeper for my own personal enjoyment.

Her lips parted on a moan as I infused endorphins into the bite—my way of praising her for adhering to my demands. The crystal glass in her hand shook, and her head fell back against my arm.

No terror now, just pure, unadulterated bliss, and it was seductive as hell. If it weren't for our audience, I would have pushed her further. They'd more than received a show tonight—one that would only solidify my plans for her.

I eased her return to reality by slowly withdrawing my incisors and healing her marks with my tongue. Some of my kind preferred to leave the wounds open as a way of declaring ownership, but I wanted her healthy and unmarred. Her creamy skin was too beautiful to damage.

Her thick lashes fluttered as she opened her almond-shaped eyes and met my gaze again. *So well-behaved.*

"You're just as sweet now as you were moments ago, Juliet," I murmured. "The alcohol only alters your mental state and, in excess, could cause weight gain. But it holds no power over your delicious blood, love. I will taste you again tomorrow if you require more proof."

I kissed her pulse once more before returning her hand to her lap. "Now eat your dinner and stop fretting about rules that hold no meaning in this house. I will tell you what I expect and you will comply. Understood?"

Her pink cheeks deepened to an appealing crimson as

she muddled her way through the cloud of desire. I imagined it was a foreign feeling, one her matron wouldn't have taught her because she wouldn't have known it existed.

As second-class citizens, humans were not promised the right to pleasure of any kind. Pain, certainly. Enjoyment, no. That didn't make my granting of gratification illegal, just not customary. Though, I suspected most of my kind allowed it in certain degrees, depending on our proclivities.

Her pink tongue darted out to wet her lips, then she nodded. "Yes, Sire."

"Then I consider this lesson closed," I replied as I removed my arm from her shoulders. "Enjoy your meal."

Because I certainly enjoyed mine, even if it barely qualified as an appetizer.

Chapter Four

JULIET

The moon shone brightly outside the balcony doors of my room. It lit up the courtyard and the thick cluster of unending trees surrounding the outskirts of the property.

I'd spent most of the early evening admiring the breathtaking view. Darius's home provided a false sense of calm that didn't exist in the walls surrounding the Coventus. Something new and quite... soothing.

Last night he had requested my presence for dinner, then excused me after dessert.

No proper feeding, nor did he offer me to his guests.

I didn't understand this game at all.

My matron had prepared me for every situation, or so I thought. But my Sire played by a foreign set of rules. He forced me to imbibe alcohol, something expressly prohibited. And yet, I enjoyed it. Perhaps too much.

Or maybe that was his bite.

My thighs clenched with the memory of his mouth on my skin. Never in my wildest dreams had I expected *that*.

It was unlike all of the scenes I'd witnessed between my matron and the vampires during my training. She usually cried silently as they took her however they craved. And when she screamed, they punished her more.

Silence was an important skill taught at a young age. Vampires preferred quiet pets who allowed them full access to whatever they desired. And I'd been prepared for that with Darius. I expected him to hurt me while sating his needs. Instead he granted me *sensation*.

My lips threatened to curl in a way they rarely did.

A trick, my mind whispered. *It's all a trick of some sort.*

Yes. A pleasurable one.

For now.

A knock startled my daydreaming. I blinked at the door, waiting for it to open.

"Juliet?" The deep voice ignited a flutter in my lower abdomen.

Why didn't he enter at will?

Another knock.

Odd.

I wandered over to open the unlocked door and revealed a suit-clad Darius waiting for me in the hallway.

"Sire," I murmured, my knees bending slightly on instinct. Remembering his command not to curtsy or bow, I straightened and caught his quirked brow. "It is a formal habit, Sire." Not that it was an excuse. My body should follow his every whim on instinct regardless of former training.

"May I come in?" he asked.

"Always." I stepped aside while forcing my eyes to remain on his face rather than averted. His chiseled jaw and sculpted cheekbones were easy to admire. It was his intense stare that I had to watch out for—I could easily lose myself in those green orbs.

"Ida informs me that you've been in your quarters all evening," he murmured. "Are you not hungry?"

Last night's feast offered me enough sustenance for a week. "I feel quite satisfied at present." I used the cup in the bathroom for water earlier when I required it.

"I see." He clasped his hands behind his back as he stared down at me. "You are free to wander the manor whenever you want."

"Sire?" That seemed... inappropriate.

He arched a brow. "Do you require a tour?"

"I..." Did I? "Would you like to give me a tour?"

He studied me for a long moment before saying, "This obedient habit is already trying my patience, Juliet. Change into something more appropriate, and I'll provide you with a new task."

"Of course, Sire." I fingered my robe. "What would you prefer me to wear?"

He smirked. "What would I prefer you wear?" He scratched his jaw before palming the back of his neck. "I'd prefer you in nothing, if I'm honest."

I untied the silk rope around my waist and allowed my robe to fall to the floor. "As you wish, Sire."

His grin slipped. "That..." He trailed off as his eyes dropped to my exposed breasts and continued lower to examine every inch of my body along the way.

Nudity didn't faze me, but I'd never stood this close to a male before without clothes. And this one could touch me at will.

That should have frightened me, yet my stomach seemed to tighten in a different manner entirely. Especially as his pupils dilated with unveiled hunger.

He wants to bite me again.

I think I want that too.

An unfamiliar warmth followed his stare, caressing all of my nerves and awakening a foreign sensation between my thighs. I fought to remain still and to maintain a calm demeanor as he met my gaze once more with a decidedly ravenous gleam.

"Sarcasm," he murmured as he stepped closer. He gathered my brown waves to one side, exposing my neck to his view. "But your literal interpretation is hardly something I can chastise."

His body brushed mine as he pressed his lips to my throat. "If I told you to please me orally—right now—would you drop to your knees?"

My mouth went dry at the prospect.

I'd witnessed fellatio countless times during my training, had even undergone oral exercises for practice, but I'd never performed the act on a real male—touching a member of the opposite sex prior to my auction was strictly prohibited. I hadn't minded, as I always thought the act would repulse me, but the idea of exploring Darius so intimately appealed in a dark way.

"Is that your wish, Sire?" I whispered.

"With a mouth like yours, I imagine it would be the desire of most men, Juliet." His teeth skimmed my pulse. I quivered at the sensual memory his mouth evoked and found myself longing for his bite.

None of this was what I expected. I anticipated harsh words, painful penetration, and the very real fate of death. Not this sensual play.

I opened my mouth to ask if he wanted me on my knees, but the words froze in my throat as he grasped my hips and pulled me flush against him. My heart skipped a beat at the very real proof of his arousal thickening against my belly.

A silent demand for me to act? I wasn't sure.

Perspiration dampened my palms as I lifted my fingers to trace the edge of his belt. He caught my wrist and whirled me around, pressing my back to his chest. My pulse skyrocketed at the fast, unexpected move, then stuttered as he flattened his hand against my lower abdomen, holding me in place.

30

I couldn't breathe, not with his lips tasting my neck.

Oh, Goddess...

His tongue traced a hypnotic pattern that left me delirious in his arms. A wave of heat rolled over me, centering in my stomach and spiraling outwards.

A whimper escaped me as I fought to understand all these sensations. Hot, cold, tension in every limb...

His palm started downward.

Slowly.

The breath caught in my throat, uncertain, as he explored the freshly groomed space between my hips. I'd been shaved everywhere prior to the auction, something my matron stated my new master would prefer.

"Time for a new lesson," he whispered.

"S-Sire?" I didn't—

My knees buckled as his fangs pierced my skin.

Intense.

Sudden.

And much harder than last night.

But also, really good.

He held me against him with one arm wrapped around my chest and a hand on my stomach. I shuddered at the possessive hold and the warmth swimming through my veins. Most vampires didn't infuse their bites with endorphins, but Darius did. And I was very thankful for it.

His name almost slipped from my lips as he drew my essence into his mouth. It burned in an intense way that caused my thighs to squeeze in response and my eyes to close.

This was my purpose, and it felt so right in his arms.

The fear I expected in this moment was replaced by a passion I never knew existed. Humans weren't meant to feel like this, or perhaps *allowed* was the more accurate term. The forbidden nature of our embrace only enhanced my enjoyment.

His hand ventured lower, to a place I didn't realize I wanted to be touched until now. I knew he belonged there and understood that he owned my body, but the reality far surpassed my assumptions.

I grabbed his forearm, needing something to hold on to as he parted my slick folds. My limbs shook as he slipped a finger inside me and penetrated me from above and below.

It was so overwhelming and powerful.

I didn't know how to think, couldn't remember how to breathe.

All I could do was feel.

His mouth.

His hand.

His heat.

I rocked against him wantonly, unable to stop myself from seeking more, *needing* more.

"Darius…" My legs trembled uncontrollably, his arm around my breasts the only thing keeping me upright.

I felt caged, protected, and owned.

He took a dangerous pull from my neck, so hard that I saw stars, while pumping more of that euphoria back into me, both with his bite and his fingers.

I couldn't move, so captivated by all the sensations that my entire body just seemed to freeze. And then I broke on a rapturous wave that left me panting and pleading and crying.

He'd ripped me in half.

Torn the air from my lungs.

Seared my skin and left me shaking wildly.

"That's it, Juliet," he whispered, his lips brushing my ear. "Feel."

I shuddered against him as my limbs refused to function. My mouth remained open on an unending moan as fire singed every nerve.

It seemed to take forever for the overwhelming sensations to subside.

And several more minutes afterwards for me to realize Darius had lifted me into his arms.

We were on my bed with me curled in his lap.

His mouth brushed my forehead and temple as he continued to whisper reassurances in my ear.

I blinked, dazed.

What just happened?

Darius tucked my hair behind my ear and cupped my cheek. "You orgasm beautifully, darling." He traced my lower lip with the pad of his finger while he spoke. "I look forward to feeling it when I'm inside you."

My pulse thrummed in my ears. Did he intend to do that now?

His finger slipped into my mouth, introducing me to a musky flavor I'd never experienced.

Me, I realized.

This was the hand he'd used to pleasure me.

My legs clamped together, arousing a quake from deep within.

His eyes smoldered as I sucked my essence from his skin. "I will very much enjoy having you on your knees," he whispered darkly as he outlined my lips again. "But not yet."

His mouth captured mine, shocking me to my core.

Vampires did not kiss humans.

But this one was definitely kissing me.

Darius's tongue slid through my defenses, coaxing me to respond. I'd never experienced anything like this but found it quite pleasing—especially the way his lips caressed mine.

I tentatively returned the movement, learning his preferences with each stroke. My essence mingled with his, thickening our kiss and creating an intoxicating atmosphere of addiction.

His fingers wound in my hair, holding me to him as he devoured my mouth, and I groaned with satisfaction. No one had ever touched me in this manner, as if I meant something.

Although I understood this was all a result of my

temporary purpose here, a small part of me hoped that this could become my permanent reality.

Darius tore his mouth away from me and pressed his forehead to mine as our heavy breaths filled the air. Would he finish the task now and rid me of my maidenhead? Or did he have something else in mind?

I no longer knew what to expect from him.

He broke all the formalities.

And he fed without hurting me.

"Pleasure," Darius murmured. "You've now experienced it." He kissed me again, softer this time, before pulling back to hold my gaze. His irises had darkened to a forest green—so hypnotic and beautiful.

"Juliet." He uttered my name with an authority that required attention.

"Yes, Sire?" I thought perhaps I said his name out loud before, but couldn't remember. Another shattered rule.

"You are only to offer yourself to me when you crave pleasure, not because you wish to adhere to a command. Do you understand?"

I blinked at him. His words were clear, but the meaning behind them confused me. My duty was to provide blood and sex. Why would my desire play into our arrangement?

He arched a brow, waiting.

"Yes, Sire." The words were out before I could stop them as my training took over. *A displeased master was an angry master.*

"Good." He brushed his lips against my forehead and set me down to the side. "Now wear an outfit of your choice and meet me in the hallway. I want to show you something."

Chapter Five

Darius

That went well.

Shit.

I rubbed a hand over my face and used the wall for support while waiting for Juliet to join me in the hall. She had better put on some fucking clothes, or I would lose it.

When I heard she hadn't left her room all evening, I thought a conversation regarding expectations might be needed. I should have let Ida handle it. But no. I decided a tour would be a good way to warm Juliet to the idea of trusting me.

Instead I nearly fucked her.

"What would you prefer me to wear?"

I'd said the first thing that came to mind, and she took it quite literally.

Exquisite didn't even begin to describe a naked Juliet. Her subtle curves and creamy skin were designed with the male gender in mind.

And those lips… I meant what I said. I couldn't wait to have them wrapped around my cock. Which was hard as a rock in my pants right now.

So much for easing her into my needs.

The door creaked as Juliet turned the handle.

I held my breath.

What did a woman bred to model translucent gowns prefer to wear when given a choice? I'd left Ida in charge of Juliet's wardrobe. Who knew what she'd purchased.

"Is this acceptable, Sire?" Juliet asked softly as she joined me in the corridor.

I preferred when she called me Darius in the bedroom. It'd been the first slip in her polite façade, and I intended to continue down that path. Perhaps in the form of more orgasms.

Hiding my internal amusement at that promise, I turned to survey her outfit choice. A black strapless dress that ended just below her ass and hugged every curve. Great. Just what my dick requested.

At least it's not transparent.

I cleared my throat and nodded. "This is acceptable." I would have to find cause for her to bend over at some point just to see what she wore beneath it, as I bet she went without.

And now that thought would torture me throughout our tour. Fantastic.

Note to self: request Ida purchase a more appropriate wardrobe for Juliet.

"Shall we?" I didn't wait for her to agree as I started in the opposite direction from the staircase. Her bare feet moved quietly over the wood floor as she followed dutifully. The rumble in her stomach told me she either lied about her hunger or was just now realizing she needed food. I would address that matter after our first stop on the tour.

"This"—I gestured to the door closest to hers—"is the entrance to my quarters."

Her dark eyes rounded as I twisted the handle.

"Nervous?" I couldn't help the taunt as I entered the sitting area. Standing naked before me proved no issue, but showing her my private rooms stirred a fiery blush on her cheeks. Intriguing.

"Yes, Sire," she whispered as she paused beside me. Her succulent scent wrapped around me, causing my incisors to ache with need. The bite in her room had been about her—not me. I craved so much more, but I required her understanding first. Without it, everything would fail.

That didn't stop me from having a little fun with her, though.

I curled my palm around the back of her neck and stepped into her personal space. Her breasts brushed my chest on a sharp inhale. Surprise mingled with fear and something decidedly feminine in her gaze.

Desire.

I pressed my lips to her ear. "You're welcome to enter my room whenever you please, darling."

I nuzzled her neck, right over the spot I nipped her earlier. The skin had already healed thanks to my ministrations. One day, I would mark her as mine, assuming she met my expectations.

"But I should warn you," I added as I drew my teeth over her tender skin. "When you visit me here, I'll assume you're in need of pleasure, and I will require the favor to be returned." My tongue traced her escalating pulse to punctuate my warning.

I grinned as Juliet arched her neck in silent invitation. She had no idea what she was inviting out to play, but she would. Soon.

"Come, Juliet," I whispered. "We still have several stops on our tour." I placed a lingering kiss against her throat and skimmed my nose over her blushing collarbone.

Possessing her would be worth the wait.

I released her nape and left her standing in the center of my sitting room. She finally caught me at the staircase, her feet padding softly against the wood. I glanced at her flushed cheeks and fought a smile. The woman wore arousal beautifully.

"As I mentioned earlier, you're allowed to wander the estate as you desire," I murmured as we ascended to the foyer. "If I need you for a social engagement, I'll provide notice. And as for attempting to escape, I wouldn't recommend it."

Acres upon acres of land and trees surrounded the manor, and beyond it, small colonies of lycans. They would not be very kind to a wandering blood virgin.

"Escape?" Juliet repeated, her voice quiet. "Where would I go?"

"Where indeed," I agreed as I led her into the kitchen. Gladice had left a dinner plate on the counter for Juliet. I lifted the top to check the heat and decided it would do. "Eat something, then we will continue." I pulled out a stool and arched a brow, daring her to argue.

She studied the offering with a curious expression as she slid onto the cushioned seat. Her dress sat high on her thighs, not that she seemed to notice or care. I again wondered what she wore beneath. It would be so easy to find out, but the mystery almost entertained me more.

I secured a set of silverware from a drawer and handed them to her as I took the seat across from her at the kitchen island.

"Thank you," she murmured as she picked at the chicken on her plate.

I folded my arms on the marble countertop. "You never need to thank me for anything, Juliet." I meant it.

The world she knew didn't resemble the one I remembered. Juliet had been told her whole life that her sole purpose on Earth was to be fucked and bled. And while the predator in me understood this, the man in me was appalled.

Vampires and lycans were the superior race—no question—but with that status came a sense of responsibility that my brethren seemed to have forgotten. Even pets deserved rights.

She ate silently, but questions radiated from her gaze. I continued to break the formalities drilled into her head, yet she never argued. It hurt to see a woman so crippled by society's teachings, and Juliet not knowing or realizing her broken nature pained me even more.

Still, nothing compared to what I had to do next.

It was almost cruel, but I needed to shatter her bubble, and I only knew one way to do that.

By telling her the truth.

"I'm not well versed on your education, aside from the dossier I was provided during your auction. You speak several languages, your arithmetic skills are adequate, and you favor biology—all items I admire. What I don't know is, how well versed you are in history."

She finished chewing and set her fork against the half-eaten plate. Her eyes darted around, searching for something before landing on the sink.

Realizing what she needed, I stood and found a glass to fill with water. Her curious eyes held mine as I handed it to her. Another formality ruined; I'd served the servant.

Juliet took a longer than necessary drink before setting it aside. "Thank…" She bit her lip, halting the rest of the words I'd just told her weren't necessary moments ago.

"You're allowed to thank me," I clarified. "But it's not mandatory."

Her rounding eyes suggested we needed to start here rather than with the history lesson. Twenty-two years in the Coventus had molded her into the perfect pet by vampire standards. Obedient, subservient, and dutiful. I needed to rearrange her perception of the rules.

"Are you finished eating?" I asked before she could speak. She had consumed the same amount as the night before, but I wanted to be sure.

"Yes, Sire."

"Excellent." I pushed away from the counter. "Follow me."

She didn't wait to be told twice and trailed right behind me. "My education included a thorough understanding of the Blood Alliance. I am also well versed in geography, the vampire royal families, royal clans, and general government affairs."

I glanced over my shoulder. "Making you a perfect pet for someone of class." And exactly why I chose her. "But none of that is history, Juliet. Has no one taught you about the world prior to lycan and vampire rule?"

Her frown answered my inquiry.

"No, of course not," I murmured as we walked by the grand ballroom. "The Coventus wouldn't want you to know such things. It fortifies your training to believe this has always been the way."

"I... I don't know how to reply, Sire."

"I suspect you wouldn't." I paused outside a set of glass doors and turned to stare down at her. "You exist to serve and please vampire aristocrats. Your blood, specifically, is why you were chosen for this path. But life wasn't always that way, Juliet."

I pushed the doors open to the library and walked backwards, my gaze on hers. "Before I give you a task, I want to make a few things clear between us."

Her attention flickered to the floor-to-ceiling bookshelves surrounding every available wall in the room before spying the windows overlooking the vibrant garden patio behind me. She swallowed as she found her way back to me, her cheeks reddening with remorse. I held up a hand before she could apologize for being distracted. I understood; it was a magnificent sight. That's why I built it.

"Fear is a beautiful training mechanism. It's what my kind instills in humans to guarantee a certain behavior." I stepped into her personal space and grabbed her chin to tilt her head back. "I do not wish for you to be afraid of me, Juliet. While I appreciate your compliance, I also seek your willingness."

I brushed my thumb over her lips, silencing whatever programmed response she had planned.

"My rules are simple. I do not care for formalities in my home, and I expect you to look after yourself. You are free to roam my estate at your leisure, which includes anything and everything within my property lines. When I require you for something, I will inform you. Otherwise, your time is your own. Do you understand?"

She studied me, her pupils dilating with uncertainty. "I… I think so, Sire." The hesitancy in her tone coupled with those telling eyes did not leave me with great confidence in her comprehension.

Rather than explain more, I released her chin and turned toward a section of the library containing some of my favorite books. Tasks were something she could appreciate, and I had a horrible one for her.

I plucked a few older texts from the shelves and set them on a table near the fireplace. That would be enough to start her reeducation. When I turned to explain, I found her studying the item beside the fireplace near the oversized couch.

"A television," I explained from beside her. "This technology isn't created anymore, but humans used to love the cinema." Mine still worked with the attached media player. I only used it when my nostalgic side required it. "From what I understand, they are still quite popular with the lycan community."

"What does it do?" she asked, her head cocked to the side.

"It plays a movie, like a book come to life. Perhaps we will watch one sometime."

She blinked up at me. "Is this something that requires permission?" So I'd finally found something that intrigued her.

"No," I murmured. "But it does require a tutorial." One I had no patience for this evening. "I have a task for you first."

She eyed the books on the table. "You wish for me to read."

"Yes." I clasped my hands behind my back to keep from touching her. No amount of soothing on my part would soften my intentions for her. "You may know how the Blood Alliance operates today, but not about how it came into existence."

Juliet picked up the first text—a global history book. "There was a council before it?"

"There were many before it, including several human governments."

"Human governments?" she repeated, her eyebrows in her hairline.

"Read," I murmured. "When you're done, come find me, and we will discuss more." I made to leave her but paused as I passed another shelf and thought better of it. "When you finish with those, select a few books from this row. They should provide you with the evidence required to believe." The manuscripts contained various pictures, all of which depicted the various world wars and a few regarding the attempted purge of immortal bloodlines.

The humans failed. Miserably.

"I have no travel planned for the next three weeks, Juliet. Nor do we have any engagements. So, feel free to take your time and come to me when you're ready." I started toward the door, then paused again. "And you can read wherever you feel most comfortable, and do not forget to eat. Remember, you're allowed to explore my estate without an escort."

"Yes, Sire," she said, her focus on the book and not on me.

Let the retraining begin.

Chapter Six

Darius

"Where's the doll?" Ivan asked as he strolled through the glass doors.

I lowered myself to the ground and back up. "You mean Juliet?"

"*Doll* seems more appropriate, but yes." He came to stand beside me, his hands tucked into the pockets of his trousers.

I completed several more push-ups before hopping to my feet. Exercising wasn't necessary, but I needed the distraction today. "She's in the library. Reading."

Ivan snorted. "That's what you said last week."

"And she's still in there." I stretched my arms over my head and rolled my neck. "Want to go on a jog with me?"

My best friend looked me over and shook his head,

bemused. "Why don't you just go fuck her? Isn't that why she's here?"

Leave it to Ivan to think with his cock over reason. "You know why she's here."

"Yeah, I do, and part of that requires fucking her." He waved a hand over my track pants. "I mean, this is absurd, mate. You don't even like to run."

True, but I needed a physical distraction to keep myself from seeking out the delectable scent calling to my every instinct.

Juliet had been in the library for ten days now, rarely leaving even to sleep. I had to stop myself several times from stalking in there to remind her to eat. Fortunately, Ida had managed that part for me.

When I mentioned three weeks, I never anticipated Juliet taking that long. I merely meant for her to read a few books, then come to me with questions. But no, she just kept flipping through the pages without the slightest hint of concern. I had wanted to use the truth to fracture her conditioning, but it did not appear to be working at all.

Which meant I was starving myself for no reason.

I could walk in there and fuck her—as Ivan so eloquently put it—then compel her to do my bidding, and I would if it came to that.

Ivan folded his arms in that condescending way he favored. "Have you tried talking to her?"

"My words won't be enough, not with the training she's undergone." I ran my fingers through my hair and blew out a breath. "Blood virgins are broken at a very young age and servitude is ingrained in their psyche. That sort of brainwashing is not easily overcome."

"But you think a few textbooks will do it?"

"It provides Juliet with a historical context of what humans used to mean to this world and creates doubt." Once I had that, I could rearrange her thinking and spark a need for revenge. "But she's read over fifteen books now and hasn't asked for any clarification."

"Does she think it's all fiction?" Ivan wondered.

I'd considered that possibility as well. "If she does, I don't know how to convince her otherwise."

Vampires and lycans had completely restructured the world to hide all hints of humanity's rule. Hope no longer lived here. All of my textbooks were considered illegal propaganda, not that I had any intention of ever giving them up.

"Will you discard her for a new one?" Ivan's tone suggested he didn't give a damn, but I knew he cared deep down. "Assuming she's defective, I mean."

"If she proves untrainable, then we'll have to determine an alternative," I admitted. The new plan wouldn't require a replacement so much as a more drastic approach. "But my goal is for it not to come to that."

"Right, because you want her compliance, which I still say is a waste of time." His dark eyes glinted in the moonlight as he narrowed his gaze. "You have the means to complete this task, but you're refusing to do what needs to be done. Just force her to drink a few times and fuck her, Darius. Then she'll be your *Erosita*, and you can control her."

I palmed the back of my neck to keep myself from punching him. The bastard was right, of course. I could solve this problem in a handful of nights if I put my mind to it. But I craved her consent. I didn't require it—I owned her—but I wanted her to be a willing party, not a coerced one.

"You're playing a mind game when you don't have to," Ivan continued, "because you're bored."

"Or perhaps I want to be better than the men I intend to kill," I suggested as I rolled my neck again. "Seriously, I need to go for a run." Anything to distract myself from walking into that library and doing exactly as my friend suggested.

"No, you need to feed," Ivan growled. "I just enjoyed the company of a pretty little blood whore, and yet, my fangs are aching at the scent of your *Juliet*."

"Aww, you're worried about me. That's cute." I jogged away, knowing the dolt would choose to follow me. He always did.

"You're an ass," he muttered as he met my pace. "A fucking lunatic too."

"You curse too much."

"Fuck you."

I grinned. "Point taken and ignored."

"As if that shocks you." He rolled the sleeves of his expensive sweater to his elbows, more out of habit than necessity. "And you can run all you like, mate, but we both know what you need to do."

My hands fisted. "The coronation is in six months. I have plenty of time to reprogram her. It'll be fine."

"Fine," he repeated. "I'll admit, Juliet is gorgeous and smells divine, but she's a shell of a woman and nowhere near capable of what you need to get this done. You'll end up compelling her anyway."

I increased the pace and pounded my frustration into the ground.

Ivan wasn't saying anything I didn't already know. Juliet had the assets, but if I couldn't convince her to use them the way I needed, I'd have to force her. She was too expensive of an investment to just throw away, and purchasing a replacement would create speculation I couldn't afford.

I had to proceed with the process.

The first step was breaking her conditioning.

The second step would be convincing her to work with me.

And the third would be retraining all her instincts.

In six months.

Not the best timeline, but it could be done. Assuming I had picked the right blood virgin.

I ducked as I hit the trees lining the edge of the courtyard and found my preferred forest trail. Ivan cursed beside me about his shoes but didn't back down.

Neither of us required the workout. We were forever frozen in our thirties thanks to vampire genetics, but I still enjoyed a good bout of physical exertion. It expunged unnecessary energy and kept my reflexes in check.

"I swear you're part lycan," Ivan muttered as he jumped over an extended root. "Next thing I know, you'll fucking shift on me."

"You complain too much. Next time I'm calling Trevor."

"Oh, right, like he'll muddy his shoes for you."

True. Trevor would just wait at the forest edge for me to return. "At least it would be a quiet run."

"You didn't call me here for quiet."

And this was why I considered Ivan one of my best friends. He knew me almost as well as Cam had, once upon a time.

I ran in silence for a few minutes before admitting, "I want to talk about the secondary plan."

"No shit."

"I haven't given up on Juliet yet," I continued, ignoring his commentary. "But I've found the right scapegoat."

He jumped over a log and landed deftly on his feet. "Lycan or vampire?"

"Neither. A rogue." I maneuvered around a wide tree and started up a steep incline without breaking my stride. One of the many benefits to vampirism was increased speed and agility, and the ability to carry on a conversation while running.

"Making it a rogue hit takes the blame off of us and would free up the sovereign's seat again," I added.

"And keeps your name in the dark," Ivan pointed out. "Thereby defeating the purpose."

"Not necessarily." I jumped over a massive rock and used a hint of my enhanced vampiric speed to propel me onward faster. "It prolongs the game a bit, but there are other ways to work my name into the masses."

Ivan whistled. "You're talking years down the road, mate. Our royal friend wouldn't be happy about that, and neither would the others."

"It's a backup plan," I clarified. "To be used if Juliet doesn't come through." But I had every intention of winning her over. "She's still our best option."

"Which is why I say to just get it over with, so we can begin the training bit." He circled around a tree and met me on the other side. "Or give her to me, and I'll handle it for you."

A vivid image of Ivan *handling* Juliet blurred my vision. She wouldn't refuse him, may even enjoy it. Just as she did my bite while in her room...

Her body had moved sensuously against mine as she surrendered to the pleasures of my touch. I could still hear her little moans and the way she said my name while in the throes of climax. My cock twitched with the sensual memory, then died at the thought of Ivan's suggestion.

I could picture it clearly—his body taking hers while his fangs penetrated her creamy neck...

Fuck no.

Negative energy zipped through my veins, heating my blood and clouding my better judgment.

Mine.

No one, other than me, would touch Juliet's innocence.

I elbowed the jackass mid-stride, sending him cascading to the ground with a grunt.

To even think he had the right...

My hands fisted as I considered hitting him again, only harder. Part of my violent need was a result of bloodlust and unnecessary starvation. But the other part was all possession.

"She's mine, Mikhail," I warned, using his surname. "The only one handling Juliet will be me."

"Proprietorial ass," he grumbled as he pushed off the ground. "It was an offer, not a request."

"I refuse."

48

"Clearly." He shook some leaves from his hair. "Do you want to spar or continue running?"

Aggression tinted the air between us. Ivan had known full well how I would react to his "offer," suggesting the bastard was testing my possessive instincts on purpose. It seemed he wanted to fight. I could use the exertion, and he would provide a decent challenge.

"Both," I decided. I would kick his ass, then continue my run.

"Great. Hit me, then," he taunted. "Or try."

I smiled. "The last time you dared me like this, I rearranged that pretty face of yours."

He shrugged. "I healed."

"You cried."

"Bullshit." He fell into a fighter's stance. "Now I want to put you on your ass just to prove a point."

"Yeah? And what would that be?"

"That I'm well fed and you're starved. Maybe afterward you'll finally feed."

I snorted. "Even half-dead, I could best you."

"That's Trevor," he corrected. "You called me because you wanted an actual opponent, in addition to the pep talk."

I couldn't deny that. "Stop talking out your ass and hit me, Ivan."

He smirked. "Gladly."

Chapter Seven

JULIET

Seventeen books were sprawled out over the library floor—all describing a world where humans ruled.

Yet none of them mentioned lycans or vampires.

Except for the one in my hand.

I'd found it buried in the shelves, the masculine scrawl across the cover having caught my eye.

The Formation.

It seemed to be a notebook rather than a reference text, but as I flipped through the handwritten pages, I finally caught some words I recognized.

I curled into the oversized chair near the fireplace—it'd become my preferred spot over the last week and a half—and began flipping through the handwritten pages.

It started with a description of a world war between

humans, something I'd read about five or six times now in the other textbooks. It's where most of the books ended, but this one began—another sign that I had picked something new.

I skimmed the familiar words concerning nuclear weapons and agreed with the stark comments regarding humans clearly wanting to destroy the world. Then I slowed as I read a new passage regarding lycans.

The Cyrus Clan outed us first. They were discovered in the late twenty-first century by a paramilitary unit searching for a missing woman from a nearby town. Apparently, the Alpha took a liking to the Governor's daughter and kidnapped her. So, truly, everything changed because of a woman.

This was definitely a journal.

I continued reading about how humans attempted to experiment with lycans in various ways, all of which resulted in failures to understand their biology. A few governments attempted to use their genetics for militaristic means, but failed.

Meanwhile, lycans and vampires met in secret to discuss the future of humanity. Several of the clansmen were furious about the treatment of the Cyrus Clan and demanded retribution, thus giving those who craved a reformed world a platform to stand upon. Hence, the Blood Alliance was formed.

The cadence of the words reminded me of Darius. Considering the notebook was stuffed in his shelves, it seemed appropriate for it to belong to him.

I turned the page, learning more about the uprising, where the superior species organized an attack that destroyed over half the human race and successfully took control of the world.

Humans were divided into camps to be tested. Spirit, strength, intelligence, beauty, and bloodline all contributed to the fate of each lesser being. Most were exterminated, leaving only 300,000 in existence for official sorting.

The Blood Alliance drafted legal requirements that suited both lycan and vampire and divided mortals into their requisite camps. All moral rights were removed, demoting humankind to property, and thus proclaiming them as objects to be owned and possessed as desired.

I shivered at the very real description of my purpose in this world. Vampires saw me as living food, to be enjoyed at will and otherwise ignored.

Although, Darius opened my eyes to a whole different regard of my kind. He allowed me to look at him, to talk to him, and he granted me pleasure.

But it could all be ripped out of my hands with a mere word from him.

I drew my nails down the page, considering the purpose. He asked me to review the textbooks, stating I should come to him when I finished reading the items on the floor and several from the shelves. I'd done as he requested, but still didn't understand why he gave me this task.

Did he mean to torture me with the history of my kind? How humans have been belittled to toys used for vampire and lycan enjoyment?

Or was it meant purely as informational, and a way to enhance my overall training?

I flipped to the next section defining the various mortal sectors. Blood farms, academies, immortal selection competitions, royal harems, clan breeding dens, human procreation camps—my eyes narrowed on a paragraph pertaining specifically to me.

Blood virgins are perhaps the most intriguing development. Their bloodlines are unique and considered to be almost lethally addictive. A special provision was made to allow for their genetic reproduction for the sole use of vampires, and in exchange lycans were given their own mortal line for full-moon games.

But what is truly fascinating is these blood virgins are being groomed for elite society. Both males and females exist in separate confines and are trained in the arts of intellectual affairs—unlike most humans—to better mingle with high society.

They are also groomed to be the perfect sexual pet, though most are only used once before being discarded. The lucky ones return to the

Coventus to train future virgins, while the majority of them are sent into the breeding cycle to procreate, then eventually the farms.

My lips parted on that last line of the page.

Breeding cycle—to create more blood virgins.

My matron always said the majority returned to the Coventus. Darius's notes implied that wasn't the case, that my fate would be to fornicate until I no longer proved fruitful.

Ice drizzled down my spine.

I existed to serve my master by providing him unlimited access to my blood and body. That was the sole purpose for my being. I meant nothing otherwise; just a pet to be used however he desired.

And then I was to be thrown away to create more for future pleasure.

But these books depicted a history where humans used to rule—not well, considering all the battles and wars, but they at least *lived*. While all I did was serve.

I blinked tears from my eyes as confusion poked holes in my bubbled existence.

Why me?

Why was this my fate?

Because of my blood.

And as a curse, I would be forced to produce more of my kind. Then that child would be sent to the Coventus to be trained, just as I was, to serve a new master before continuing the cycle.

My stomach churned, reminding me that I had forgotten to eat again today. But what did it matter?

I tossed the journal to the ground and found the history book depicting a strong female leader—human. She didn't smile, but her eyes bespoke of intelligence and determination. Mine would never resemble hers. When I looked in the mirror, I saw a soulless being who knew nothing about life. Because I resided in a shell shaped by my vampire betters.

They were more powerful, stronger, and immortal.

That granted them the ability to control everyone beneath them and to own a person like me.

Humans used to have rights.

Why would Darius require me to learn all of this?

It served no benefit other than to prove my place while removing all hope. Was that what he wanted to show me? In case I garnered any ideas about what we were doing here?

I preferred my state of ignorance where the Blood Alliance always existed as the superior power. Where humans were never in a position of authority. Where I had no inkling of an optimistic future.

He'd taken all that from me with this library of books.

Why?

I set the female leader aside and stood, determined.

What did I have to lose? He intended to use me and throw me away anyway. I might as well demand an explanation. Maybe he would kill me as a result. That had to be better than forced breeding.

My hands curled into fists as I stomped out of the library and turned toward the foyer. He told me only to visit him in his quarters for pleasure. He also told me to find him when I finished. Well, I was more than done.

Damn the rules and etiquette.

I required answers, and I wanted them now.

"Juliet," Ida called as I reached the bottom of the staircase.

Normally, I responded to her with a demure smile or a polite greeting, but my mouth revolted against both actions as I turned to face her. If she noticed my lack of courtesy, she didn't show it.

"If you're looking for Master Darius, he is out back with Master Ivan." She winked and wandered away in that oddly chipper way of hers.

Darius obviously hadn't given her the same reading assignment as me, or she wouldn't be nearly as content with her fate.

Then again, she wasn't going to be sent to the breeding camps to produce more blood virgins.

My lips thinned.

Outside.

I'd yet to venture beyond the doors of this large home. Darius had given me permission to wander at will, but I feared it might be a test. Now I no longer cared if I passed or not.

Something sweet tickled my nose on my way through the kitchen to the dining area. A few of Darius's servants mingled around, giving me curious looks as I went straight for the glass doors that led to the oversized patio beyond it.

I hesitated. This could be exactly how he wanted me to react and might be out there waiting to punish me.

He also said to find him when I finished reading.

The hairs along my arms danced as I considered breaking the one rule my matron warned me never to breach. Demanding the audience of a vampire typically earned the human a harsh punishment, even death.

But he instructed me to locate him after I completed my task, and I was done with those books.

I'd rather die than be forced to breed.

And the farms?

I shuddered. The term alone painted a picture I didn't want in my head.

Not my future.

I refused.

Because you have a choice?

The human's eyes flashed in my mind again from the photo of the female leader who clearly *lived*. What would I look like if I stood up to Darius? A warrior? Or would I stare lifelessly up at the evening sky?

Would it even matter?

My lips flattened as I twisted the handle.

I had nothing to lose. No life to value living. Just rules that dictated my every action. Darius had shattered several already. What was one more?

The stone patio chilled my bare feet as I wandered outside. It took me several steps before I realized the gravity of what I'd just done.

The only other time I had ventured outdoors was when the guards escorted me to Darius's waiting limo. And yet I'd just walked outside as though it meant nothing.

No alarms.

No guards.

I blinked.

If I'd even managed to reach a door at the Coventus, I would have been surrounded as soon as I touched the handle. Not that I ever considered trying. It just wasn't done. Why would I escape? Where would I go?

The moonlight illuminated a path to the trees, almost beckoning me to follow. I knew from my window view that the forest went on and on, but it had to stop eventually. Where would it take me? To a worse fate? A better one?

I stepped forward and paused at the new texture below me.

Grass.

How... quaint.

I knelt to touch the cool blades when a whisper to the left jolted me upright.

"Juliet..." The murmur caressed my ear, announcing Darius's presence just as he materialized behind me. Heat enveloped my body as he pressed his chest to my back and wrapped his forearm around my lower abdomen.

"Hello, darling." He pressed a kiss to my neck just as Master Ivan appeared before me. I'd barely even considered running, and already two powerful vampires had trapped me between them.

Ivan stood close enough to touch but didn't. Lust shone bright in his brown gaze as he stared down at me with an arrogance I could never match. He knew he could overpower me with a flick of his wrist, and he thrived on that knowledge. His lips quirked up in a grin, drawing my attention to the blood glistening on the corner of his mouth. It lent a ravenous appeal to his otherwise handsome face.

"No bowing and eye contact," he mused. "Even with a guest. I'd call that progress, Darius."

His words dumped ice water over my head, freezing me in place. I hadn't meant to look at his face, or meet his gaze, but I'd fallen into a casual cadence after spending however many days in the library. I'd been lost in a haze of history and forgotten all my training.

Or perhaps I *chose* to forget it.

"Indeed." Darius's lips brushed my pulse with the single word. "Have you ventured outside to feed us, darling?"

"F-feed?" I repeated, my throat dry.

Ivan ran his fingers through his dark hair and appraised me thoroughly with his flaring pupils. "I think your Juliet had other intentions. Pity."

"Is Ivan right? Did you seek my audience for a different purpose, Juliet?" Darius pulled my curls to one side, exposing the full column of my throat while I fought to remember how to breathe. "Have you finished reading?" His teeth scraped my sensitive skin, causing my abdomen to clench.

I knew the sensations that accompanied his bite now, and a dark part of me craved another. It seemed like just yesterday he'd held me in my bedroom, but I knew that wasn't right. Maybe a week ago? I'd been—

"Juliet." He nipped my neck in warning, bringing me back into the moment. "Did you complete the task I gave you? Is that why you've joined us?"

I swallowed—or tried to, anyway. His warmth at my back dismantled my resolve. I'd wanted to demand answers, but the intention and inevitable recourse didn't resemble one another.

He could snap me like a twig.

Or send me away to create more humans...

"I read," I said slowly, my voice hoarse. "Blood virgins go into the breeding cycle prior to being sent to the farms." I swallowed again before adding, "That is my fate." A sour note crept into my tone, one I'd never heard before. He didn't give me time to contemplate it.

"Mmm, you found my journal." He whirled me in his arms with that lightning-fast speed and twined his fingers in my hair. The moonlight cast eerie shadows across his face while highlighting his green irises. They blazed with a hunger I could almost taste, and he appeared to have a fading bruise on his right cheek. It rather satisfied me to see it there, though I couldn't determine why.

"You sound displeased with your fate, Juliet," he continued. "Any particular reason why?"

"Displeased," I repeated, trying the word. "That I am to be forced to create more of my kind? That my progeny will be offered up to the highest bidder, then forced to continue the cycle? And that I will inevitably go to a farm?" Each word strengthened my voice, raising me from a whisper to a pitch I'd never heard from my mouth before. "After learning that humans used to have rights?"

Why would he teach me this?

Did he mean to torture me?

To poke fun at my fate?

To taunt the poor human girl with a false hope that no longer existed?

"I'd say she sounds displeased," Ivan remarked, a smile in his voice.

My hands curled into fists in response. A violent reaction I'd never before considered...

"It would seem that way," Darius agreed, grinning.

That smug amusement drove my nails into my palms. How cruel they were to pick on the weakling and laugh at my plight. I *never* had a choice.

I was more than *displeased*.

My head spun with an inferno of details that clouded

my thoughts in a haze of red. Foreign emotions streamed through my conscious, heating my blood.

It consumed me.

Took hold of every nerve, demanding something I couldn't articulate.

My chest hummed with the need to scream.

And my fists clenched with the desire to hurt.

I couldn't do this. I couldn't breathe. Not with him so close.

I tried to dislodge myself from his hold, but he didn't budge. Instead he chuckled.

My eyes widened as a fire blossomed in my heart, causing my instincts to spiral out of control.

I wanted to hurt him.

Kick him.

Punch him.

Kill him.

All of them.

I'd never once even considered it an option, but knowing that humans had once fought for their lives against his kind encouraged all manner of thoughts.

"Yes," he murmured. "There's the emotion I wanted."

"Yeah, good luck taming it, mate," Ivan said as he started toward the back patio. "I don't envy you the task."

Chapter Eight

Darius

The moment Juliet's scent hit my senses, I'd phased back to the estate with Ivan on my tail. I rarely used the teleportation-like ability, but I'd wanted to know what brought her outside.

And I couldn't be more delighted with the furious expression on her face now. It painted her cheeks a lovely shade of rose and deepened the allure of her plump lips. But it was the blaze in her dark eyes that intrigued me most.

This was the woman I wanted to invite out to play.

"What else did you read in my journal?" I wondered. "About the immortal bond?"

Her nose flared. "You intend to use me for my purpose and send me to a breeding camp."

I smirked. "That is the usual path, but tell me what else you read."

She tried to move away again, but I held her in place. "I do not wish to procreate!" she shouted, shocking me.

"Juliet—"

She squirmed violently, her body trembling with unsuppressed emotion as tears pricked her eyes.

Okay, the rage I enjoyed.

This, not so much.

I'd wanted to destroy her training, not the woman herself.

"Stop," I demanded, tightening my grip. "Juliet."

"No," she whispered brokenly. "I'd rather die." Her legs gave out, leaving her limp in my arms. I lifted her with ease, cradling her against my chest as she wept silently.

My resolve faltered at the sight of her training kicking in even as she mourned. Displays of strong emotion were punished by my kind, hence her attempt to mask her sobs by remaining quiet.

I shook my head. "You didn't read beyond the part about breeding, did you?"

Her lips moved, but no sound escaped.

I interpreted that as a confirmation that she'd not finished my notebook. She'd probably been too shocked to bother with the next page. A pity considering it would have given her a glimpse of the hope she so desperately needed.

Ivan had meandered into the house at the first sign of emotion and met me at the back door as I approached. He didn't say a word as I carried Juliet past him and the staff.

I considered taking her upstairs to her room but decided a detour to the library would benefit us both.

She didn't move or utter a sound as I walked through the threshold of the room she'd practically lived in these last ten days.

I wandered over to her bizarre arrangement of books on the floor. A familiar photo of a former female president glowered up at me, reminding me of a time where humans ruled unsuccessfully. Juliet must have found that fascinating since she left it on the chair for everyone to see.

Holding her with one arm, I bent to retrieve my notebook from the ground. "You didn't finish reading."

"I don't care," she managed on a choked whisper. "Punish me. Kill me. I don't care."

Those last few words were mouthed more than voiced, but I understood the resolve in her expression. She preferred death to her future. I couldn't blame her. Most would feel the same in her position.

I settled in the chaise lounge with her in my lap. "I have no desire to kill you, Juliet." It would be a waste of an exquisite blood virgin. I pushed the hair away from her pretty face with my free hand and held out my book with the other. "Finish reading."

She balked at the notebook and curled into my chest. "No." A pleading note colored her tone as she tucked her chin to hide her face.

"No?" I repeated, minutely impressed by her refusal.

She appeared to be both denying me and seeking comfort from me at the same time. An odd combination that stemmed from having her world turned upside down. I wouldn't apologize, but I could be lenient with her. To an extent.

"I'll read to you instead." And hopefully the additional explanation would help our situation.

I thumbed through the familiar pages, searching for my retelling of the sorting process.

This notebook had been my way of dealing with the formation of our new world.

As a former professor, I lived in a land of textbooks and research. Documentation came naturally, but I stopped writing when the Blood Alliance reached a status quo nearly a century ago. Their operation was seamless due to a hundred years of sharpening the edges and removing all those who opposed the movement—such as

Cam.

Whispers of a revolution had died with my maker's proclaimed demise, leaving me with nothing new to document.

Until recently, anyway.

I found the section I wanted, ending with the line about the farms. Juliet hadn't confirmed it, but I felt certain this was where she had stopped reading, so I flipped to the next page.

"Then there are those select few who are gifted with an eternity of servitude. Some may consider death a preferable alternative beneath these new customs, as the ceremony that once required mutual agreement has now been tainted by enslavement. While society scoffs at the notion of bonded mates, it's still deemed an acceptable practice under the Blood Alliance laws."

I paused to ensure I had her attention and found her studying the book in my hand. Her shoulders still trembled, but the sobs had stopped. I took that as a sign to continue.

"Once a blood virgin—or any human for that matter—undergoes the ceremony, the human is considered valued property and is granted certain allowances. One such concession is the ability to attend social events with his or her master. Although elite society mocks the ritual, it is inevitably revered and garners a certain prestige that inspires envy from many. To touch another vampire's blood virgin, especially one granted ceremonial rights, is punishable by immediate death."

And that last bit was what intrigued me most. For some males couldn't resist the forbidden, particularly one of Juliet's caliber. Marking her as my *Erosita* would make her irresistible to my brethren, especially those who craved power.

I lowered the journal and focused on the gorgeous woman curled in my lap. She wore another one of those short dresses, causing me to wonder what Ida had purchased for her. Surely a pair of pants and a normal shirt?

"I..." Juliet licked her lips, her brow furrowed. "I don't understand what you're trying to tell me."

Yes, I supposed she wouldn't. Or perhaps she suspected but didn't wish to hope. I set the notebook on the side table and wrapped my arms around her waist to hold her close.

The comforting move likely confused her even more, but it was more for me than for her. I enjoyed the feel of holding a woman, specifically one who smelled decidedly edible.

"The purpose of reading all these books was to give you insight into the history of humanity." I glanced over her array of items on the floor. Everything from ancient mythology to the last of the world wars stared back at me. "Did you read all of these?"

"Yes," she whispered. "But I didn't finish the notebook."

I determined as much already. "You read more than enough to understand that lycans and vampires have not always ruled, and that the world has not always operated as it does today."

She nodded as some of that fire sparked in her alluring eyes.

Good. That's what I craved from her, that anger. It would help this conversation flow to my advantage.

"If you think the treatment of blood virgins is unjust, then you should witness a Blood Day." I gently rubbed my palms over her bare arms to help temper my yearning to possess her. Knowing that I could do whatever I wanted without retribution didn't help matters. But I knew her agreeing to help me would be so much sweeter than compelling her into action.

"So the purpose was to show me that my life could be worse?"

I grinned at the hint of irritation in her tone. "No,

darling, the purpose was to give you context. You see, I have a proposition for you, and I couldn't offer it without the history lesson."

She twisted in my lap to fully meet my gaze. I'd required her to make eye contact whenever we spoke, but this felt different. Stronger, more confident—as though she felt she had the right to study me. It demonstrated a flaw in her conditioning, and that thrilled me.

"A proposition," she repeated, her brow pinched. "I'm yours to command, Sire. Why would you wish to offer me anything?"

I palmed the back of her neck and brushed my thumb over her steady pulse. She'd calmed down considerably since arriving in the library. Her flushed cheeks and puffy eyes remained, but her breathing had returned to normal.

"Hmm." She had the most alluring lips. I tried to ignore them, but being this close to her, with her supple body in my lap, I couldn't resist. "Your purpose has always been to serve a master, with the intention of it being temporary, yes?"

Juliet's heart rate escalated—just a little—but the usual fearful glint in her eye didn't appear as she nodded. *Intriguing.*

"From what I understand, they teach you to expect death." It served as a way to train the humans not to react to the inevitable. It also functioned as a brainwashing mechanism to remind them of their place at the bottom of the food chain. I observed her closely as I added, "I don't want your service to me to be temporary."

Her tongue darted out to dampen her lips as my words hit their mark. "You refer to… to the ceremony? From your journal?"

"Yes." I traced the column of her neck with my thumb and tracked the move with my eyes. "But I want something in return."

"What would you have from me?" she asked softly. "I'm already yours."

"Mmm, true." I threaded my fingers in her hair and pulled her closer, leaving a scant inch between our mouths. "I own your body and blood, but what I desire is your soul."

"You wish to kill me, Sire?" she breathed against my lips.

"No, darling, I wish to mold you into the perfect poison." I skimmed my nose along her blushing cheek before pressing a kiss to her throat.

Temptation personified.

My incisors ached to bite her. Ten days without her blood had been too long. I'd taken from some of the donors living in my estate, but it hadn't whetted my appetite in the slightest. If anything, I only craved her more.

She swallowed. "A poison?"

I smiled against her neck. "Yes. A lethal one."

"I'm not sure I follow, Sire."

"You're irresistible, Juliet," I breathed against her ear. "By making you mine through the ceremony, I'm creating a forbidden fruit that my kind will be unable to resist. And I will use that temptation to my advantage." She was the perfect poison, and I intended to exploit her accordingly.

"But how will you use me, Sire? What will be requested of me?" Arousal thickened her tone as her body instinctively responded to my unsuppressed yearnings. That kind of training could not be taught; it was all related to her bloodline and its natural response to my nearness. Some considered it a mating mechanism, while others a gift from the heavens. I thought of it as an opportunity.

"I could answer that in so many ways, darling." But I knew what she meant. "If you agree to the ceremony, I will use you to destroy my enemies. They'll never know what hit them. And I will most definitely use you to sate my every need as well." Because having her here and not enjoying the luxury of her company would be a waste of a perfectly good bedmate.

"I've only begun to demonstrate what I can offer you, Juliet." I placed an openmouthed kiss beneath her ear and grinned at her responding shiver. "And I believe I've shown that living here can be quite pleasurable for us both, yes?"

"Would...?" She cleared her throat. "Would this c-continue?"

"My seducing you?"

"And the other things?" she asked.

"You mean pleasure?"

She whimpered as I explored the column of her neck with my tongue. "Y-yes." I couldn't tell if she meant that as an invitation to continue or in response to my clarification. Perhaps both.

"As I mentioned during your tour of the estate, you're welcome in my room any time you desire more pleasure." I shifted to meet her gaze. "But tonight, I require it."

Her chest rose and fell in quick succession. So beautiful. I wanted to tug down her dress to reveal those gorgeous breasts and nibble every inch. This time I would take as well as give.

"My purpose is to sate your needs, whatever they may be," she said softly.

"Mmm, but I insist you give me everything, Juliet." I pulled away from the temptation of her blood to capture her hypnotic gaze. "You're trained to mingle with high society, to converse in various languages, and to seduce with a glance. All admirable traits, but what I desire to teach you is vastly different from what you already know."

She gazed up at me with an innocence I planned to destroy. I supposed that made me the villain in her story, or perhaps, her savior.

"Will you agree to learn more, Juliet?" I loosened my hold in her hair to run my fingers through her thick locks. "In exchange, I can offer you the initial ceremony. It will grant you unique privileges within society and mark you as mine, thus protecting you from any alternative future. And it will stop your aging." At least temporarily. The blood exchange had to be repeated several times prior to my claiming her body, but even the initial stages would gift her certain rights and strengths.

"Stop my aging?" she repeated.

"Yes. The bond between us will grant you immortality, darling."

Her pupils flared. "Immortality?" A note of awe touched her soft voice. She clearly hadn't understood my comment regarding eternal servitude from the journal. "And, er, what does the ceremony require?"

"Your willingness to meet my needs," I replied. "As for the ritual itself, you'll drink from me." *And I'll eventually fuck you to oblivion and back.*

Her eyes widened. "That's forbidden, Sire."

I smiled. "No, only the turning is outlawed. The ceremony is very legal. You'll understand after we attend our first social outing."

Several would ridicule my actions, but most would envy them. Blood virgins, especially one as tempting as Juliet, were rare and coveted. Purchasing her was the first step in drawing attention to my reemergence into society. Keeping her would be the second. Sometimes one had to play the game before destroying it.

I gathered her curls over one shoulder and forcibly relaxed into the chair. Touching her was an obsession, and I needed to focus.

"Immortality, pleasure, and safety, Juliet. That's what I offer. In return, I want your compliance and cooperation in everything I desire. It won't be easy, and you will do things for me that you will not enjoy, but I believe the benefits will outweigh the negatives in the end. The decision, however, is yours."

Chapter Nine

JULIET

"The decision, however, is yours."

False. Nothing in my life was ever *my* decision. I existed to provide sex and sustenance to a master—something I always accepted. It wasn't a debate or an opinion, merely a fact of life.

Except the books sprawled out around us painted a different world, one where humans were given choices and allowed to live as they wanted.

That world no longer prevailed.

I had no rights here.

No choices.

I lived for Darius's pleasure for as long as he wanted me. My matron prepared me for the inevitability of being discarded, though she never mentioned the alternatives.

The notebook clarified everything. Blood virgins weren't necessarily killed by their masters, so much as sent elsewhere to procreate.

And a select few were offered the ceremony.

Darius didn't explain what all that entailed, but I inferred enough to understand his proposition.

If I refused him, he would return me to the Coventus or send me somewhere worse. Or maybe even kill me. He could, and no one would care.

Yet he claimed the decision was mine.

A lie.

Accepting the ceremony was the only option, even if it did require me to give him everything. But my very purpose was to please him, with or without the offer of immortality. That made his proposal more of a gift since he owed me nothing at all.

And living with him thus far hadn't been nearly as horrible as I originally expected. He provided pleasure where most elicited pain. Even now, his gaze held a voracious hunger that he controlled with admirable ease. The vampires of my limited acquaintance didn't wait, they took. Yet Darius possessed a patience I admired, and a touch I craved.

There was no choice.

I would accept.

Saying no earned me nothing, while agreeing granted me opportunity, even if temporary.

It would never truly be consent, not without any other feasible alternative. But humans didn't possess the right to decide; we merely did as we were told. Which made my response easy.

"I'll do anything you wish, Sire." *It's why I'm here.*

"Mmm." He tilted his head to the side and drew his thumb over his bottom lip. "You will, yes, but that's not entirely what I wanted." His pupils dilated as he studied me. "Well, I suppose it's a start. We can revisit my requirements after I teach you more about what I *wish* for

70

you to do."

"Of course, Sire." I doubted it would convince me otherwise. Even if he chose to turn me into a poison—whatever that meant—I'd do whatever he requested. Because there was no other option, unless I wanted to breed or be sent to the farms. Hopefully, I wouldn't disappoint him.

"Then we'll initiate the ceremony," he murmured, his hands settling on my hips.

I swallowed. "Now?"

"Yes." He tightened his grasp. "Straddle me."

Electricity zipped down my spine as I shifted on his lap to place my legs on the outside of his thighs. It stretched the fabric of my dress, causing it to bunch closer to his fingers.

"You won't need to drink a lot from me." He ran his palms up and down my sides, creating a trail of fire through the thin fabric. "But I'll demand more of your blood in return, especially as I've not fed well in the last two weeks."

I studied the hollows beneath his eyes. Most vampires required daily nourishment, but the older and stronger ones could survive on little. That he hadn't come to me every day for a meal said a lot about his status. I'd not considered it until now.

But if he hadn't fed much, as he said, then he would indeed necessitate a lot from me. It would intensify his bite and, potentially, the pleasure that accompanied it. He did mention requiring the latter tonight.

A quiver worked its way over my limbs as I considered what that would entail. Surely he meant to deflower me as well.

It would hurt.

But I also might enjoy it.

There is something very wrong with me.

All the reading and unexpected conversations had derailed my being. I no longer knew what to anticipate, but one thing was certain.

"I'm ready, Sire." Pleasing him would not be a hardship, even if he did inflict pain. I gathered my hair to one side to expose my throat for easy access. It was my way of inviting him to feed, not that he needed it.

His hands fell to my exposed thighs as he relaxed into the chaise and gazed up at me with hooded eyes. All vampires were attractive, but my breath caught at the desire radiating from Darius's handsome features. He truly was one of the most beautiful men I'd ever seen.

No, this definitely would not be a hardship at all.

He traced the edge of my dress with his thumbs and inched the fabric upward. The hairs along my arms danced as he skirted the crease of my bottom.

I swallowed.

He's going to touch me again.

Pleasure...

Cool air met my intimate flesh, eliciting a tremble from deep within.

Yes.

"Mmm, as I thought," he murmured as the material gathered around my waist. "You're not wearing anything beneath this dress." His gaze fell to the apex between my thighs.

"I was instructed never to wear undergarments," I whispered.

"A rule that can remain," he said as his hand explored the zipper along my spine. It slowly loosened, bit by bit.

My breath hitched as he hit the base. I'd been naked in front of him before, but this felt different. My pulse didn't beat out of fear, but out of yearning.

Bite me, I nearly said, catching the words before they could escape on a groan.

He tugged the dress down, exposing my breasts. My nipples pebbled to painful peaks as I waited for whatever came next.

But he removed his hands and relaxed into the chair

instead. "Gorgeous."

My skin heated beneath his slow visual inspection. Sensation stirred between my legs, begging me to find friction while I fought to remain still.

Oh, Goddess…

I wanted to squirm.

To lie against him.

Seek comfort.

Something. *Anything.*

"Sire," I managed, my voice sounding foreign to my ears.

"Yes, Juliet?" He folded his hands behind his head. "What do you desire?"

"I…" I licked my lips. "I wish to please you."

One eyebrow inched upward. "Do you?"

I nodded. "Yes." It would give me a distraction from the ache forming inside and also allow me to touch him—to explore him. "Oh, yes. Very much." The words flowed without my permission, but I couldn't take them back even if I wanted to. Amusement radiated from him.

"Very well. On your knees, Juliet." The command in his voice soothed me and provided the guidance I craved.

I slid from his lap to the floor and assumed a submissive position, as requested. This was the training I understood. He shifted to place his feet on either side of me, bracketing me between his strong thighs.

"You may please me in two ways," he murmured as he loosened his pants. They weren't his usual suit trousers, but of the athletic variety. I thought he meant to remove them, but he lifted his wrist to his mouth instead and bit down hard enough to draw blood. "Drink."

"For the ceremony," I breathed.

"Yes." He lowered the wound to my lips. "Now, before it closes."

"Yes, Sire." I couldn't refuse him, not when he used that tone. I grasped his hand and tentatively licked the area he desired.

His sweet essence touched my tongue, surprising me.

That... isn't horrible.

Actually, it's quite pleasant.

I closed my lips over the laceration and drew more into my mouth. His hand fisted in mine, as his opposite palm clasped the back of my head to hold me against him. I interpreted that as a sign to continue drinking and complied.

A humming simmered in my mind, causing my eyes to fall closed. It compelled me to take more, to suck harder. I responded instinctually, pulling more and more of his blood into my mouth and swallowing, until he threaded his fingers in my hair and yanked me away from his wrist.

My breaths came in pants as my body desired more, but he held me with ease.

"I want you to do that to my cock." His sharp tone snapped me from my daze and forced me into action. He released me to tug down his pants. My heart skipped a beat at the sight of his prominent erection. Not all men were created equal, and Darius put many of the others I'd seen to shame.

And he intends to put that inside me...

My thighs clenched in response.

"Your mouth, Juliet. Now."

"Yes, Sire," I managed roughly.

I can do this.

My matron taught me several techniques both through demonstration and by having me practice on similarly shaped items. But I'd never held a man in this manner.

I grasped the base and gave him a hesitant stroke.

So hot... I hadn't expected that, or the soft skin.

He pulsed in my palm, encouraging me to glide my hand over him again, this time with more pressure than before.

"Stop teasing and suck my cock," he demanded.

I leaned forward to take him deep into my mouth the way I knew he would enjoy. His head fell back on a groan of approval that I felt through every fiber of my being. I swallowed as much of him as I could before retreating and starting again.

"Fuck," he growled, his hands grabbing my head to help guide my ministrations.

An intense craving built between my legs as I pictured him entering my body as he did my mouth.

Oh, Goddess, I never thought I would want that, but I did.

My thighs clamped together as I moaned around his thick shaft.

"Do that again," he said, his voice hoarse. "Moan my name."

I did, not because he told me to, but because I *needed* to. "Darius" rolled off my tongue onto his bulbous head before I sucked him so hard he hit the back of my throat.

He fisted my hair on both sides and shoved himself into me even farther, making it impossible to breathe. I grabbed his hips for support as he began roughly plunging himself between my lips.

Darius grunted my name and a string of curses while I fought for air. Each harsh thrust taunted the ache throbbing inside me, stirring a yearning for him to take me in the same savage manner. It would hurt, but so did this, and I enjoyed it.

Tears stung my eyes as his fingers curled even more harshly, tugging at my strands. His movements sharpened in a sign I recognized.

"Breathe deep, Juliet," he rasped.

I inhaled as much as he allowed and relaxed my throat as best I could to accept his pleasure. He went impossibly deeper, forcing my lips to hit the base of his shaft as he emptied his seed with a possessive groan.

My legs trembled as I endeavored not to choke on his ruthless invasion. He loosened his hold just enough to give me room to gasp and swallow while remaining in my mouth.

I met his gaze as I finished, causing his lips to curl. "You're worth everything I paid for and more, darling." He combed his fingers through my hair as he slowly eased my mouth off of him. "But I still need to feed."

"Yes, Sire," I whispered through my aching windpipe.

He smiled. "Remove your dress."

I gathered the fabric at my waist and pulled it over my head to set on the floor while I remained kneeling before him. He stood and tucked himself back into his pants, only inches from my face.

His palm caressed my cheek as he stared down at me. "You looked so beautiful with my cock in your mouth. We will be doing that again very soon."

I was about to agree to his wishes, but Darius pressed his thumb to my lips, silencing me.

"Lie down on the chaise with your legs spread," he murmured. "On your back."

My knees protested as I tried to rise, and he held out his hand to help me from the ground. I accepted with a murmured "Thank you" before moving into the position he requested on the cushions.

He admired me for a moment, his gaze touching every exposed angle. "Slide farther up."

I moved until my head hit the upward cushion of the chair as he knelt on the bottom of the chaise. His palms clasped my calves before slipping higher to force my legs farther apart.

My shoulders hitched as he settled on his elbows between my thighs, placing his face directly above my dampening folds. "Mmm, you're glistening for me. I approve, darling."

I jolted as he placed an openmouthed kiss against my most sensitive area.

"Oh…" My nails dug into the cushions. "S-sire…" My pelvis bucked into his mouth as he suckled my intimate nub. "I…" I had no words.

It felt…

Amazing.

Hot and cold.

I shivered even as a fire blossomed inside. His fingers trailed up my inner thighs and joined his mouth to torture me more. Two digits entered me at once, causing me to yelp and moan simultaneously.

Never in my wildest dreams had I expected something quite like this.

His tongue... I didn't know they could move this way. Darius flattened and curled it, right where I desired him most. My legs trembled beneath his assault as my veins heated with some exuberant fluid.

His teeth scraped my delicate nerves, sending a shock through my system. He couldn't mean to bite me there. It would hurt far too much, and—

A scream caught in my throat as he pierced my skin just above, not enough to feed, but enough for me to bleed.

"D-Darius," I whimpered as flame overwhelmed every aspect of my being. He'd done something, sent some sort of wave of ecstasy through me with that nick, leaving every part of me throbbing uncontrollably.

"Embrace it, Juliet." The words vibrated my tender flesh, making me convulse. Then he suckled me hard into his mouth, and stars exploded behind my eyes.

I no longer cared how loud I yelled or that it was his name rolling through the air. He'd done something so incredible, so powerful, that I couldn't even begin to comprehend.

My soul detached from my body, returned, and escaped again. It left me shaking and moaning and crying. I couldn't stop. Wave after wave of euphoria hit me, and I barely even registered that Darius had moved from my center to my thigh. His thumb circled my inflamed nub while he drank directly from my femoral artery, weakening me by the minute.

But I couldn't focus enough to care.

I just felt.

And floated.

And luxuriated.

"Darius," I breathed as darkness dimmed the stars. Some part of me knew we were heading down a dangerous path. I struggled to emerge enough to warn him, to beg him...

"D..." My mouth felt dryer than it should. Heavy. I tried to lick my lips but couldn't move my tongue.

Everything felt so much cooler than moments ago.

Numb.

Darius.

Midnight consumed my vision as I blinked into a starless night.

So alone.

I always expected to die...

I never expected to want to live.

Until today.

Until Darius inspired hope.

Another cruel vampire joke.

I should have known—

Chapter Ten

Darius

"Sleep," I whispered as I covered Juliet with a blanket. She looked so pale, but her heart beat healthily in my ears. The marks on her thighs had already healed. "My gorgeous Juliet."

I brushed the curls away from her face and bent to kiss her forehead. We'd only just begun the ceremonial process, but it would be enough for now. In the morning I would start her training. Perhaps after I fucked her beautiful mouth again.

Taking her virginity would have to wait. For now. I wanted to test her first, to determine just how far she would be willing to go to *please* me.

Regardless, I would keep her. She more than proved her worth on her knees, but if I could train her beyond the bedroom, her worth to me would be infinite.

"I'm impressed you've gotten this far," Ivan said. He leaned against the wall of my bedroom with his arms folded. "But you still have a way to go, mate. She's a beautiful doll, but looks are not everything for this job."

I ran my finger down her arm and back up. "She has spirit."

"Yes, but is it enough?"

"Only time will tell," I admitted. "But with the proper motivation, I think it will work."

Ivan scratched his jaw. "If you pull this off, you'll have earned that seat."

"We both know this is about more than power."

His brown eyes blazed. "Yes, but it's a side benefit."

"The side benefit," I repeated, my gaze falling on the beauty resting in my bed. "Will be watching our enemies fall at the hands of their very own creation."

It would be the sweetest revenge, and so very deserved.

"If anyone can pull this off, it's you," Ivan said as he pushed away from the wall. "You always did fancy the impossible."

I grinned. "I prefer to call it a challenge."

"Sure, mate." He left with a backward wave, leaving me alone with my future *Erosita*. Poor Juliet wanted to please me yet had no idea what I truly desired from her.

"You'll learn," I murmured as I ran my knuckles over her cheek. "And when I succeed, you'll be the most lethal weapon in my armory."

Both alluring and deadly.

And mine to train.

Fuck the Blood Alliance.

Part Two

CHASTELY CLAIMED

Chapter Eleven

DARIUS

Six Weeks Later...

"She's not ready." Ivan pitched his voice low for my ears alone.

I sipped my bourbon while observing the room. "Yes, that's the point."

"You're risking her life, Darius."

"Which is my prerogative and choice, Ivan." Besides, she'd be well within my sight, and when she found herself in trouble, I'd save her. Tonight was about introducing Juliet to our future together, not harming her.

I fixed my tie while Ivan shook his head. "When does the show start?"

"As soon as Viktor expresses his interest," I replied.

"Well, considering he's salivating all over her, it won't take long."

I smirked, agreeing.

Juliet's translucent gown left nothing to the imagination, yet she wore it beautifully. It wasn't confidence so much as acceptance. Putting her body on display for a room full of vampires barely fazed her. She kept her dark eyes downcast, using her perceived obedience to her advantage.

And her blood...

Fuck, it aroused the entire room. Everyone would sense her chastity, as well as her purpose here—to entertain and provide sustenance.

And no one could touch her without my permission because she belonged to me.

To fuck.

To please.

To devour.

To share.

Anything I wanted.

Her dark gaze lifted to mine, then fell again. I suppressed a smile at her blatant show of defiance. To meet a master's stare without permission was expressly forbidden even though I allowed it at home. Here, however, was a risk to us both.

Maybe she would surprise me after all.

"He's interested," Ivan muttered beside me. "Lecherous prick."

I grinned against my glass tumbler. "You're just sour that I've taken on the task of killing him."

"No, I'm pissed that you're risking her life for a job I could do in my sleep," he retorted.

I snorted. He was right, of course, but there would be consequences involved if Ivan assassinated a prestigious member of the Blood Alliance. Juliet, however, afforded us a unique opportunity.

Touching another vampire's property without

permission resulted in dire consequences. Harming the property enhanced the crime, making death a more than acceptable outcome. Even for high-ranking political members.

"Look at him," Ivan added darkly. "He'll have her on her back in seconds. She doesn't stand a chance."

I studied the blond male over the rim of my glass and shrugged. "I gave her a knife."

"That she barely knows how to use," Ivan countered.

Semantics. I demonstrated the key motions with her earlier. "All she needs to do is create a scene, maybe cut him in the process, and I'll take care of the rest."

"Because *that* will be easy for a woman with her history." Ivan shook his head. "You seriously overestimate her abilities."

"On the contrary, I'm well acquainted with her talents." Innuendo deepened my voice as I observed Juliet. I'd left her there to help the other human in the room hand out appetizers and drinks, something I had hoped would put her at ease. It also gave her a grander purpose, one that allowed her to mingle freely with the guests while being ogled to the fullest extent.

"None of which have anything to do with helping to assassinate a vampire," my oldest friend growled. "Let me handle this one."

"No." A flat command. One that few would be brave enough to dare contend. "I can't break her conditioning until I fully understand how it works. So you will not intervene. I have this handled."

Ivan's lips tightened just enough for me to notice. He clearly did not approve of my methods but remained quiet.

"Careful, old friend," I teased softly. "Or I'll start to think you might actually care about the girl."

He scoffed at that. "She's a fuck doll." Ivan and Trevor's favorite term for my pretty little toy. "I just think you're wasting a significant investment."

True. Juliet did cost a small fortune, but that was

exactly the point. Owning her added to my prestige, something that gave me leverage in the political arena. Vampires admired wealth over all else because it equated to age and power, and I possessed all three traits in abundance.

"Darius," a deep voice spoke from the left. Not my mark for the evening, but an important society member.

"Sebastian." I held out my hand. "It's been a long time."

"It has," he agreed as he pressed his palm to mine. "I was beginning to think you'd decided to hibernate for eternity."

Ivan chuckled. "No, just a century."

I feigned amusement. "It's difficult to hibernate with Ivan constantly stopping by to irritate me."

"Cheers." Ivan knocked back the rest of his drink and set the glass to the side. "Someone had to ensure you were alive."

"Clearly, I'm fine," I replied dryly. "I've merely enjoyed my privacy of late."

"Yes, when I heard you had stepped out for the most recent auction, I thought for sure it to be a mistake." Sebastian eyed Juliet with interest across the room.

"As you can see, it's not," I replied. "I decided it was time to indulge more in the finer parts of society and desired something delectable to accompany me."

"I'd say you succeeded." Sebastian hadn't taken his eyes off her yet, something I couldn't entirely fault him for. That was her purpose, after all.

"Yes, I believe I did," I murmured, pleased with his assessment.

"It's good to have you back." Sebastian's tone held no hint of a lie and neither did his gaze as he finally refocused on me. "At least, I assume that is the purpose of your attendance tonight?"

"I'm easing into it slowly." I finished my bourbon and placed the tumbler on the table beside Ivan's discarded glass. "This seemed a reasonable event in which to socialize. Maybe I'll attend the coronation later this year as well." The absolute truth considering I intended to be crowned the new sovereign of this region. Not that anyone outside of my circle knew that—yet.

Sebastian's eyebrows lifted. "You mean to involve yourself in politics?"

I allowed myself a small grin. "*Involve* is such a strong word. Let's just say, I'm interested in mingling with old friends." And winning over their favor in the process. Starting with tonight. Viktor was one of the candidates up for consideration, and I intended to rectify that by using Juliet as bait.

"Hmm, well, should you decide you want to play, be sure to talk to me. I think the alliance could benefit from a man with your skill set."

I hid my resulting smile. Sebastian carried significant weight in the political arena. Having him on my side would certainly be a benefit, and exactly the kind of support I intended to recruit.

"I appreciate the vote of confidence," I replied smoothly. "And I will take your suggestions under advisement."

"Do," he encouraged, handing me his card. "We should catch up formally, perhaps over dinner sometime this week?" His gaze shifted to Juliet as he spoke, his underlying request clear.

"Of course," I murmured, pleased. Already Juliet was serving her purpose in helping me recruit allies. And all she needed to do was exist. "I'll give you a call to arrange."

"Brilliant." He held out his hand and I accepted it. "I've missed you."

"Likewise," I lied.

Ivan stood silently beside me as Sebastian took his leave, then asked, "Am I invisible?"

I grinned. "Only to a man of status."

"You're a man of status and you seem to notice me just

fine."

"Because you refuse to leave my side." Like an irritating gnat who buzzed permanently around my personal space. Except I actually liked him.

"Jackass," he muttered, causing me to smile. Very few would dare to call me such a name, but Ivan did it with a skill I greatly admired. It was why I'd selected him as a best friend.

"You seem to be getting on well," Trevor said as he joined us in the corner. "And your little fuck doll is causing quite the stir."

"Is she?" I mused, following his gaze to Juliet. She stood beside the bar, holding a tray of drinks, all of which were laced with blood. "I hadn't noticed."

Trevor chuckled. "Liar. You'll have her naked over your lap the second you depart."

True. "She does wear that dress rather well."

"Is that what it's called?" Ivan asked. "Because it reminds me of lingerie."

"It flows to the ground," I pointed out. "It just happens to be translucent and slit up to her hip on both sides. Easier access to the femoral artery that way."

I snapped my fingers and her head lifted immediately, her dark eyes catching mine for a split second before she started toward us with the tray. No one tried to stop her, but several of my kind observed her ambulation across the room.

When she reached me, she curtsied. "Sire."

"Are you all right, darling?" I asked softly as I took a flute from her tray. Ivan and Trevor followed suit.

"Yes, Sire," she whispered.

"Then you're ready?" I pressed, already knowing she wasn't anywhere near prepared for the task at hand.

But she nodded anyway. "It's what you wish, Sire. So yes."

Ivan rolled his eyes beside me while Trevor grinned wickedly. He was clearly looking forward to Viktor's future demise. I met my mark's gaze and read the inquiry in his expression.

"It seems he's ready too," I murmured as I inclined my head discreetly toward the door beside me. Beyond it lay a hallway that led to several private quarters. I'd already informed Juliet which one I intended for her to use. Viktor would be able to find her on scent alone.

I pressed a kiss to her temple as I passed her tray to Ivan.

"Don't fail me, Juliet," I whispered against her ear. To Viktor, it would appear that I'd just given her a command while the rest of the room merely witnessed me conversing with my pet. This was all a very delicate dance. If anyone caught the subtle exchange between me and Viktor, the plan would fail.

Which was why I had Trevor and Ivan there to observe. They both gave me understated nods of approval, confirming no one had noticed.

"Y-yes, Sire."

"Remember my warning," I added, my lips brushing her pulse. "Now go."

"Sire." She curtsied again before disappearing through the door.

I fixed my tie and smiled good-naturedly at my closest friends. "Punishing her failure later will be fun."

Ivan swirled the contents in his flute, his gaze hard. "You're a sadistic ass, D."

"More like a genius," Trevor corrected.

"Don't worry, Ivan. I'll ensure she enjoys it too." Or I would try, anyway. It depended on just how badly she fucked this up.

Viktor approached, his gaze darkening with ravenous hunger. My smile fell slightly as I considered what I was about to unleash on Juliet. If that look was anything to go by, then it would take significant effort not to act too soon on her behalf.

"Thank you," he whispered as he passed me on his way

toward the exit.

I lifted an eyebrow as he wandered through it, both an act for the room and in response to his perceived rudeness. "His conversational skills leave a lot to be desired."

"He appears to be in a hurry for something," Trevor replied, playing his role perfectly. His voice was pitched just high enough for a few to overhear, but not too high that it was obvious.

"Rude," Ivan agreed, sipping his flute casually.

I joined him in enjoying my own flute of bubbly liquid, feigning an ease I didn't quite feel. My senses were tied to Juliet's, waiting for any ounce of panic to ripple through our tentative bond. The ceremony linked us initially, just enough for me to feel her emotions. Such as the rising panic and self-doubt spiking through our connection.

Yes, it seemed she would fail miserably.

Oh, my darling Juliet.

I slowly finished my drink and set it on a nearby table. Then I made a show of loosening my tie and eyeing the door Juliet and Viktor had escaped through. "If you gentlemen will excuse me, I'm in need of a different kind of refreshment."

Ivan smirked. "I knew you wouldn't be able to last the night without indulging in a little foreplay."

"Can you blame him?" Trevor asked.

"I certainly can't," a male commented from nearby, his lips curled in amusement.

"Neither can I," his companion said. "She smells fantastic."

"Well, I'm glad you all approve," I remarked dryly as I started for the door. *Because you're all in for quite a show.*

Let the games begin.

Chapter Twelve

JULIET

Breathe in.

Breathe out.

My hands shook.

You can do this.

There was no other choice. Darius commanded it, therefore I would complete the task. Even if it meant taking a life.

My lips curled in an inviting smile while my insides turned to ice.

"Well, you are a tempting morsel, aren't you?" The deep tenor sent a shiver down my spine, and not the good kind. I demurely stared at the vampire's shoes, as was the etiquette by one in my position.

A blood virgin. A possession. A human without rights.

"So pretty…" The male's smoke-laced breath lingered over my lips as he traced a finger along the deep V-neck of my sheer black dress. Darius had chosen the outfit and piled my dark hair up on my head to better expose my throat. I wore nothing beneath the thin, see-through fabric—something the vampire touching me appreciated thoroughly.

"How generous of your master to share you with me," he continued with a sharp pinch to my nipple. I bit my tongue to hold in the yelp his touch inspired.

The blade strapped to my inner thigh begged me to act, but my instincts held me steady.

Not yet, I whispered to myself.

Coward, my conscious replied. *You're not ready for this.*

"Straddle me," the vampire demanded.

My body moved of its own accord, adhering to his will as if I were a puppet. All the while my brain rebelled, dared my new learnings to override the old, but my every action felt entranced by his command.

Humans obey.

Then obey your master's command.

My eyes threatened to close as a war raged through my heart and mind.

To harm a vampire was strictly forbidden. As was to disobey a master. Either way, I broke a cardinal rule.

The vampire's palms ran up my sides as I slid onto his lap on autopilot. His arousal settled between my legs—a hot invitation I had no desire to accept. But if he took me, I'd have to comply.

Master Darius put me here.

To challenge the being beneath me.

Not to pleasure him.

A test.

One I would fail if I didn't slide my fingers beneath the fabric of my dress, find the dagger, and plunge it into this vampire.

Oh, Goddess… How had this become my life? The

92

auction seemed like a lifetime ago. I was meant to be a new master's blood virgin—to provide sustenance and sex— not to become an accomplice to murder.

My stomach revolted as the vampire drew his fangs across my collarbone and up the column of my neck. It felt wrong. Only my master—Darius—was allowed to touch me there. Except he had given me to this blond male without a name and left me with a single demand to create a scene.

Use the blade.

Goose bumps pebbled across my flesh.

No. It's only there for protection.

Hot air seeped into my skin, the vampire readying my pulse for his bite. Darius had told me not to let the male strike, to defend myself as needed...

Grab the knife.

Oh, Darius would be so angry with me if I failed. I'd yet to earn his wrath and punishment, but it would ensue if I didn't pull the weapon out and wield it.

What if I missed?

What if I wasn't fast enough?

What if someone caught me?

Hot and cold fused in my blood, paralyzing me. Then the prick of a fang pierced my skin, and I fell victim to the compulsion to obey.

Twenty-two years with the Coventus overruled my master's two-month tutorial. Muscle memory was a powerful tool.

Succumb.

Allow.

Yield.

Pain flickered through the fog of my mind as the vampire deepened his lethal kiss. Darius was the only other ever to taste my blood, and he always infused it with euphoria... This was not Darius.

My lips parted on a scream I forcibly swallowed. Showing signs of pain only encouraged them. I knew this from observation during my many lessons.

Rough hands went to my dress, ripping the fabric from my chest to my waist. His mouth followed, clamping onto my breast in a cruel bite that scalded my insides.

No pleasure.

Only excruciating pain.

A preference most vampires seemed to share.

Not Darius…

My hands scrambled for the knife, but the vampire took too much too fast. My limbs had gone cold in a matter of seconds, leaving me helpless on his lap.

And very, very alone.

One command.

To reject the male's feeding by screaming or fighting back. Something, *anything*, to garner attention, and now I could barely scream, let alone yell.

I'd failed.

Hadn't even removed the dagger from its sheath around my thigh.

And this would be my punishment—to endure the fate I always feared—death by overzealous vampire. My blood was intoxicating, and from the fanatic way the male suckled at me now, he'd definitely fallen beneath the spell.

No one would care.

Not even Darius.

I was property. A broken toy my master had failed to retrain. It didn't matter that he'd essentially thrown me into the fire with no experience. I should have done better. He would most certainly allow me to succumb to this death.

Splinters fractured along my chest, whether from the pain of failure or the vampire, I couldn't tell.

Everything hurt.

Warm liquid seeped over my skin, drenching me in the life being cruelly sucked from my body.

A knock to my head caused light to flicker behind my eyes—the vampire trying to bring me back to lucidity, no doubt to admire his handiwork.

Or to deflower me.

Because Darius never had, and now I'd failed him.

He would start over with another.

Replace me at a new auction.

I never meant anything to him.

Don't let that hurt, I chastised. *You know better.*

But he was a kind master, far better than I ever anticipated, even with his intention of molding me into his personal poison.

"Juliet," Darius's voice traveled over me in a warm caress that nearly pulled me from my reverie.

Even post-death he would haunt me.

"Juliet." Harsher now, followed by a shake that confused my senses. I felt heavy. Covered in a warm muddy substance that weighed down my chest. It hurt to breathe.

"I'd say it's justified," a male voice advised. Flat. Unfamiliar.

What's justified? I wondered.

"Clearly," Darius snapped. "As if there was any question."

"Hmm. Well. I do hope she's not thoroughly defiled. Would be a shame." Same flat male voice.

My eyelids fluttered but remained unseeing.

Too much… something.

"If she is, I'll be seeking retribution on his entire line," Darius growled.

"Fair enough." Fabric shifted—suit pants, maybe?—as the voice grew fainter. "I'll provide my report of events to the alliance. You won't be held accountable."

"I'll do the same," another man declared. It reminded me of Trevor…

"Me too." And that was Ivan.

Where am I?

"Thank you all," Darius replied, sounding somewhat mollified. "Now, if you wouldn't mind, I'd like to tend to my future *Erosita*."

Erosita? Had I heard that right? What did it mean?

"Of course," the cool voice said. "If you need anything, you know where to find us."

"Noted," my master murmured, his fingers on my neck.

Everything seemed to shift around me. Savory foods and liquor melted into the crisp evening air. Then leather. New or freshly cleaned.

My head swam.

Something warm touched my lips.

Decadent.

Liquid.

Addicting.

Gone.

My world continued to change, floating in a haze of foreign sensations and scents, until silence overtook the buzzing in my ears.

"Ah, Juliet," Darius whispered. "I had hoped for better, but at least I know where to begin." His lips feathered over mine. "Now. Wake up." The command in his voice pulled at all my nerve endings, forcing my eyes to open.

Even in the subdued lighting of the limo, I could discern the stern lines of his handsome face. High cheekbones. Long, dark lashes. Lush, brown hair. Square, masculine jaw. Smoldering green irises.

"What the fuck happened, Juliet?"

I swallowed. "I…" My mouth reminded me of sandpaper. Not because of my brush with death, but because of his intense expression. "I couldn't kill him."

"Meaning you disobeyed my command," he replied as he gripped my chin to hold my gaze. "What happens when a blood virgin disobeys her master, Juliet?"

"Punishment," I whispered.

"Louder, darling. I want to ensure you understand the ramifications of what you've done."

My throat bobbed as I struggled to repeat myself.

"Punishment." It still came out raspy.

"Hmm." His palm slid to my throat and squeezed just enough to threaten. "What will I do with you?"

Only then did I realize he'd seated me over his lap, my legs dangling off to one side as he held me steady with one arm around my lower back. Normally, I wouldn't mind being this close to him, but danger lurked in his tense form.

"Whatever you wish, Sire," I replied softly, meaning it. He owned me. Mind, body, and soul. My purpose was to appease him and I'd failed. I deserved to be punished.

"Indeed." His thumb traced my jawline, his voice silky and menacing. "He bit you, Juliet. Do you know how that makes me feel?"

Lead rocks weighed down my insides. Since I'd broken the number one rule, I had no doubt he was… "Angry."

"Possessive," he corrected. "He touched what's mine, and why? Because you failed to act as I instructed."

I licked my suddenly dry lips. "I—I'm sorry, Sire."

"Are you?" he asked in that same velvety tone. His hand slipped over my exposed chest. My pulse jumped as he pinched the stiffening peak between his thumb and forefinger. "He had his mouth here. Drinking the essence that belongs to me."

I bit back a pained moan as Darius harshly squeezed my tender skin. Normally, his touch elicited pleasure. This was not meant to please—not entirely, anyway.

"Darius," I breathed as he twisted his hold.

"Do you know what it does to a vampire to see his possession caressed by another?" More agony shot through my breast at the subtle hold. Goddess, how did his forefinger and thumb *do* that? "And all because you allowed it. Why, Juliet? Why did you allow it? I warned you what would happen if you let another bite you, didn't I?"

I nodded, and he slapped my breast so sharply I gasped. *Holy…*

"Words, Juliet. Give them to me."

"Yes!" I cried, shaking both from his tone and the odd sensations his touch inspired. Agony... mingled with arousal?

What is wrong with my body?

"More," he growled, his fingers switching to my unabused nipple. "*Why* did you allow it?"

"Habit," I admitted as he applied pressure. "I... I'm trained... Submission."

"And reason is not enough to break the binds to the Coventus?"

Too much... It hurt too much... "It's not that easy," I said, tears in my eyes. "I don't... The rules... I can't."

My whole body thrummed beneath his touch. It burned between my legs, and heated my bare skin, even as numbness tingled along my chest.

"Darius, please..." I begged, not knowing what I wanted. Him to stop? To continue? "I'm sorry I failed you!" Anguish rippled through my voice—a convoluted response to this sensual torture coupled with his obvious irritation.

I'd never fought anyone before, nor had I ever desired it.

Even knowing that vampires and lycans had destroyed humanity, relegated humans to specific factions, removed all our rights, and essentially created my bloodline specifically for vampire enjoyment...

"I'm not a fighter, Darius," I whispered, my eyes closing. "I can't do it."

Chapter Thirteen

Darius

"That's where you're wrong, Juliet." A warrior lurked beneath her skin; I just had to coax her out to play.

Testing her tonight was the first step.

Her punishment would be the second.

I released Juliet's breast and suppressed a smile as she squirmed in my lap. Even pained, she still sought to please.

Perfect.

Gorgeous.

Mine.

Yet, despite all my warnings, she'd readily allowed another to bite her. Had I not been waiting for Viktor to lose control, she would have died.

I caught the exact moment when her indoctrinated thoughts took over, forcing her to succumb to Viktor's needs. I could have stopped the feeding then, but I needed his aggression to stage the scene properly. Which wouldn't have been needed had she merely reacted the way I instructed her to.

Killing a vampire without appropriate cause created a mountain of unnecessary paperwork. Having Juliet nearly bleed out in my arms gave me a just reason to act. I did so swiftly, severing Viktor's head from his body even while he continued feeding. A gory scene, sure, but strong messages were best served bloody.

But not even assassinating Viktor could chill the burn inside of me after seeing him mull Juliet. Worse, she'd simply accepted her fate.

I pinched the bridge of my nose.

This beautiful creature was crafted and molded into the perfect temptress. She could speak several languages, hold intelligent conversation on a variety of subjects, walk naked through a room of men without breaking her stride, and she had the mouth of a goddess.

And she was a submissive in every manner of the word.

With a snap of my fingers, she would fall to her knees and suck my cock for as long as I desired. She'd please whomever I gave her to, including a complete stranger, all because the Coventus ingrained this sense of duty into her pretty little head.

I fucking hated them and loved them at the same time.

Such a conundrum. I wanted her to think for herself, yet my sinister side luxuriated in all the ways her body could please mine. Over and over again.

My dick throbbed beneath her, begging to be allowed out to play. But now wasn't the time. Her life relied on her ability to follow my orders to the fullest extent.

If she couldn't fight, she was worthless to me outside the bedroom.

I slid my fingers into her long, nearly black hair and wrapped the strands around my fist. She yelped as I tugged, hard, forcing her gaze once again to mine.

"I gave you my blood, Juliet. That's the only reason you're alive right now." My immortality healed her quickly and efficiently, but that belied the whole point of this exercise. "You would have happily died beneath his fangs. Pleasing another master. How disloyal of you."

"No!" Her dark eyes flared as they met mine, the first spark of challenge flashing in their depths.

I cocked a brow when she didn't continue. "No?"

"You gave me to him." The breathy, slightly sullen quality of her voice suggested her wavering resolve, but the words were clear.

"To fight. Not to fuck and feed." She'd been naked in the vampire's lap, her breasts exposed to his mouth, and she'd not even screamed for him to stop.

Because she expected it. Accepted it. Embraced it.

Fucking Coventus.

It had been a miracle that Viktor hadn't seen the knife strapped to her thigh. It'd been the first item I had grabbed before killing him. The whole scene was a nightmare.

"I'm a blood virgin," she whispered brokenly. "That's our purpose."

"That's not *your* purpose, Juliet." I loosened my grip slightly. "But if all you wish to do is please me, then get on your knees."

She stiffened. "Now?"

"Yes." My cock would enjoy the attention while I taught her a lesson. I released her completely and raised a brow. "Are you going to make me wait?"

"No, Sire." She scrambled off my lap to the floor and placed her shaking palms on my thighs.

Having her like this between my legs helped tamper some of the fury rioting inside me. I meant what I said about possessive instincts. She belonged to me. No one else. And that vampire had touched her in places only meant for my hands and lips.

We would be rectifying that error right now.

"Do your job, Juliet." Cruel words, but effective.

"Yes, Sire." Her blood-coated chest heaved with a deep breath as she trailed her fingers up to my belt. The clasp came undone beneath her expert touch, followed swiftly by the button and zipper. My dick practically leapt out to meet her, but I withheld all emotion from my face. This lesson was not meant to be enjoyable.

Her tongue darted out to dampen her lips as she stroked my shaft from head to base. I relaxed into the leather seat, not giving her the satisfaction of a response, other than the one she held in her palm. If she wanted this to be her sole purpose, I'd make her work for it. The lack of lighting in the limousine aided my plight. She wouldn't be able to see me nearly as well as I could see her.

"Deeper, Juliet." She knew what I liked after several weeks of providing oral pleasure. I'd yet to take her fully because I desired her true consent, not the compliance her Coventus had instilled in her.

My cock hit the back of her throat as she sucked hard. I nearly growled, but I swallowed it at the last minute. Fuck, the woman possessed the most talented mouth I'd ever experienced. No gag reflex. No hesitation. Just pure, unadulterated understanding of exactly what I craved.

It took considerable effort to remain relaxed and unfazed on the surface, especially when my blood started to boil from her ministrations.

So perfect.

So hot.

So damn amazing.

Electricity hummed through my veins, heightened by her constant eye contact. Yearning brightened her gaze, giving her a goddess-like appeal. The woman was gorgeous even when covered in another man's blood.

Shit.

I focused all my energy into remaining neutral even as my groin throbbed. Maybe Juliet truly did belong on her knees, servicing me. Because fuck if I wanted her anywhere else.

My fingers itched to curl in her hair, to force her to take me to the hilt, hard, over and over again. I would come powerfully down her beautiful throat. And she'd swallow every drop, just as she always did.

Mine.

She was crafted for my pleasure.

Trained in all the arts of sex, including the darkest desires.

I couldn't wait to explore them all. In time. Soon.

Now.

I gave in to one of my urges, threading my fingers through her hair and shoving myself all the way down her throat without warning. Her eyes widened a fraction, but she didn't fight me. Just waited for me to let her breathe again.

Submissive to her core.

Trusting.

Not wavering.

Tears gathered at the edges of her irises, the only indication she needed air.

But still no other reaction, not even a plea. Such a turn-on, and yet, so infuriating. How could I break one so obviously broken?

By putting the pieces back together in a new pattern.

One befitting a warrior.

I allowed myself one thrust out and back in again before yanking her off me completely. My other hand wrapped around my shaft, giving it a violent pump as my balls tightened at the pending explosion.

"You're mine," I growled. "No one else touches you."

"Yes, Sire," she agreed, her pupils enlarged as I glowered down at her. With one final jerk of my cock, I unloaded onto her chest while gripping her hair in a way that forced her to watch.

Her name teased my tongue but didn't meet the air. I refused to indulge her when I felt so fucking unsatisfied.

"Rub it into your skin," I demanded as soon as I finished. I wanted it to erase the other man's presence. To mark her in the most degrading way as *my* property.

But she didn't move or respond.

I tugged sharply on her hair. Not enough to hurt, but enough to capture her attention. "Now, Juliet."

Her palms flattened against her breasts, massaging and smearing my essence all over her skin. I observed beneath my hooded gaze, watching as my cum branded her.

"Don't stop." It came out sharp and a little gruff, causing her fingers to move faster over her nipples. She obviously understood my desire since that was the spot Viktor had bitten her. Each swipe of her thumb reaffirmed my place there, my ownership.

Such a good little blood virgin.

I yanked Juliet forward and her mouth opened without my command, her tongue darting out to lick the liquid coating my slit. She hummed in approval before taking me deep into her mouth and drawing every last drop from my shaft.

My grip didn't loosen. If anything, it tightened as she devoured my cock in a manner few others could fathom.

Her hands continued to massage her breasts while she sucked me off, but slowly and more intensely now.

She had adopted an erotic rhythm, one that intensified her arousal.

I stole a deep breath, luxuriating in her intoxicating scent.

Mmm... So, so good.

Damp heat radiated from her, no doubt dripping down her thighs.

She relished in this—my owning her body. My dominance.

And now my darling little Juliet wanted to come.

Perfect.

I let her continue, reveling in the slight squirm of her hips as she fought for the friction she needed. Her nipples were hard little peaks now, begging for my touch, and her pupils overshadowed her irises.

"You enjoyed that," I murmured.

"Yes, Sire." The words were spoken around my still-solid erection. Her attentions had only taken the edge off. I craved so much more from her, but not until she learned her lesson.

"Zip me up, Juliet." We had reached the manor a few minutes ago, but I'd allowed our moment to extend just long enough to ensure her sensitive state. If she spread her legs, I'd no doubt find a very swollen, wet, and ready pussy to sink into.

Not yet.

Her fingers didn't fumble as she secured my hard-on into my pants. I'd tend to it later.

The door opened not a second later, my driver clearly sensing my next move, and I stepped out into the night with a hand for Juliet. She pressed her palm to mine even as her brow furrowed in confusion. Every time we indulged in these types of activities, I returned the pleasure.

But not tonight.

Unless she requested it.

I tucked her arm into mine after she stood. Her bare feet probably didn't appreciate the cobblestone, but that was the point. I wanted her hot, bothered, and uncomfortable.

She moved at my side without flinching, following me into the house and upstairs, and not seeming to mind at all that she wore nothing but semen-laced blood. Her confidence, at least, was intact.

I pushed open the door to her quarters and her nostrils flared as excitement tinged the air. She thought I meant to devour her on the bed. Poor darling. No. That was not the game we were playing tonight.

Instead, I led her to the bathroom, and flipped on the shower.

"You have my permission to bathe, Juliet. I suggest you use the opportunity while it's offered to thoroughly clean yourself." I let that insinuation hang for a moment before continuing. "Then get some sleep. We have a long day tomorrow."

"Y-yes, Sire," she said, her lips curling downward.

"Unless there is something else you require?" I prompted, one eyebrow raised.

She blinked. Frowned. Shook her head. "N-no, Sire. I will bathe and sleep."

Hmm. Disappointing. "Good," I said instead. "See you tomorrow."

I turned and left without looking at her, and ignored the hitch in her breath, too.

The rules in this house were clear. Juliet had an open invitation to join me in my bedroom whenever she desired pleasure. Given the way her arousal taunted my nostrils as I left her room, it was a safe bet to assume she yearned for me tonight. Badly. It would be up to her if she chose to seek me out.

Hence, tonight's primary lesson: living.

A gift not many humans received in this world, but one I happily bestowed upon her. Unfortunately, I couldn't force her to accept it.

Twenty-two years of training to accept fate regardless of personal satisfaction was a difficult mentality to alter.

I needed the fighter hidden beneath her skin to surface and play. Once I coaxed her out, we could well and truly begin the retraining.

Until then, I really only had a shell of a woman to work with, and I desired so much more.

"Join me, Juliet," I whispered into the empty hallway. "Please."

Chapter Fourteen

JULIET

My body was on fire.

Not literally, but it burned so fiercely I couldn't sleep under the bedcovers. And the fan above did little to cool my hot skin.

I could still feel Darius on me, even after the shower. His essence scorched my very being, imprinting on my soul.

He well and truly owned me. I knew that from the beginning, but to feel it in such a way was intoxicating. Addicting. Frustratingly arousing.

I kicked the remainder of the blankets off of the bed and huffed in irritation.

How had I gone from expecting to be used within an inch of my life to anticipating Darius's pleasurable attentions?

I was here for his needs, not my own. Yet, he'd always returned the favor.

Except tonight.

Why? Because I'd failed him. Was this his version of punishment?

I bolted upright. The Coventus introduced me to various methods of reprimand, all of which resulted in severe pain and sometimes death. None of those applied here.

A test, then?

"For what?" I whispered to myself. "What do you want?"

I examined our ceremonial bond, curious to see if I could sense anything from him.

It was there—a psychic connection shrouded in darkness—as if we were on the verge of linking our thoughts, but not quite.

Darius had mentioned it wasn't yet complete, that it would require several more rounds of exchanging blood to hold. Perhaps that's what he meant?

Still, I *knew* he was awake as if he were a part of me already. But his emotions were shut off.

He's waiting.

I frowned at the thought. A guess or an instinct?

Does it matter?

He told me I could enter his room whenever I pleased.

"But I should warn you," he had said. *"When you visit me here, I'll assume you're in need of pleasure, and I will require the favor to be returned."*

I shivered at the vivid memory of his incisors brushing my pulse with those words. A promise and a threat rolled up into one.

My sex pulsed with craving, urging me to take him up on the standing offer. If this ache between my thighs was meant to be a punishment, would he send me back to my room unfulfilled? Or reward me for asking him to care for my needs?

I bit my lip, considering. There was only one way to find out.

You're insane, a small voice whispered. *He can kill you with a flick of his wrist, or worse.*

True.

However, in our nearly two months of knowing each other, he'd never truly hurt me. His version of pain always mingled with pleasure. My core ached with the memory of the limo. Some of it had hurt, but it had also created an inferno inside of me that still burned.

I moaned as my nipples hardened against my flimsy nightgown. Even silk felt too heavy right now. I hadn't bothered with underwear. There was a whole drawer of untouched undergarments I chose not to use, likely because they were forbidden at the Coventus. The only ones I even considered were the sexy pieces. Darius would like those.

My eyebrows lifted.

If I went to his quarters wearing one of those sets, he might be more inclined to indulge me.

Maybe.

I pushed off the bed to look for the most enticing lingerie in the drawer. Darius seemed to prefer darker colors. A black negligee caught my eye with its translucent material. I swapped my silk shirt for the thin fabric and shivered as it tickled the top of my thighs.

A pair of matching panties completed the set, but they suffocated my aroused center to the point of discomfort. I tore them off, gasping at the relief that small action afforded me.

My legs quivered as desire overwhelmed my being. Goose bumps filed down my arms despite the heat boiling within, and a moan parted my lips.

I could handle this on my own, or try to, anyway, but I coveted Darius's expert skill. Only he would be able to truly relieve me of this incessant throbbing. His touch was an addiction my body now required. Without it, I would continue to burn.

A pair of four-inch heels and a silk robe completed my outfit. I'd lose the latter as soon as I stepped into his room, assuming he granted me entry.

With a deep, steadying breath, I started down the hallway toward his quarters. The words he spoke during my initial tour bolstered my steps, reminding me that I had an open invitation to seek him out for this very reason.

He might still be displeased with me for earlier, but he never told me I had to stay in my room.

Just bathe and sleep.

Which might have been a command...

Stop. We're doing this.

I paused before his door, hand raised and ready.

Knock.

Run.

Introduce your fist to his door. Softly.

Go back to your room.

You were a coward once tonight; don't do it again.

Choose sanity.

Choose pleasure.

My knuckles tentatively tapped the wood as my thighs clenched. I needed this—him. Strength infused my muscles as I solidified my resolve and knocked with slightly more force.

"Come in." His voice carried through the door and seemed to caress every fiber of my being.

I twisted the handle and stepped inside. He sat shirtless with a notebook in his lap, his back pressed against the pillows and the headboard of his oversized bed.

"Juliet," he murmured, setting his pen down. "What can I do for you?"

I quietly closed the door and moved into the soft light streaming down from his high ceilings. "I can't sleep," I admitted, dropping my robe. "I'm... I *need.*"

His green eyes trailed over my form, taking everything

in before meeting my gaze. "What do you need, darling? Tell me."

"Pleasure," I whispered.

He arched a brow in challenge. "Louder, darling."

"Pleasure," I repeated, my throat dry and my thighs trembling. "Please, Sire. I'm so hot it hurts."

"Are you wet for me?"

"Yes." It came out on a moan as I clamped my legs together. Any more and I would surely collapse in agony.

"Show me." His low voice coupled with the request stirred a volcano of sensation inside me. It was so intense I couldn't breathe. Couldn't move. Couldn't think.

His muscles flexed as he moved the notebook from his lap to the nightstand and resettled onto his back.

"I'm waiting, Juliet," he murmured, hands tucked behind his head. He resembled a dark angel, his gaze devious and his lips inviting.

The meaning of his request slammed into my gut, forcing my feet to move before the words caught up with my brain. By then, it was already too late.

I knelt beside him on the bed, lifting the lace for his inspection.

"Closer, love." His tone was an erotic caress that tantalized every nerve. My body succumbed to his every wish, doing exactly as he required without question.

The pillows beneath his head dipped as I pressed my knees into them and positioned the hottest part of me directly over his face. His palms slid up beneath the translucent lingerie to grab my hips while I gripped the headboard for balance.

"Mmm, you're so aroused you're swollen." His breath teased my damp flesh, stirring a groan from my throat that sounded nothing like me.

"Please, Sire," I begged. "Please."

"Only because you asked so sweetly." His grasp tightened as he guided my core to his mouth. The first touch of his tongue against my clit elicited a guttural scream from me that resembled his name.

My body shook uncontrollably above him, his hold the only thing keeping me steady.

I needed this, craved it.

Oh, Goddess...

His mouth was pure magic. Just the right pressure.

"Darius," I breathed, my legs quaking violently.

His headboard creaked beneath my palms. It was almost too much, but I couldn't stop the pleasurable assault. Not when it consumed me so completely.

Fire churned inside my lower belly, shooting sparks through my limbs. My indecent position above him only heightened the sensation. It gave me a false sense of power, some semblance of control never before experienced. His hands anchored me, his lips possessed me, and I felt like a queen.

His queen.

Molten heat pooled between my legs, frying my insides and creating a cyclone of energy focused on one single point.

"Oh," I moaned, my body screaming for release. Something sharp—Darius's incisors—skimmed the center of my pleasure, piercing me ever so slightly and vaulting me into a sea of dark bliss.

His name rent the air, sounding suspiciously like a growl, as I came undone. Every sensor exploded at once, my body breaking on a crash of such extreme ecstasy that I could no longer think.

My forehead hit something hard.

My hands squeezed impossibly tighter.

Savage spasms shot through me over and over.

"Darius," I managed, my brain shattered, my heart in tatters, and my soul crushed.

How could something so phenomenal hurt?

"Shh," he murmured, coaxing me back to him, to reality.

I still straddled his face, my shoulders curled in

torturous pleasure, and my head pressed against the cool headboard. Light slowly filtered into my vision. The heat of his palms registered against my thighs. His mouth against my intimate flesh.

"Beautiful." Praise deepened his voice, sending a shiver down my spine. His hands skimmed my legs all the way to my ankles where he deftly removed my heels. The pads of his fingers massaged the bottom of my feet, sending tingles up my calves.

So, so good…

"What did I tell you about coming in here?" he asked softly.

My dry throat convulsed as I tried to swallow. "Reciprocation," I rasped.

"Good girl." His irises darkened to a forest green as he smiled. "Slide down. I want to feel your arousal against mine."

It took far too long for me to adhere to his command, but he didn't push me. His hands acted as a guide as I shuffled backward across his body to his bare waist and lower.

He's not just shirtless; he's naked.

I'd yet to see Darius nude. He always kept his clothes on, even when I serviced him. My palms went to his abdomen for balance and also to *touch* him. Solid muscle. Gorgeous. Sleek. A predator encased in hot, tan skin.

All vampires were good-looking, but Darius redefined the meaning of the word. He perfected it. All lean, exquisite lines, handsome face, athletic figure, and beautifully proportioned. His erection was no different. It slipped between my damp folds, molding flawlessly to my body as if we'd been created for each other.

"Fuck," he whispered, his back arching slightly off the bed. "Ride me, Juliet. I want you to soak every inch of me."

We'd not done this yet. It felt intimate, right, and slightly terrifying. His hard member would more than fill me. It would rip through my maidenhead and definitely cause discomfort.

I had to be ready for him, especially if he intended to finally take me tonight. My body belonged to him, to be fucked as he required, and I would allow it. Whatever he wanted.

My hips shifted, drenching him as he commanded, spreading all of my subsequent pleasure over him and dampening his hot arousal. Every time his head met my cleft, I flinched. He'd left me too sensitive, too used, but I had to give him what he desired. His fingers danced up my sides, beneath my negligee, and wandered to my breasts.

"You're so perfect." A note of reverence touched his voice, granting me immense satisfaction. His lower body moved with mine, the friction intensifying with every thrust. I half expected him to reposition me and force his cock inside, but he seemed lost in our movements.

My lingerie disappeared with a rip, and I found my hair wrapped in his fist as he forcibly pulled me down to ravage my mouth with his. I forgot how to breathe beneath the onslaught and lost all touch with reality as he rolled me onto my back.

This is it, I thought, terrified and aroused.

He kissed me hard, his shaft continuing to slide through my damp folds with sharper thrusts. My clit throbbed from the abuse of his bulbous head, but I no longer flinched. No. I was starting to feel hot again.

I bowed off the bed as his fangs pierced my neck.

I hadn't even felt him move. He just struck, his vampiric kiss claiming my essence as his.

"Darius," I whispered, threading my fingers in his hair.

"Mine," he growled as he lowered to my breast and bit me in the same place the other vampire had just hours before. It occurred to me then that he'd done the same to my throat.

He's remarking me.

Except this bite didn't hurt.

Electricity surged down my spine, centering in the place where our arousals connected, heightening the sensations.

Then his member disappeared, his hips lifting slightly as he grabbed my wrist and forced my hand lower. "Stroke me, Juliet. I want to come all over your clit."

I wrapped my fingers around his thick arousal. The effects of my orgasm had drenched his skin, just as he had desired, enabling me to easily fondle him. Up and down, applying pressure where I knew he enjoyed it. My opposite palm joined the action, cupping his heavy balls as I worked his throbbing member with purposeful pumps.

"More," he demanded, his teeth scraping my nipple. I shuddered as he pierced me again, drinking my blood as I massaged him intimately below.

He was close. I could feel it as his sack tightened in my palm, and the way his cock grew impossibly larger. The temptation to put him at my entrance slammed into my gut, forcing my hand to angle his head toward my weeping slit.

It would be so easy.

One thrust.

But it wasn't what he requested.

I continued my task, moving in a way I knew he couldn't resist, and grinned when I felt his growl against my breast. Hot spurts of semen met my intimate flesh, striking me with the force of his orgasm and branding me indefinitely as his.

My hips rose to meet his of their own accord, desiring more, wishing he was inside me and not just hovering above. His scorching essence blended with mine, creating spasms of delight. I squeezed out every drop with my hand, relishing the feel of him.

Darius lifted onto his knees, his gaze between my spread legs. He swiped his thumb through my slick folds to my clit and then back again. "You look amazing like this, drenched in my seed."

I shivered from both his touch and the view of his very naked body crouched so close to mine. Muscle and strength radiated from him, as did an aura of danger. Darius wasn't just a vampire, but an old one too.

He smeared his essence around my entrance, awakening a hunger deep within me. Then he pressed inside, introducing his pleasure to mine and mating them in the world's oldest dance.

"Soon," he whispered darkly. "But not yet."

Why? I wanted to ask, but only a moan escaped instead. He applied just the right amount of pressure to my sensitive nub, massaging our combined euphoria into my flesh.

Lava slithered into the pit of my stomach, growing with each swipe of his thumb. Darius played my body with such expertise, his gaze always attentive and his focus on my reactions. He pinched me, kneaded me, and teased my nerves. I shook beneath him, completely lost to his will.

One hand.

That's all he used.

And I was already coming undone.

When he leaned down to capture my nipple with his mouth, I bucked against him. My breathing stopped. The whole world blacked out around me. Everything focused on Darius.

"My seed owns you now," he whispered. "And soon, so will my cock."

His words increased the intensity building inside me, cresting the volcano threatening to erupt. I trembled from the potency of it all, my mind losing its grip on reality.

"So close." He nibbled my breast. "I can feel it bubbling beneath the surface, awaiting my command. Your body is so beautifully trained, Juliet." He trailed kisses up to my collarbone and along my jaw.

My nerves were linked to a live wire, sizzling with energy and waiting to combust. I felt imprisoned, frozen in time—a slave to my master's desire.

"Please," I whispered, aching from the force of it. "Please, Sire."

He grinned against my throat, his tongue tracing my pulse. "You beg so prettily, darling."

My nails dug into my palms as waves of excruciating need rolled over my being. I was gasping his name, writhing beneath his attentions, dying for the release he held in reserve.

His lips brushed my ear, his exhale heavy and intoxicating. "Come for me."

Agony coupled with gratification exploded inside me, destroying my ability to move and think.

Flashes of light.

Fractures of my consciousness.

A world of discomfort and euphoria.

My lungs burned from my screams while my limbs melted into a puddle of repletion.

"Glorious," Darius murmured, his lips against mine. "Fucking perfection."

I trailed my fingers up his strong arms to hold on to him while he kissed me. He tasted sweet, with a hint of sex, his tongue masterful as he explored my mouth almost tenderly.

"Sleep, Juliet." He nuzzled his nose against mine. "We'll continue your training tomorrow."

Chapter Fifteen

Juliet

I stretched my arms over my head and sighed in contentment at the warmth flowing through my veins. A foreign feeling, one I wished to enjoy for a few minutes more.

Most nights were so cold that I awoke to the feeling of ice drizzling over my flesh. It numbed me before the day began, helping me to endure whatever new trial the Coventus threw at me.

Waking with Darius was different.

New.

Intoxicating.

His lips were on my neck, his bare chest pressed to my back, as he slowly coaxed me from my dream state. I wiggled my hips, loving the sensation of his hot erection pressed into my backside.

"Careful," he murmured. "Or I'll accept that invitation, darling."

I might enjoy that, I thought. But I stopped moving for the sake of my sore body.

Darius had used me so completely last night that I felt exhausted today despite the decent sleep. When he took me for the first time, he wouldn't be gentle. No vampire ever was, and Darius had more than shown his penchant for rough sex. I expected it to hurt. A lot.

He caressed my chin and tilted my head back to meet his kiss.

Mmm. Long, fluid strokes of his tongue against mine.

I could become addicted to this treatment. So gentle, caring, almost reverent.

"Good morning," he whispered when he finished. "Or I suppose I should say 'evening' since it's well after midnight."

Yes, a typical vampire schedule. The sunlight didn't particularly bother them; they just preferred the night. Lycans, however, embraced the day. Or so I'd been told. I'd yet to meet one.

"Hi," I managed, my throat sore.

He nudged me onto my back to lie beneath him and smiled down at me. "I'm proud of you, Juliet."

I blinked. "Me? Why?"

His mouth brushed mine. "Because you came to me last night and told me what you needed. I want that to happen more often."

So, it was a test.

Or rather, a lesson of some kind.

Everything Darius did seemed to have some sort of motive.

He kissed me again, this time with slightly more force as his erection pulsed between my legs. I dampened for him automatically, had probably slept in that state most of the night on instinct alone.

"Mmm, hold that thought." He pressed his palms into the pillow on either side of my head and lifted himself up while holding my gaze. "We need to discuss your comments about not being a fighter."

Ice slithered through my veins, freezing me beneath him. "I'm not."

"I agree that you're not," he replied. "Yet." He rolled off of me and held out his hand. "Come with me."

His tone brooked no argument. My palm met his as he assisted me from the bed. Rather than head toward the hallway, he directed me to his oversized marble bathroom and flipped on the shower. I stood beneath the already warm water, awaiting his instructions.

"Your survival instincts have been beaten out of you," he murmured as he ran his fingers through my dampening hair. "I'm going to help you find your spirit and resolve." He selected a bottle and poured some of the clear liquid into his palm.

"Vampires and lycans are superior beings," he continued as he massaged the shampoo into my hair. "There is no question on that front, but that does not mean all humans are weak. With the right training and mindset, you have the capability to be my lethal counterpart. The Coventus taught you how to tempt. I will teach you to fight."

Darius pushed me under the water, his hands running over my damp strands until the last of the bubbles went down the drain. Then he started over with the conditioner.

"We have four months until the coronation." His voice lowered with the words. "I need you to help me eliminate the competition."

My eyes widened both at his words and the inherent trust underlining them. Not once had he mentioned *why* he wanted my cooperation. "You intend to run," I realized.

"No, I intend to win." He fondled a stray piece of my hair that had fallen over my breast. "The best way to defeat an enemy is to become the enemy."

"You refer to the alliance?" I pitched my voice low, uncertain.

"Yes." He nudged me beneath the water again and repeated his actions from before. Then rotated us so he stood closer to the showerhead. "The vampire you helped me assassinate last night was Viktor Armintrov." He ducked beneath the spray while my jaw dropped.

"He's aristocracy." It came out on a shocked whisper that of course Darius heard.

"Yes and an utter bastard who deserved his fate." He shook the droplets from his dark hair and stepped forward. "His favorite establishment is the whorehouse. I'm sure your Coventus explained that to you?"

Yes. The vampires in charge had used it as a potential threat should anyone misbehave. "It's a place where humans with less worthy bloodlines are sent," I said, quoting my texts. "The average age of death is twenty-five."

"Because of men like Viktor," Darius replied as he lathered his head with shampoo. "Trust me when I say he deserved a far worse fate than beheading."

I considered that while he rinsed and applied conditioner. "Why do you wish to join the alliance?" I wondered out loud. "You do not strike me as having political motivations." Perhaps that was out of turn for me to say, but given all of my learnings, Darius did not fit the mold.

His lips curled into a dangerous smile. "I want to destroy it and reinstate our rightful leader."

All the breath left my lungs. He'd mentioned the tidbit about enemies, but this...

The alliance was the glue that held our society together. Without it, lycans and vampires would go to war, leaving the humans as collateral damage.

Everything would collapse.

Darius pressed a bar of soap to my breast and began massaging it in small circles.

"Tell me, Juliet, are you happy?" he asked softly. "With this life, I mean. Do you enjoy being relegated to slavery? To being a source of food and pleasure for my kind?"

My mouth opened and closed, no sound escaping. They weren't questions I knew the answers to as I'd never even considered them. My purpose was defined at birth. I never had a choice. What other means of happiness was there for a blood virgin?

"Humans used to have a higher place in society." His hand moved south as he lathered more soap into my skin. "I showed you the history books when you first arrived so you would understand. It's not something the Coventus teaches. The information is considered irrelevant, which is really a fancy way of classifying it as illegal."

He turned me away from him and lifted my hair over one shoulder to better access my back while he continued speaking.

"There are those who disagree with the way our government works today. It favors the old aristocracy and degrades those of lesser bloodlines. Ivan and Trevor are two examples—they don't qualify for a judicial position merely because they were born into the lower class as humans. It bars them from certain career paths as well, disqualifies them from events such as your blood virgin auction, and even prevents them from entering certain social circles without a representative."

Darius's palm ran down my thigh as he kneeled behind me.

"As you've no doubt ascertained, blood is very important in vampiric hierarchy. And it's the foundation of the alliance. Turn."

I did as he asked, placing my most sensitive body part before his eyes. He placed a kiss on my shaved mound before gently washing the area of his attentions from last night.

"How much do you know about lycans?" he asked, his green irises meeting mine.

"Bloodlines are important to them as well," I replied. "They have royal houses and hierarchy in their packs."

"A crude assessment, but true," he agreed. "The alpha males control everything, including the females in their territories. Property can be exchanged for a woman of choice, and they very much believe in forced breeding. And as that's how they treat their own kind, you can imagine humans have it far worse."

I shivered. Lycans were never the predator I had to worry about, so I hadn't spent much time studying them, but I knew their kind to be violent. There were rumors about what happened to humans chosen for the full moon. None of them survived.

"My point is that our system is flawed and there are those—myself included—who do not agree with how everything is run, and we wish to fix it." He stood. "Rinse."

I stepped beneath the water again as he soaped himself off in a far more efficient manner and then traded positions when he was ready to wash away the suds. They pooled at our feet, creating a swirling motion over the drain as I observed numbly.

Of all the masters, I had been selected by the one who desired change.

A world without the alliance. I couldn't even begin to imagine what that would look like.

Darius lifted my chin, his gaze capturing mine. "My bloodline is purely aristocratic, identifying me as an ideal candidate for ascension."

"What happened to the former sovereign? Adrian Loughton?" The name was a guess based on his comment regarding Viktor. I remembered his region from my studies and knew he resided beneath Adrian.

"I'm impressed," Darius praised. "And to answer your question, Mister Loughton met an unfortunate end at the hands of a few misguided lycans. Tragic."

He didn't sound all that upset about it. "You

orchestrated it." Another guess, one I knew was correct by the gleam in his green eyes.

"As I said, tragic." He turned off the water and pulled an oversized towel from the rack. The warm cotton covered me from my shoulders to my knees. "There are several in this region who qualify to replace him, myself being one of those candidates. But I've avoided politics for nearly a century, choosing instead to live alone."

"Why?" I asked, curious.

His smile was sad. "A story for another day, darling. We have other activities to tend to that take precedence, including a dinner with Ivan and Trevor."

"Dinner?" I repeated.

"Mmm." He wrapped a towel around his waist. "Yes. It'll be a practice run for later this week."

"What's happening later this week?" The words were out before I could stop them, an indication of an error in my conditioning. To question a master was wrong, not that Darius seemed to mind. If anything, he appeared amused.

"An engagement with Sebastian Cromwell."

My eyes rounded. "The Regent?" He was second in command to a sovereign and notoriously powerful. That couldn't be the vampire he meant...

"The very one," he replied. "He requested it."

"Why?" I just couldn't seem to stop my mouth from moving or speaking.

Some of his amusement dissipated as he stepped closer, forcing me to back up against the wall behind me. He placed his palms on the marble on either side of my head, caging me between his muscular arms.

"A ceremony is rare, Juliet. So rare that the last one on record occurred over five decades ago. And while ours isn't complete yet, the initial stages have begun, which has inspired a certain amount of curiosity among my brethren."

"Meaning he's coming because of me," I inferred.

"Yes." He let that response settle between us, his

expression patient as though waiting for an additional inquiry, but he'd finally silenced me. "Do you know what purpose a mated blood virgin typically serves at a dinner party?"

I recalled all my texts and came up blank. None of them had ever discussed the ceremony, let alone the etiquette that followed it. "No, Sire."

"Sharing," he murmured.

My brow furrowed, not understanding. "Sharing what?"

"You, darling. Sebastian wishes for me to share *you*, and given my innate response to Viktor last night, I need to practice my patience where that is concerned. So, we'll begin with Ivan and Trevor. Today."

Chapter Sixteen

Darius

"You told her about the endgame?" Despite his elegant suit and tie, Ivan appeared ready for a fist match, with my face being his primary target.

"Yes." I didn't elaborate because what was the point?

Sharing my desires with Juliet suited the moment. Her understanding my objective was crucial to her training.

"Yes," Ivan repeated, pacing. "That's it, is it?"

"Yes." That time I said it to piss him off, and it worked. My old friend rounded on me, his nose inches from mine.

"She could go to the fucking alliance and have you slayed. You do realize that, right?" His anger was founded in his concern for me, which was the only reason I didn't respond outwardly to his physical proximity. "Fuck, where is that damn royal when I need him? If anyone could talk some sense into you, it'd be *him*."

I ran my fingers over my tie and held his gaze unwaveringly. "No one would believe a blood virgin's babbling over a vampire of my status, not that she would ever have access to anyone of aristocracy to inform them. Above all of that, she is mine and she will not repeat a word to anyone." As for his comment about "the royal," he'd understand as my oldest friend and ally. After all, most of this was his idea. *For Cam.*

Ivan's eyebrows popped up to meet his dark hairline. "You trust her?"

"I own her," I clarified. "Trust isn't required with property." A harsh statement, but true nonetheless.

"I don't like it."

"You don't have to like it to accept it."

He picked up his glass of bourbon and downed the contents before slamming it on my desk. "Fine. But if she ends up endangering you, don't expect any pity from me."

I chuckled. "Duly noted. Now, where's Trevor?"

"Probably sating himself in some redhead," Ivan muttered.

"When I offered him my blood virgin for the night?"

"*Because* you offered her."

I smiled. Trevor clearly worried he might lose control. Well, that wouldn't be an issue, because I planned to be in charge of every detail. No one would harm my Juliet.

"Is she terrified?" Ivan asked.

"Yes." I'd scented her terror when I mentioned sharing her earlier and again when I dismissed her to ready herself for dinner. The outfit I'd requested she wear didn't help matters. Rather than black, I'd opted for a dark red tonight. It would look beautiful against her pale skin.

"Then you clearly didn't tell her how this is going to go."

I snorted. "Of course not. What would be the fun in that?"

"Still a jackass, I see."

"Why would that ever change?" I asked, smirking. "Now, shall we go have a little fun?"

"You're an evil man, Darius."

"Another fact that will never change," I pointed out as I led the way to the foyer. Juliet's scent had grown stronger—indicating she'd left her room—and I wanted to observe her reactions as she descended the grand staircase. Her glittery dress caught the light from the chandelier above, illuminating her curves as she paused at the top.

"Shit," Ivan growled beside me. "I fucking hate you."

"We both know that's not true," I replied softly as Juliet started toward us on her four-inch stiletto heels. Never once did she falter despite her obvious nerves over what dinner would entail.

Her breasts swayed with each step, making me quite pleased that I had chosen this dress for her to wear tonight. Thin gold chains held the fabric up on her shoulders, and the neck split to her belly button. There was no back, the slits on her skirt went up to midthigh, and, as with everything else she wore, the sheer fabric revealed everything beneath.

"Juliet," I murmured, kissing her cheek as she joined us. "We're going to pretend this is a traditional affair—just for dinner—to practice for future events. So I'll need you to bow as you normally would as I properly introduce you to Ivan."

They'd already met on a few occasions, but tonight was about preparing for our meal with Sebastian. And to do that, we needed to pretend a little.

Her dark eyes slipped from mine, her subservience immediately taking over. "Yes, Sire."

I lifted her chin, wanting to hold her gaze for a moment longer. "I'll be here the entire time, love. And I'll coach you through it, all right?"

She swallowed. "Yes, Sire."

I cupped her cheek and kissed her on the mouth. "I

won't let anything happen to you that you won't enjoy," I whispered against her lips. "You'll see."

"All right." She didn't appear all that convinced, but I would prove my point by the end of the meal.

I released her and took a step back. "As much as it pains me to say, please bow for Ivan." Such a ridiculous formality, but humans were considered to be the lowest echelons of society. They ranked on the same level as cattle.

Juliet lowered to the ground with a practiced ease, her gaze again on our shoes. She wouldn't stand again until I granted permission.

"When Sebastian arrives later this week, you will descend the staircase with the same confidence and bow as soon as you reach the foyer."

"Yes, Sire." Her voice held no hint of fear, this type of formality no doubt being typical for her.

"Ivan," I prompted.

He gave me a look that expressed his irritation before eyeing Juliet's submissive form. With his hands in his pockets, he circled her, eyeing every asset on display while purposely brushing against her as he moved. She didn't flinch, her posture perfect the entire time.

"She's lovely, Darius." He stopped behind her. "May I?"

My instincts rioted while I replied, "Of course."

I could handle this.

I had to.

"Kneel for Master Ivan," I instructed.

Juliet sat up onto her heels, palms on her thighs, head still bowed respectfully. My cock hardened at the now familiar position. She truly was a gorgeous woman.

Ivan brushed his knuckles over her cheek before trailing them down her neck to the gold chains gracing her shoulders. I monitored her heart rate as he continued his exploration and admired the steady rhythm, especially as he moved to press his legs to her exposed back.

He gripped her chin to force her head back, meeting her gaze with a smoldering one of his own, and smiled seductively. "Hello, pet."

"Master Ivan," she greeted. "Welcome."

Such a natural. No trembling or hiding, just utter compliance in a dangerous situation. The Coventus had certainly done their job well. Too bad I had to undo all their hard work.

Oh, on the surface she would remain the same, but not beneath. And her reactions today proved it all to be possible. Juliet had questioned me openly without fear—a leap forward in our arrangement whether she realized it or not.

Ivan drew his thumb over her lips, tracing them slowly and thoroughly. "You have quite the fuckable mouth. Perhaps your Sire will allow me to experience it later."

I swallowed my choice response to that statement and maintained my air of indifference. An improvement from the Viktor situation.

"Oh, I've missed the introductions." Trevor's voice carried through the foyer as he entered my home without knocking—an indication of our friendship. Very few could do that without risking their lives.

"You're just in time," Ivan replied, his palm on Juliet's cheek. "Come meet Darius's pet."

Trevor wandered over in a black tailored suit and stood in front of Juliet while Ivan continued to slowly stroke her jaw. Trevor trailed his gaze slowly over her low-cut neckline to her waist, down to her slightly parted thighs, and back up.

"She's delectable, Darius," Trevor praised, playing his part appropriately.

"Would you like to touch her?" I offered.

"Mmm, yes, I would. With your permission." His blue-green eyes lifted to mine in polite question.

"It's given." The words tasted sour in my mouth but sounded normal. An indicator that I might be able to complete this evening without killing one of my best friends. Of course, this was the easy part.

Trevor touched her shoulder before tracing the line of her dress down over the swell of her breasts and back up again. "So soft," he mused, his attention focused on her hardening nipples. "And responsive."

Her body reacting to a vampire's touch—yet another impulse driven into her through years of conditioning. Was that why she submitted to me so easily? Or was it something else?

Does it matter?

Yes.

"Shall we move to the dining room?" My steady voice sounded nothing like the one rioting in my head.

"I'm certainly famished." Ivan released Juliet but didn't move away from her. "Your pet is exquisite."

Meanwhile, Trevor continued his exploration, moving from her collarbone to her jawline. "May I escort her?" he asked with a glance my way.

I forced a smile. "Absolutely."

"Excellent." He held out his hand, palm up. "Beautiful?"

Her eyebrows lifted a little in surprise at the nickname he'd bestowed upon her while Ivan smirked at the clear social mishap. Not that Trevor cared. He more than embraced being snubbed by aristocracy.

Juliet accepted his help up from the ground and slid her arm through his as he offered it to her. "A pleasure, little one."

"Thank you, Master Trevor."

He chuckled. "Oh, how I do enjoy hearing those words from a woman's mouth, especially one as gorgeous as yours."

"I doubt Sebastian will be nearly this good-natured," Ivan drawled as he followed the couple down the hall. I remained a few steps behind, my goal to show trust and respect.

Trevor snorted. "Certainly not. The man has a dick up his ass."

"Stick," Ivan corrected.

"No, I definitely meant a dick." Trevor led the way to the dining room, a grin on his face the whole way while I shook my head.

"I told you he wouldn't last more than five minutes," Ivan said conversationally. "Do you think perhaps it's the blond hair? Bleached it too much during his surfing days?"

"Seriously, a blond joke?" Trevor tossed back. "I suppose I shouldn't expect much from a former Brit."

"Poor Mister America doesn't understand our dry sarcasm, D," Ivan murmured. "Do you think it's because his former political system didn't value education the way ours did?"

"Absolutely," I agreed, even though I didn't grow up in the same era. Both of my friends were born much, much later than me.

"What do the nicknames mean?" Juliet asked, her gaze meeting mine unexpectedly in the dining room.

Everyone stopped smiling, the air cooling to a frigid level. Juliet's eyes grew wide as she realized her social faux pas, her lower lip trembling.

Hmm. If Sebastian were here, I'd have no choice but to publicly punish her for such an outburst. However, since Trevor had already broken all formalities, I could let this slide.

Besides, this was the type of behavior I desired—a fracture in her conditioning that I could exploit.

Trevor stepped away as I moved forward, and Juliet immediately fell into a formal bow. I bit my tongue to keep from chastising her for it. She thought we were still practicing, which meant I'd enforce her penalty now. But no. I had no desire to reprimand her for showing curiosity.

Both Ivan and Trevor gaped as I knelt before her, my palms going to her face to lift her gaze. "America is a former country and technically where we live now. Brit is short for British, which relates to Great Britain or the United Kingdom. They disappeared with the fall of humanity. Now everything is divided into regions."

Her brown eyes gazed deeply into mine. "I read about those in the history books. So many wars."

I hid a smile. "Yes, they participated in several, but most humans did throughout the centuries. Remind me to let you read about the Crusades some time." A devastating period that I did not enjoy living through.

"You are British?" she asked softly.

"Actually, no." I smiled as I stood and held out my hand for her to join me. "I was born in the Gaul region, which later became Western Europe. I'll show you on a map later, but my ancestry is Roman. I later moved to the Britannia province when it was otherwise known as Roman Britain."

"What he's trying to say is that he's fucking old," Trevor translated.

I ignored him and focused once again on Juliet. "Nearly three millennia, to be precise."

She didn't appear shocked by that information in the slightest, suggesting she'd either anticipated it or been numbed to eternal beings. Likely both. "You look very good for your age," she replied, shocking me yet again.

"Was that...?" Ivan trailed off.

"A joke," Trevor finished. "Oh, I knew I liked her."

"You keep calling her a fuck doll."

"Which she is, but a clever one."

"Enough," I snapped, tired of the side conversation interrupting the moment.

Juliet flinched, her gaze falling. "I'm sorry, Sire. I meant it as a compliment."

"I know," I whispered. No way had she suddenly adopted a sense of humor. "Thank you." I kissed her forehead and folded my arms around her in a hug. Ivan and Trevor both gaped at me as if I'd grown a second head.

"What? You fucked up the practice round back in the foyer, Trevor. We'll start again in a moment." It wasn't like they cared about decorum. We never followed it here.

I kissed Juliet soundly on the mouth to display my pleasure at her breaking the confines of her training. So beautifully disobedient. I wanted to see more of it, but only in the confines of our home.

"You can't act like this around society members, Juliet." I held her gaze, ensuring she understood the importance of my words. "Only here."

"Yes, Sire." She frowned. "I didn't mean to speak out of turn; I'm not quite sure why I did."

"Because you're learning how to live," I advised softly. "Now go take the middle chair. Trevor and Ivan will sit on either side of you, and I'll be across the table."

We were nowhere near done yet.

I still had to share her.

Physically and sexually.

Chapter Seventeen

JULIET

"Open," Trevor demanded.

I parted my lips while keeping my eyes closed, as instructed. Something warm and decadent slid over my tongue, and I fought a responding moan.

They told me not to speak or utter a sound—a demand they seemed to be testing through a game of feeding me sweet desserts. Breaking the rules resulted in punishment, and these men clearly wanted me to disobey their commands.

"I think she likes it," Ivan mused. "Give her another bite."

Ohhhh, I sighed mentally. I was so full already. After years of eating food only of nutritional value, it was hard to enjoy meals in the way Darius and his friends did. My stomach couldn't tolerate the rich flavors.

"Only one more," Darius advised, voice flat.

"Spoilsport," Trevor grumbled.

"Here, love, open," Ivan said as the edges of a spoon met my mouth.

I obeyed dutifully. Another sweet slice of heaven tortured my underdeveloped taste buds as I forced myself to chew and swallow.

"Gorgeous," Trevor praised as someone trailed a gooey substance along my collarbone. I almost glanced at it but remembered their order for me to shut my eyes.

Something wet—a tongue—met my skin as one of them laved up whatever had just been applied to my body. They'd done this a few times during dinner, their hands and mouths finding one reason or another to touch me. But never beneath the dress, and always with Darius's permission.

"Mmm, I'm craving something else for dessert." Ivan's words flowed over and through me, the insinuation in his voice punctuated by his palm sliding over my thigh. "Darius?"

"Yes." The sound of a chair scraping over wood, then footsteps.

My heart skipped a beat.

The stroking and licking throughout dinner hadn't bothered me nearly as much as I expected because Darius sat close by. They were all busy eating as well, lost to their conversations in politics while using my body as a side amusement.

But now I was under the spotlight.

I felt it with every fiber of my being, all three gazes on me—voracious.

Oh, Goddess.

It was like the first night in Darius's home, when I thought they'd all intended to devour me. Except this time, I *knew* that was the plan.

To share.

Three men.

Can I manage it?

I could barely handle Darius…

A warm palm slid beneath my hair, curling around the back of my neck as Darius's familiar scent overwhelmed me. "You've done so well, darling. But now it's time for the real test." His thumb stroked my thrumming pulse. "Stand."

Finding my footing while blind wasn't easy, but I managed. The chair disappeared as Darius pressed his chest to my back.

His hands found my hips. "Open your eyes."

I did and found nothing had changed. Trevor and Ivan both sat in the same chairs, their expressions predatory.

"Gentlemen, you've ensured Juliet's appetite is well sated. Would you like her to return the favor?" Darius asked, his tone dark and sensual.

My heart fluttered. *Return the favor…*

Ivan stood and ran his hand over his tie, his caramel-colored irises a thin line around his oversized pupils. He looked hungry. Very, very hungry. "I would adore that."

"Me too," Trevor added, standing.

"Excellent." Darius pressed a kiss to my neck—a show of open possession—and splayed his fingers along my sides. "Shall we adjourn to the great room?"

Ivan's heated gaze danced over me, his lips quirking. "I suppose that would be more comfortable."

Trevor smirked and turned to lead the way, Ivan right behind him.

"Follow them," Darius whispered when my feet refused to move.

I swallowed, my throat dry. "Yes, Sire."

It took a moment for my legs to work, my limbs frozen with trepidation. The Coventus had well prepared me for what came next. While I'd never experienced it for myself, I'd witnessed several threesomes and foursomes throughout my training days. So much blood, and not all mortals survived.

Darius needs me alive. Or that's what he had said, anyway. Hopefully, he and his friends remembered that.

Trevor and Ivan stopped on either side of an oversized chaise lounge in the mansion's ornate living area. Plush chairs and couches decorated the immense room, leaving multiple other options for seating, suggesting they chose this spot with purpose. It provided ample angles for devouring their dessert—me.

I refrained from the urge to wipe my clammy palms against my dress and stood with my eyes downcast, awaiting Darius's instructions. His fingers lightly traced my arms, eliciting a row of goose bumps in their wake as his hands settled on my shoulders.

Trevor slid out of his jacket and draped it over the back of a chair. "What was the name of tonight's wine?" he asked while rolling up the sleeves of his crisp white dress shirt.

"An old French wine that isn't made anymore." Darius's thumbs brushed my collarbone while his fingers toyed with the gold chains of my dress.

Ivan mimed Trevor's movements as he murmured, "That's a shame."

"Indeed." Darius drew the metal across my shoulder slowly, his lips near my neck. "Shall I reveal your dessert?"

My heart slammed a chaotic rhythm against my ribs. They could already see right through my dress, minimizing the impact of my pending nudity. Yet, the idea of Darius removing the only barrier between me and these three men—

"Yes." No hesitation from Ivan, not that I expected any.

"Absolutely," Trevor added, his tone taking on a low growl that rippled across my skin.

Darius chuckled darkly as he drew the straps down my arms, exposing my breasts inch by inch. My nipples pebbled in reaction to both the cool air and the sexual tension igniting throughout the room.

"Gorgeous," Ivan murmured as the fabric reached my stomach. I could *feel* their gazes on me, memorizing my flesh, or more likely, determining where to bite me first.

My blood heated and cooled, my body at war with how to respond. Darius's vampiric kiss always elicited pleasure, but I knew that wasn't how most of his kind fed. How would Trevor and Ivan feel? Would it hurt? Would I like it?

Darius's thumbs skimmed my hips, the dress following his lead and slowly slipping from my body to pool at my feet.

"Leave the heels on," Ivan said, his tone laced with yearning. "Please."

"Of course. Just one thing first." Darius twisted me in his grasp so fast that I would have fallen if his arm hadn't wrapped around my lower back. His opposite hand lifted to grab a fist full of my hair. A sharp tug forced my gaze to his—two smoldering orbs of the deepest green.

His mouth sealed over mine in a punishing kiss that left me wondering what I'd done wrong. Had it been the goose bumps? My thundering pulse? Both were considered mortal faults. The Coventus tried to break my kind of those instinctual reactions through hours of forced observation. Alas, I never managed to master the art of hiding my body's responses. Just as I couldn't deny the heat Darius provoked in me now with the dominating swipes of his tongue against mine.

I gripped his jacket for balance as he deepened his claim. My head stung from how tightly he held my hair, while my stiff nipples luxuriated in the feel of his fine wool jacket abrading my bare skin. It evoked pleasure and pain simultaneously, leaving me off-kilter. I didn't know whether to scream or to moan, and that convoluted swarm of emotions only worsened as blood filled our mouths.

My breaths came in pants against him, uncertain of this possession. The sticky essence coated my tongue and throat, causing me to gag. That only seemed to spur him on more, his arm squeezing me tighter as the fingers knotted in my hair loosened to trace my face.

"Take a deep breath," he instructed, causing my heart to jump.

Why? I wondered even while I complied. Then he gripped my nose while resealing his lips over mine.

My eyes flew open.

I couldn't breathe.

More blood filled my mouth, drowning me, forcing me to swallow in heavy gulps while my lungs burned with the need for air.

Tears flooded my vision, my body aching, my heart beating a mile a minute.

Why? I blinked. *What did I do wrong?*

My nails dug into his jacket while I gulped the thick substance lining my throat. I didn't dare inhale, but I would be forced to soon if he didn't release me.

Domination.

Darius owned me. Each subtle sweep of his tongue over mine confirmed his power, and the erection against my lower belly said he enjoyed his dominion. I was his to do with as he pleased—to fuck, to bleed, to suffocate, to kill. That notion of complete and utter control calmed me despite the inferno etching a path through my lungs.

He'll let me breathe.

The confident thought pierced my haze of fear and stirred a quiver deep in my belly. So contrary to the act at hand. I should be screaming and fighting; instead I relaxed. My body yielding to his desires and trusting him in the most crucial of ways.

I'm broken. Shattered. His. Just as the Coventus trained me to be. A human toy.

Darius's lips slipped from mine as his hand drifted to my hair again, his grip far gentler than before.

The unexpected reprieve sent a jolt through my system, shooting electricity to my nerve endings and heating me to my very core. I inhaled deeply, completely, my body shaking uncontrollably from fright and a lethal need for *more*. Fire laced my veins, setting my skin ablaze with conflicting messages while my lungs wept with joy.

Arousal deepened Darius's irises to a dangerous forest-green color as he studied me intently. "You enjoyed that."

I shuddered, my body enflamed from his touch and kiss. *What did he just do to me?*

He brushed his mouth against mine and smiled. "Yes, you definitely enjoyed that."

I licked the blood from my lips and shuddered again as I swallowed. *So sweet. So addicting. Like life in liquid form.*

My eyebrows drew down at those errant thoughts and shot upward as understanding dawned.

Not my blood.

Darius had forced me to swallow *his* essence, not mine. "Why?" I mouthed. Would this further the ceremonial bond between us? He mentioned after the first time that we would have to consume each other again.

"Protection," he whispered, brushing his knuckles over my cheek. "Now go lay on the chaise and spread your legs for us."

Chapter Eighteen

Darius

Juliet resembled a goddess with her dark hair fanned out against the lounge pillows. Her perfect breasts rose and fell with each breath, her pulse a constant thrum in my ears.

She behaved so beautifully—so submissively. Her long, creamy legs were parted just as I requested, revealing every intimate inch of her to our gazes. Hunger radiated from Trevor and Ivan, their stances predatory. One signal from me and they would pounce, but not a second before. I controlled this moment, this room, this woman.

My blood sang as my essence settled inside her, coating her in yet another layer of immortality that deepened our bond. I could have asked her to feed from my wrist, but it seemed too chaste. The possessive man in me demanded a show, a declaration to those in the room that I owned her.

That regardless of what would transpire in the coming minutes, Juliet was *mine*.

I removed my jacket and added it to the pile on top of the chair. "This is going to hurt, Juliet." A warning she likely didn't need. The look Ivan flashed me also said it went against protocol. So did my eternal kiss. Fuck if I cared. This was a test run for a reason.

"Yes, Sire." Her pulse sang an entirely different tune from her tone.

I knelt beside her and kissed her temple. "Your fear is intoxicating, darling." I nuzzled her jawline, her neck, and nipped her thundering pulse. *Mmm, divine temptation.* I glanced at my friends. "Ivan, Trevor, care to join me?"

Fuck you, Ivan seemed to say with his brown gaze. "I thought you'd never ask."

Oh, I definitely considered that option, I thought, grinning. "Be my guest. Please."

With an arrogant lift of his brow, he lowered himself to the chaise and settled between Juliet's splayed thighs. Far too close for my liking, but we'd already agreed that he could feed from her femoral artery.

Trevor remained standing, his focus on Juliet's breasts. Her breath hitched as he drew his finger between them. "Jumpy," he murmured.

"Something to work on before Sebastian's visit." Ivan grasped her thighs, his attention shifting to her shaved mound. "Although, her arousal will please him." He dropped a kiss to her hip, then slightly lower, and smiled at her responding shiver. "Oh, yes, it'll please him very much indeed."

I fought the urge to punch my best friend and instead focused on Juliet's breathing, her heartbeat, her dilated pupils. She inhaled sharply as Trevor palmed her breast, then exhaled slowly. He pinched her nipple—hard from the looks of it—and smiled when she didn't outwardly react.

"That's better, gorgeous," he praised while settling

beside her. His blue-green eyes met mine, seeking permission to explore more. It was his way of deferring to his elder and superior before playing with the delectable toy.

If I told them to leave, they wouldn't hesitate. Of course, Ivan would give me hell later for it, but my dominance in this room was absolute. Both males were waiting for me to give them permission to continue.

We reviewed the ground rules in depth while discussing this exercise, and I trusted them not to cross the boundaries I set. That's why they were here. I would entrust Juliet with no one else. Not yet. Perhaps not ever.

I circled Juliet's throat with my palm, my thumb resting against her artery, and squeezed. "Look at me."

She complied immediately, her big brown eyes locking on mine with a relieved expression. Had she craved my gaze this entire time? Pride blossomed inside me at the prospect—another crack in her conditioning.

"Sire," she breathed, her cheeks flushing.

I lifted my opposite hand and drew my fingers through her thick hair. The thudding against my thumb slowed, her body surrendering to my will. We were developing trust, an important component to our future plans. I held her gaze for a moment longer before shifting my attention to Ivan and Trevor.

"You may proceed," I said quietly.

Juliet didn't tense or make a sound as both men bent to run their mouths and hands over her exposed skin— Trevor at her breasts, Ivan near her femoral artery.

I held her gaze, my grip on her neck tightening a fraction to keep her in the present. My friends wouldn't be gentle. It was the only way to ensure she understood the future expectations of my counterparts. I couldn't afford for her to react negatively to Sebastian or anyone else.

Her lips parted, her expression clouding with a mixture of pleasure and pain. I brushed my thumb over her pulse again before glancing down her naked body to my feasting friends. Trevor had her nipple in his mouth, his fangs firmly lodged into her skin. A deep flush crept its way across her chest, leading back to her neck and up into her cheeks. My Juliet enjoyed a little roughness in the bedroom. Whether that was truly her or a result of her upbringing, I would never know.

She gasped as Ivan's incisors pierced her femoral artery, his mouth pulling hard and sharp. A typical vampiric kiss providing no ecstasy for the victim, only for the predator. My kind notoriously thrived on cruelty, luxuriated in the agony of others. Fear was intoxicating to a predator, sometimes more so than a being writhing in the pleasure of climax.

Tears glistened in Juliet's gaze, but her body remained relaxed, her breathing even. Such an impressive pain tolerance.

Her lips trembled. I caught her bottom one with my teeth, hiding her reaction from my friends.

Juliet could not show any weakness in front of my brethren. Kept humans were used to excruciating games, blood play, harsh sex, and domination. To be fazed by a mere bite would raise questions regarding our relationship that we couldn't afford.

Part of this exercise was for me to learn how to help her survive in my world. Mated blood virgins were rare for a reason, and I fully intended to keep mine alive.

I traced her tongue with my own, wiped the tear from her cheek, and tightened my grip around her throat. It wasn't meant as a punishment, but as a reminder of my presence—a way to hold her here with me and provide comfort. Despite the two males feeding from her breast and thigh, I was the one in control of her fate, and hopefully by now, she realized I had no intention of losing her.

She returned my kiss with graceful strokes, her body melting beneath my command.

Very good, sweetheart, I praised with my mouth. Her heart

rate accelerated for an entirely different reason now, her blood singing an alluring song that prompted a delicious idea. I smiled against her lips, more pleased with her than words could express, and trailed my mouth along her jaw to her ear.

"Needy little pet." I nipped the tender lobe in mock reprimand. She shivered in response, her throat working beneath my palm. "Mmm, I can taste your arousal, Juliet." It sweetened the air, taunting my carnivorous senses. "Naughty darling," I whispered before tracing my lips down her neck to the breast closest to me.

Trevor had moved to her opposite nipple, his fangs imbedded deep into her skin. Two puncture marks highlighted her rosy peak, both dribbling blood thanks to my friend's clumsy bite. But that was typical, the lack of care for a human.

I sliced my tongue across my own lengthening incisor—just as I had earlier before kissing Juliet—and licked each abrasion to help her heal faster. Her eyes held mine, her pupils two round black points of desire. I smiled and licked her again while my hand left her neck and traveled down to cup her sex.

Mine, I told her with a look that brought a flush to her cheeks. She wasn't thinking about Trevor or Ivan anymore. Only me. I wanted to reward her for it, for letting go, for her perfect submission.

I slid a finger through her slick folds while kissing a path up to her neck. She remained perfectly still beneath my touch, but the heat radiating from her skin confirmed her yearning.

Fuck this test. My age and stature in this society dictated I could do whatever the hell I desired, however the fuck I wanted. And I *needed* her to come.

My incisors struck her deep, pulling her intoxicating essence into my mouth and coating my aching throat with her life. More decadent than any other food, the most delicious of blood, and it was all mine. The art of sharing was an old-world practice, one that solidified relationships and sealed business arrangements. Fine. I could handle that, but it would be under my terms.

Her moan was music to my ears. It fractured the rules, playing her into my hands and my game the way I preferred, and as her back arched, I heard the hiss of frustration from Ivan. I ignored him, my fingers sliding into her waiting heat while my thumb circled her clit. Her inner walls clenched around me, causing my cock to ache with want.

Soon, I promised.

I kept my penetration shallow, not wanting to disturb her innocence—yet—and sucked hard from her neck. Three vampires feeding from her delicate body would steal her consciousness quickly, but damn if I wouldn't provide her with a little ecstasy to inspire her dreams. For that was the only place she was safe from me, this world, and the nightmares surrounding us. It was the least I could do—a thank-you she more than deserved.

Her tension intensified, her groans growing in length. A glance downward showed why—Trevor and Ivan had joined the game. They weren't touching her outside their designated areas. Rather, they'd chosen to fill their bite with euphoria while continuing to drink.

Sweat glistened across her over-sensitized skin, her body shaking with restraint. She caught her lip between her teeth and bit down so hard she drew blood. I released her neck and lifted to lick the droplet away, then nuzzled her flushed cheek.

"You look so beautiful like this," I praised. "Waiting for my command." She knew better than to let go completely without my permission. I hadn't even needed to say it or warn her; she already understood.

So fucking perfect.

Her dark eyes simmered with yearning, her body so tight I knew she would scream if I allowed it. I applied pressure to her clit and she bit her lip again, her expression one of pure agony and bliss tied up in a gorgeous box of desire.

"Come for us, Juliet," I demanded, my dick eager to join her. "And don't hold back."

My name left her lips on a scream I felt all the way to my very soul as she shattered.

So. Fucking. Hot. I doubted I'd ever tire of that rapturous expression on her face or the way she trembled beneath the pleasurable assault.

Waves of electricity radiated through our bond, her body grasping at my immortality to pull much-needed life into her being. Trevor and Ivan had begun drinking in earnest now, yanking from her reserves while she writhed in the throes of a climax that seemed unending in its brutality and ecstasy.

I stroked her through it, my touch varying between gentle and harsh while her eyelids grew heavy from the fierce sensations. Gone was the pinkness of her cheeks as her blood flowed elsewhere into the greedy mouths of the men feeding from her addictive essence.

Blue touched her lips next, even while she trembled beneath the astounding shroud of hedonism. Her pupils flared at the last instant, her brain triggering some fight-or-survival mechanism far too late, and a tear leaked from the corner of her beautiful eyes. I caught it with my tongue and pressed a kiss to her closing lids.

A few lasting sparks ignited between us as the magic of my being swept over her, encasing her in a protective shell.

Her breathing thinned, and her heart slowed.

My forehead fell to hers as a painful ache stirred inside my chest. Foreign in its intensity, unwelcome in its presence.

I hate this. These rules, these practices, this monstrous side to our tendencies. Isn't this act exactly what I wanted to stop?

I sighed. Changing the system took time, something I had on an infinite loop. This would be a long gambit, a harsh one, and there would be unpleasant sacrifices on both sides.

She never had a choice, my conscience chided.

Neither did I, I reminded on a growl.

"Enough," I said out loud, unable to bear the shuddering gasps spilling from her purple lips as she struggled to breathe.

They'd nearly sucked her dry, which was the plan. An unmated mortal would die—no, she would've died already—but my old blood thrived inside Juliet while her agony ripped at my heart.

I could *feel* her fear, her sorrow, her confusion. She thought I meant to kill her and didn't understand why. Then a hint of self-assurance chased that notion, reminding her that I needed her alive.

To see inside her soul, inside her thoughts, was part of our connection. It would increase as I deepened our eternal link, to a point where we would be able to sense everything inside each other. My determination, my craving for revenge, my frustration at the current state of affairs—all of it would become evident. This was why I'd already begun confiding in her. She would know eventually anyway. Telling her up front merely solidified our partnership, helped encourage trust, and would hopefully recruit her desire to help the cause.

"You royally fucked that up," Ivan said, his voice a low snarl. "But you already know that and don't care."

I took in every detail of her immobile form, including the lack of bite marks. My friends had already healed her. Good. I added my blood to the incisions on her neck before kissing her on the cheek. Now she just needed rest. Tomorrow she would be fine.

"Grab that blanket behind you, Trevor." I gestured to the couch with my chin.

He snatched the fleece material, arousal simmering in his gaze. "You're totally fucked."

"Thank you," I said, both for pointing out the obvious and for handing me the item I requested. I wrapped it around Juliet before lifting her in my arms. "Join me for a cigar." It wasn't a request but a demand. I didn't bother looking to see if they followed me through the manor to the seating area outside. I already knew they would.

Several plush chairs were situated around an already glowing fire—my servants knew us too well. They'd even left a package of cigars on the table, prepped and ready. Trevor lifted the bottle of aged bourbon beside it and poured himself a drink before collapsing in his usual spot. Ivan selected a cigar instead and joined him, his brown eyes smoldering from the dancing flames as I settled into a chair with Juliet in my lap. I refused to leave her alone until her skin regained its creamy color.

"She comes beautifully, Darius," Ivan remarked before taking a puff. He blew out his breath slowly, expression thoughtful. "I can see the appeal, but others won't. Especially not the Regent."

I considered his words while stroking Juliet's jaw. The icy quality left an unpleasant sensation against my fingers, leading straight to my chest. "Perhaps not," I agreed. "Perhaps, I don't care."

"Clearly." Trevor knocked back the contents of his drink. "Pretty sure that won't help you win the sovereign's seat."

"Or maybe it will." Ivan scratched his chin. "It's all a show of arrogance and prestige, yes? Darius breaking from decorum will shock them and inspire intrigue. It's one way to ensure his name hits the masses."

"Says the former politician," Trevor muttered.

"I was a political advisor," Ivan corrected, tone irritated. "Far more useful than a shitty surfer."

"Back to that again. One of these decades, you'll get more creative."

"And perhaps you'll grow a brain. We all can dream."

"Enough," I cut in, not needing to witness another of their bickering matches right now. Sometimes I wondered why I chose them as my best friends. "I will figure out our strategy for the Regent's visit. A lot of our brethren seduce their unwilling victims. Perhaps I'll play into that lifestyle notion."

"By telling him you enjoy forcing orgasms from her?" Ivan asked, gaze astute. "That might actually work."

"Or you could tell him the truth." Trevor shrugged. "Not all of us prefer resistant partners."

"No, only the old ones," I replied, sighing at the reminder of why I indulged this friendship with Trevor and Ivan.

The ancient of my kind had given in to their harsher selves ages ago, choosing to embrace the darker parts of our nature and thrive at the top of the food chain. Trevor and Ivan still remembered what it was like to be human. They preferred consensual sex, not that it really existed anymore. One of the many aspects of this world I desired to change.

I traced Juliet's cool lips with my thumb. Testing my resolve was the primary reason for tonight's interaction. Juliet behaved admirably. I did not, at least not according to the rules governing higher society. But I was older than most, a direct descendant of the royal bloodline, and therefore a power in my own right.

"The Regent may hold a position higher than me now, but if I win the sovereign's seat, he'll bow to me." I uttered the words out loud despite them mostly being for myself. "Why should I bend to his will?"

"He has the trust of numerous sovereigns and royals. Winning him over will ensure your election." Ivan—the constant political voice of reason. "And, to be blunt, there is the matter of your ties to Cam."

My blood cooled at the familiar topic. "Severed ties," I corrected flatly. "And I have support from other royals." Including the one who desired me as his new sovereign.

"True. However, your rivals will point out the direct lineage, which means you can't afford to have anyone question your treatment of Juliet. Not if you want them to believe this charade."

"Any other obvious points you'd like to mention, Ivan?" I asked, bored.

We had discussed this part a thousand times. Cam met his *Erosita* by chance and fell in love. By contrast, I bought my future *Erosita* through the proper channels and treated her as everyone expected in social situations. Very different approaches.

"I've done everything to prove I'm willing to play by their rules, including denounce my blood ties," I added bitterly. "Even as Cam's sole progeny, they have no reason to suspect me of being a sympathizer."

"Right, because you resolved the issue by denying his royal throne a century ago," Trevor added, waving his hand theatrically. "I'm with Darius here, mate. Move along, puppet master, so I can enjoy my blood high."

Ivan narrowed his eyes at the blond. "Political mastermind."

Trevor's lips twitched. "Sure."

"I'm working with children," I muttered, my focus shifting to the gorgeous woman in my lap. Juliet's heart beat steadily against my palm, the only indication of the life thriving inside her. I drew a line across her collarbone with my thumb. So delicate and beautiful, and far too fragile for the games ahead.

Fewer than four months to coronation...

Ivan cleared his throat. "You've done everything right so far by purchasing a docile, obedient slave. She behaved admirably at the event over the weekend, at least in terms of their standards. But that brings us to the matter of sharing, specifically with the Regent. I don't think you'll have to, at least not yet."

Hmm, words I wanted to hear. I met his knowing gaze. "Keep talking."

His lips twitched. "She's still a virgin. Use that to your advantage. It shows a restraint very few possess—"

"I certainly would have fucked her by now," Trevor

interjected, his electric gaze on the woman in my arms. "Probably killed her by accident too."

Ivan snorted. "Crudely accurate, and honestly, I'd do the same. Regardless, tell the Regent you're savoring her, perhaps offer to pour him a drink yourself, or give him a wrist. She's not afraid to dance naked, so give him a show, but keep his fangs off her. If anything, it'll encourage him to come back for more, thereby giving you cause to develop that relationship."

"A clever plan," I murmured, considering. "It'll also grant me time to feel out his proclivities and human interests." Something I did with everyone in my acquaintance, for the desire for change expanded well beyond Trevor, Ivan, and me. I just happened to be the first pawn to move into place after decades of preparation, and we would need at least another ten to twenty years to move the rest into their respective positions, if not longer.

"Well, at least this wasn't a complete waste of time." Trevor relaxed with a yawn, his eyes fluttering closed. "I don't regret tasting your delicious little fuck toy. At all."

Ivan chuckled. "I don't normally agree with the idiot, but on this matter, I certainly do."

"You're both assholes." I couldn't help the growl in my voice. They both deserved it and worse.

"And you're far too protective of your property," Ivan tossed back. "Should probably work on that, mate."

"'Cause it's only going to get worse," Trevor added softly, his eyes closed in contentment from his recent feed. "Especially after the mating."

I admired the gorgeous woman in my arms. "Yes. I know."

Ivan cocked a brow, his gaze assessing. "The man brings up a good point, Darius. All it takes is a good fucking now."

I feigned a boredom I didn't quite feel, not with the pleasant weight settled across my lap. "Any other comments or questions about our trial run?" I asked, ready to move on from this conversation.

"Yeah." Ivan puffed his cigar and relaxed with a sigh. "Juliet's blood is fucking heaven, mate."

"Mm-hmm." Trevor looked half-lost to sleep, the glass of bourbon loosely held in his hand. "Starting to understand the whole cost thing."

"Right?" Ivan chuckled, his eyes shifting upward to the starry night. "We might have to crash here, D."

"You already have rooms waiting for you." My staff had prepared them knowing they would need a place to sleep during daylight.

Juliet's blood served as both an aphrodisiac and a drug, especially in younger vampires without any tolerance. Trevor and Ivan were only a few centuries old. Their tastes and temperance were still being refined—as was currently evident by Trevor chuckling at whatever he saw dancing behind his closed eyes. Ivan joined him, making them resemble a pair of drunken lunatics who would no longer provide any meaningful discussion tonight.

Fair enough. There wasn't anything left for us to deliberate anyway.

"I'll leave you both to your... personal fascinations." I stood, holding Juliet close to my chest.

"So you can go luxuriate in your own?" Ivan asked without opening his eyes.

"Fuck toy," Trevor added, grinning. "Go get laid."

I didn't bother pointing out that she was still half-dead. "Good night, lightweights."

"Fuck you," Ivan growled. "Ancient one."

Trevor laughed. "So fucking old."

I shook my head. "You're both high as kites."

"And not sorry at all," Trevor replied. "Maybe next time I can play with the fuck doll more. Her tits are fantastic."

"Her pussy is even better." Ivan sounded almost wistful. I walked away as he started detailing all the things he wanted to do to Juliet. If I stayed, he'd probably die.

Because no one would be touching her except for me.

"Mine," I whispered as she snuggled into my chest, her body naturally seeking my warmth. "I'll never share you again, Juliet."

A forbidden promise, one that felt far too right leaving my lips.

Societal obligations. The words ghosted through my thoughts, leaving a trail of doubt across my mind. I pushed it back, refusing to acknowledge the threat.

"Rest well, darling," I told her as I placed her in my bed. "Tomorrow we'll start your physical conditioning, and I won't be going easy on you."

Chapter Nineteen

JULIET

"Again." Darius's voice rumbled through me like a bad dream.

I hated him.

Or rather, my body did.

Yet my aching legs moved on his command, my feet hurtling over the ground outside as I forced myself to complete another lap around the grounds.

Every evening this week had started with a light breakfast and some stretching, followed by this insane series of activities Darius referred to as "conditioning." It went on for hours, until dinner. We only stopped when I needed water or food. Three days of training, and I was already done with it. Especially the running.

Sweat beaded against my skin, my breath labored from

the endless trials. I thought the Coventus had been hard on me. Darius was slowly disabusing me of that notion.

"Twenty push-ups," he said as I completed the circle. "Now."

I collapsed to the ground and considered just lying there. What would he do? Bite me? My blood heated at the prospect. He hadn't touched me since Trevor and Ivan's visit. I'd woken alone in Darius's bed with a note that said to get ready and meet him at the dining table. Then I spent the last two sleeps in my own room while he rested elsewhere. Despite spending most of our nights together exercising, I missed him.

"Push-ups, Juliet."

My gaze flicked up to his as a denial tickled my lips, but the threat in his gaze sent me into motion. Vampires loved to punish, and Darius was no different. Although, I usually enjoyed his brand of castigation.

How would he react if I refused? He couldn't force me to run. Well, not entirely true. He could compel me. That might hurt more than operating at my own pace. Still, it could be fun to deny him.

Listen to yourself! a logical part of me chastised. *You've clearly lost your mind if you think challenging a vampire is a good idea.*

Not a vampire, but Darius…

"What are you doing?" he asked, his voice holding a touch of irritation.

"Um..." I started doing push-ups again. "Sorry, Sire."

"Twenty more," he growled.

I narrowed my gaze at the ground and fell back to my knees to stare up at him. "Why? What purpose does this serve?"

His eyebrows shot upward. "Are you questioning my command?"

"No, I'm requesting a purpose." I could hear the obedient version of myself screaming in my head, but I ignored her. "I want to know why we're doing this."

He crouched before me in his jeans, elbows braced on his knees. "You're defying me."

"I'm…" I swallowed from both his nearness and the intensity smoldering in his green irises. "No, Sire. I—"

He grabbed my ponytail—something he insisted I wear—and yanked me to him. "You're. Defying. Me."

I trembled at the lethality lurking in his tone. *Oh, Goddess.* I'd managed to anger him, and on the night of the Regent's pending visit. What had I been thinking? "I-I'm sorry. I-I, it won't—"

His lips touched mine gently, silencing me. "Very good, Juliet. You're learning."

I blinked. "S-sire?"

He kissed me again, his tongue parting my lips as he pushed me back onto the grass, his body stretching out over mine. My short-clad thighs parted automatically to embrace him, even though I didn't understand. Was this my punishment for acting out? Because it felt more like a reward.

"I like you defiant." He tugged my bottom lip into his mouth, sucking lightly, before reclaiming me with his tongue. I moaned as he pressed his erection against me in the place meant only for him. "I like it very much."

His lips trailed fire over my cheeks, my neck, my collarbone. I arched as he bit my nipple through the material of the sports bra, my heart beating rapidly. "D-Darius?"

"Yes, pet?"

"I'm confused," I admitted as I grasped his bare shoulders. "Am I in trouble?"

He chuckled darkly against my breast. "No, darling. You're learning."

I swallowed. "I'm not sure I understand."

His fangs pierced my cleavage so unexpectedly that I yelped. He took a deep pull and groaned. Adrenaline mingled with bliss shot through my veins, all inspired by his bite and the way he felt on top of me.

"Darius," I whispered, running my palms over his bare back. His muscles flexed and moved beneath my touch, stirring desires in the base of my soul.

When had this attraction grown so deep? Just moments ago I'd fantasized about killing him by forcing him to run to death. Now I wanted him to pleasure me with his tongue, his body, his hands.

He took my mouth with a ferocity that left me breathless, my breasts heaving from exertion. Trickles of warm blood flowed across my skin from the bite he'd left unsealed, and a small part of me hoped that meant he intended to return. Instead, his essence spilled down my throat, causing me to cough and sputter, as he forced me to drink from him like he did the other day.

I clung to his shoulders, accepting his immortal gift with heady swallows. It warmed me from the inside, sending tingles of energy to my limbs and fingertips. His possession washed over me, coupled with his need to keep me safe. He wanted me stronger, more athletic—a fighter. The thoughts overwhelmed me while simultaneously explaining his behavior this week.

Darius was training me to be his partner. His blood strengthened me, made me faster, less breakable, harder to kill. But not all of it was tied to his need for me to help him win the sovereign's seat.

A flicker of something else—an emotion he kept buried—spurred his need as well. I reached for it, needing to know more.

The link severed abruptly, causing my eyes to water.

What just happened? How was that even possible?

I had *felt* him inside me, connected in a way I couldn't explain. Like I knew him better than I knew myself. His intentions, his desires, his feelings—they were all clear. And now gone with a snap that ached inside my heart.

"Fuck." Darius moved back onto his knees, his breathing harsher than usual, his gaze simmering. I couldn't tell if he wanted to devour me or hurt me. Maybe both.

"Sire," I whispered, uncertain. Did he want an apology? Had I done something wrong?

He wiped his hand over his face and exhaled slowly. "I think that's enough for now. We should prepare for the Regent's visit."

"O-okay." I swallowed. "Um. Is there anything I need to do?" We had yet to discuss our trial night with Ivan and Trevor, leaving me uncertain as to whether or not my behavior was acceptable. They would have told me if it wasn't, right?

"Just get ready as usual, Juliet. I'll handle the rest." He stood and turned toward the house. "Your dress is on your bed."

I went to my elbows, my mouth opening before I could stop it. "Darius?"

He stopped but didn't turn. "Yes?"

"Am I..." I cleared my throat. "Are you sharing me with him? Like Master Trevor and Master Ivan?" I shivered at the memory, not entirely convinced I wanted to repeat it.

The pleasure had been intense, almost painfully so. I'd floated through a cloud of ecstasy while my life had slipped through my fingers, Darius's eyes the last memory I possessed before everything had gone black. I hadn't known if I would survive, and that fear nearly suffocated me in my last seconds before death overwhelmed me. Then I had awoken in Darius's bed feeling renewed and full of life again.

How many times could someone survive such an experience?

He glanced over his shoulder. "Would you like me to share you with Regent Sebastian?"

I stared at Darius. Was this another test? His way of gauging my submission after acting out earlier?

My training kicked in, my response automatic. "If it is your wish, then yes."

His darkening expression told me that was the wrong answer. "Then it shall be my wish, Juliet." The words sounded cruel on his tongue, as did the way he narrowed his gaze. "Try not to disappoint me again."

Again? "Y-yes, Sire."

He turned on his heel and disappeared into the house, leaving me even more confused.

"When did I disappoint you the first time?" I whispered, my lips trembling. I looked down, spying the blood trickling over my sports bra.

Darius hadn't closed the wound.

Another translucent dress—this one royal blue with a slit up both legs to midthigh. The silver chains on my shoulders held up the fabric while the deep V-line revealed my breasts all the way to my nipple.

Darius's bite stared back at me in the mirror, almost as a taunt to remind me to behave. I still didn't understand what I did to displease him, but I would do everything I could tonight to make it up to him.

Ida knocked on my door as she entered, her motherly grin firmly in place. "Master Darius asked me to bring you some shoes." She held up a pair of silver heels that matched the adornments of my dress.

I pulled my hair over one shoulder and walked over to accept them. "Thank you."

She frowned, her brow pulling down ever so slightly. "Are you all right, dear?"

"Yes." I slipped on the four-inch stilettos. "No. I've done something to upset Master Darius." I covered my mouth, startled by my brazen reply. I knew better than to admit that out loud.

What has gotten into me? I felt undone, a tad out of control, as if I couldn't rely on the rules any longer.

"Oh, Goddess," I mumbled beneath my hand. "I'm sorry, Ida. I…" I had nothing else to say. Here I was about to meet the Regent and speaking out of turn.

I'm going to die tonight. Painfully.

"Darling girl, you have nothing to apologize for." She picked up a comb to fuss with my hair, her eyes far too kind. "If you upset Master Darius, it was probably his own doing. He's a stubborn old vampire, but there's a good man underneath. Surely you've seen that side of him by now?"

"I—yes. Yes, of course I've seen it. But earlier, I did something. He said I disappointed him."

"Ah," she murmured, gently brushing my long, dark strands. "Well, I'm sure he will forgive you, dear. He seems quite fond of you." Her eyes twinkled with the words.

"But he didn't tell me why I disappointed him," I whispered, confiding in her.

"Then ask him," she replied, making it sound so easy to defy a master by demanding explanations.

Except, hadn't I done that during the push-up session? Demanded to know why he wanted twenty more on top of however many I'd already done?

And he had rewarded me with a kiss, saying he enjoyed my defiance. Then when I asked about the sharing, he requested my input, and I yielded the decision back to him.

Darius enjoyed my defiance.

He didn't like me deferring to him on the subject of sharing.

He wanted to know how I felt about it.

I blinked. Why would Darius care? Or perhaps "care" wasn't the right word, insomuch as he wanted me to voice my opinion. To make a decision and ask questions. To be defiant.

"I see," I said, frowning. "I see." Why I felt the need to voice that twice was beyond me. Nor did I truly *see* anything, but I sort of understood. Darius craved my disobedience, not because he wished to punish me, but because he wanted to crack my shell of deference. It took me one step closer to becoming his poison—submissive on the outside, defiant on the inside.

Fine. However, what about my desires? My needs? My aspirations? Did he care nothing of those? What if I didn't want to be the weapon he used to lure his enemies into a trap?

I stopped at the door of my room, my eyes widening. Since when did I ever consider *those* questions? Never once had I possessed a dream for myself. All I ever craved was survival.

Oh, Darius, what have you awakened inside me?

An ache caressed my heart, sending spasms to my lungs and prickling tears behind my eyes. *What is this madness? How do I stop it?*

"Juliet?" Ida prompted behind me.

I cleared my throat and blinked several times to clear my vision. "My apologies. I lost my way for a moment." *Understatement of the century.* I swallowed the remains of my emotions, forcing them back into the confines of my chest, locking them away hopefully for eternity. "Is the Regent here?"

"He and Master Darius are waiting for you in the foyer, yes."

I nodded, expecting as much. "All right. Thank you, Ida."

Time to meet my fate.

Chapter Twenty

DARIUS

Juliet's conflicting emotions flickered through our bond while I listened to Sebastian Cromwell prattle on about the most recent royal scandal.

Confusion and hurt poured through our connection, Juliet's thoughts a rolling wave through my head. I hadn't been fair with her earlier when I allowed my frustration to get the better of me, but her brainwashing was just so damn frustrating.

We finally had a breakthrough when she questioned my authority, demanding a reason for all the physical training. My rewarding response had been automatic—a kiss laced in blood. Except I gave her too much, granting her access to my mind without meaning to, and had abruptly cut Juliet off when I felt her prodding for more.

Her intrusion hadn't upset me. Not really. Just startled me.

It was her subservient response regarding sharing that infuriated me.

I asked her what she wanted and she gave me a practiced response. No trust, no truth, just a colossal step backward in our work together.

Fuck. Even now I wanted to punch a hole through the wall, but instead I grinned at Sebastian and nodded along with his words. Something about Kylan killing his entire human harem out of boredom. Typical behavior for a member of the royal family.

"He requested the next Blood Day be brought forward so he can replenish what he lost, which, of course, the Goddess denied."

"An intelligent move," I replied, my eyes on the stairs. "Breaking from protocol would set a poor precedent. Besides, he can borrow from the others or seek out a whorehouse in the interim." For the right price, they would probably loan him a new harem while he waited for his replacements.

Sebastian's eyes twinkled. "My thoughts exactly. Well, not the borrowing aspect, as the royals are quite possessive of their harems, but same principle."

True. Royals didn't mind occasionally sharing but only only temporarily.

"He's going to decimate the incoming flock," I added, hands tucked into the pockets of my trousers.

Sebastian shrugged. "Most don't survive the trials anyway, but I suspect the Goddess will select extras from this year's crop to join the harem camps."

I nodded. "Likely." This was what my kind had reduced themselves to—discussing humans like sheep.

Blood Day was an atrocious ritual where humans of a certain age graduated into their futures. They competed for their positions, all hoping for the coveted immortal cup where twelve mortals fought for immortality. Only two won—one became vampire, the other lycan—the rest died.

It was a brilliant system, really, pitting humans against humans. Only the fastest, brightest, and most gorgeous, were awarded the top honor of killing each other in the name of a future. The rest were sent to battle in other ways.

Some went to the harem camps, where they vied for a royal's attention with the hopes of prolonging their very short lives. A select few with useful skills went back to human camps to procreate—thus providing the next generation—and perform menial tasks. The list of factions went on, all divided equally between lycan and vampire needs. I personally pitied those who were relegated to the moon harvest.

A shimmer of light appeared at the top of the stairs as Juliet stepped into view, her sapphire gown dazzling beneath the chandelier. Her dark eyes captured mine briefly before she descended, her head bowed in reverence as expected.

"I thought I smelled something sweet," Sebastian said, his gaze taking in every inch of the gorgeous woman descending the stairs.

"She is quite delectable," I murmured.

Juliet's apprehension trickled through our mental link, but her steps remained steady, her body deceptively relaxed. It was almost fascinating to feel the truth emanating behind her flawless facade, providing a glimpse of the woman within. My Juliet—a jewel I intended to unearth, polish, and shine. Unless she continued to bury herself and hide.

I'll dig deeper, darling. So deep that you'll glisten and burn when I'm finished with you. Only then will I make you well and truly mine.

The mental vow stirred something ancient and dark inside me—a possessive instinct as old as time itself.

Juliet folded onto the floor in a graceful bow as soon as

she reached the bottom, her body frozen and awaiting my command to rise.

"Allow me to formally introduce my future *Erosita*, Juliet." A note of wonder traveled through my mental chain to Juliet. I'd never explained that term to her, nor had I ever used it in her presence while she was awake.

"I'm impressed by your restraint," Sebastian replied, his hazel eyes lifting to mine. "Some might assume your actions, or lack thereof, boast a certain purpose."

I smiled. "Aspirations are wicked dreams, are they not?"

He returned my amusement. "Indeed they are."

Word games always bored me, but vampires adored them, especially the political ones. It would be so much easier to admit that I was undeniably refraining from fucking my blood virgin to prove I possessed superior age, skill, and the control necessary to lead. Alas, we chose riddles instead.

"May I familiarize myself with your Juliet?" he asked, his pupils dilating with barely restrained hunger. To deny him would be an insult of the highest degree. I needed to impress him, not piss him off, but that didn't stop me from imagining what his face might look like beneath my leather shoe.

"You may." I waved him forward and tucked my hand back into my pocket. In a fist. That I badly wanted to introduce to his jaw.

Off to a great start, D, I imagined Ivan saying.

I didn't kill him was my reply. Because I certainly wanted to with the way Sebastian circled Juliet now, his expression predatory. He crouched before her, drew his fingers through her thick hair before tracing his thumb along her jaw to her chin. "Let me see your face, sweetheart."

Her mental wince told me he'd pinched her, his hand too impatient for his words. She lifted her head, meeting his gaze in a bold way that caused my lips to twitch. No fear in those dark depths, something Sebastian seemed to take as a challenge.

Tendrils of hesitation threatened her mental resolve as the Regent leaned in to nuzzle her cheek and throat, but beneath her fear was a sense of comfort. I followed that train of thought, curious, and found the source of her solace.

Me.

Juliet knew I would protect her. Her absolute faith in me caressed my heart in shocking waves, my mind instantly opening up to hers.

You're safe, I whispered to her.

I know, she replied, her heart rate steady as Sebastian kissed her pulse.

"Remarkable," he marveled, his voice one of utter respect. "The Coventus has either perfected their training or you have found yourself a rare blood virgin, Darius. I've never seen one so calm. So trusting." He stood and held out his hand. "Stand, young one. I must learn more about you."

Juliet glanced at me, her expression inquiring. "Do as he says, Juliet."

"Sire," she replied, bowing slightly as she accepted Sebastian's help up from the ground.

"No, no." Sebastian placed two fingers beneath her chin. "You're too beautiful to hide." He held her there, his eyes on hers, and smiled. "Such fire, Darius. My admiration for you continues to grow by the second."

This riddle was slightly less clear. Did he admire me more for not fucking my blood virgin yet, or was there a hidden meaning to his words? Perhaps something tied to my treatment of her? Maintaining eye contact with a vampire clearly didn't faze Juliet, thanks to our time together. Sebastian wouldn't be blind to that fact, might even wonder at it, but instead he appeared to be praising me for it.

He chuckled, his hand lifting to stroke her hair. "I adore her," he said as one would about a pet. "You're going to help your master in more ways than you realize, sweetheart. Let's chat more over dinner?"

"Of course, Regent Sebastian." Her steady voice matched the confidence in her expression, eliciting a joyful laugh from our guest.

"Utterly delightful," he praised, his hazel eyes sparkling at me. "I'm positively envious."

Age and experience had taught me how to read my competitors, search for traces of a lie, uncertainty, and manipulation. All of Sebastian's cues confirmed his sincerity and enjoyment. Something new—a fascination—had piqued his interest in the best way possible. All in the form of my beautiful Juliet.

"She's very special," I agreed, pleased with her performance. "And probably starving after the workout I gave her earlier."

Sebastian's focus shifted to the bite marks on her cleavage, his lips tilting. "I'm certain she enjoyed it."

I captured her gaze and smirked. "I'm not quite sure she did."

The subtle flattening of her lips confirmed my words and provoked another laugh from the Regent. I was referring to the running—something she knew—but Sebastian mistook it as something else.

Another word game, one my opponent unknowingly lost.

"Shall we?" I gestured toward the main hall that led to the dining area.

"We shall," Sebastian agreed, extending his arm to Juliet. "If you would lead the way, sweetheart."

"Thank you, Regent," she murmured, her steps sure as she escorted our guest. I admired her pert little ass in the translucent sapphire fabric. My cock stirred at the sight, irritated that I'd ignored my needs all week. Alas, she had needed her strength after the way Trevor and Ivan had fed from her a few days ago. And now, she definitely required the energy to handle Sebastian. He would not go easy on her, might even kill her if I didn't monitor him carefully.

We entered the dining area—a room I was beginning to dislike—and Juliet guided Sebastian to the chair Ivan had sat in earlier this week. Rather than sit down, the Regent assisted her into the seat and smiled up at me. "May I join her, Darius?"

Okay, yeah, I really fucking hated this room now. "Please, be our guest," I said waving at the space meant for Juliet.

Sebastian flashed a pair of dimples that gave him a young appeal as he settled beside my blood virgin. She didn't move as he draped a napkin over her lap, then one over his own, and eyed me as I took over the space across from them.

Raquel, one of Gladice's cooking aides, entered with a tray of salads, her head bowed in reverence. Decorum. Something I rarely expected in my home, but had to be engaged because of our guest. Another aspect of society I would love to change, but I was getting ahead of myself.

Sebastian placed his palm on Juliet's thigh. "Tell me about your education, darling girl. What are your strongest attributes?"

She flicked her gaze at me, again seeking my guidance, and I gave her a subtle nod. Her pink tongue swept over her lower lip, her shoulders squaring as she looked directly at our guest and recited her portfolio. It reminded me of the auction when the Coventus's auctioneer listed all her traits and aptitudes. High marks in linguistics, history, logic puzzles, memory games, and government affairs. All the makings of a perfect blood virgin.

"What about the arts?" Sebastian asked in fluent German—one of the languages Juliet spoke fluently.

She replied with a flawless accent, studiously recalling her scores in dance, music, and choir. Sebastian ate his salad while she spoke, his other hand still firmly affixed to her thigh. I busied myself with my own food to refrain from the desire to break his arm.

"And sexual prospects?" he prompted, his eyes darkening with curiosity.

Juliet swallowed, the only indication of her discomfort. All those years of brainwashing kept her calm and collected as she detailed every aspect of her sexual education from throat training to observation courses to female-on-female instruction. I knew all of this, but to hear it outlined so openly, to realize why she sucked cock so incredibly well, enraged my sensibilities.

And yet, compared with so many others, Juliet's experience was considered easy. No vampire could touch her in the Coventus, not as a blood virgin. She had to witness unthinkable actions around her, but never *to* her. Only the mortal matrons could touch their charges.

"Fascinating," Sebastian said, his gaze appraising. "You'll forgive me for my questions, but you're quite rare, Juliet. While blood virgins are trained for such affairs as this, very few actually graduate to this level."

Because most of them were fucked to death, sent to breeding farms, or returned to the Coventus to train the next generation. I set down my fork, finished with my wilting salad. "Eat, Juliet," I said, asserting my authority in the room.

"Yes, Sire." She immediately complied.

Sebastian smiled. "Beautifully obedient." He finally removed his palm from Juliet's thigh and relaxed into his chair, his salad long gone. "She's perfect for your platform, Darius. The royals will love her."

"Platform?" I repeated, arching a brow.

"Enough with the posturing." He waved an errant hand. "We both know you want the sovereign's seat. No point denying it."

"And here I thought we might play a few more word games," I said, amused and slightly relieved. I expected at least another hour of posturing and pontificating before we reached this point. Thankfully, it seemed my guest was done with the formalities and ready to progress to business. "Your frank summarization means you have an opinion. What is it?"

"I want you to run." No hesitation, no hint of a lie, not even a smile.

I lifted my glass of wine—a dark red laced with blood—and swirled the contents. "Why?"

The Regent smiled. "Because you're Cam's only blood heir."

A surge of shock traveled down the connection, the only indication Juliet recognized the name. Her gaze remained on her plate, her mouth slowly chewing, although she clearly understood the implication of Sebastian's statement.

"You wish for me to assume a position because of my blood ties," I mused and took a sip of the fortifying liquid.

"You're essentially royalty, Darius, and by far the most powerful of our kind in this region. There are a few who will challenge you on the basis of your century of disappearance—"

"And Cam's treason," I interjected, the bitter note in my voice coming easily after decades of practice. "Can't forget that major detail."

Raquel returned, switching our salads for the main course of roasted chicken, mashed potatoes, and a melody of vegetables. Juliet picked at those first, her old habits of eating healthily overriding her taste buds.

Sebastian murmured a few words of appreciation about the meal and suggested we eat before continuing our discussion. I maintained an air of nonchalance, as if I didn't have a care in the world, and indulged in the rich food while memories whirred through my thoughts.

Cam. My maker. A royal and the rightful heir to the Goddess's throne.

"I'm sorry to lay this burden on you, Darius, but it's the only way. You must continue what I started, or all of this will be for naught. My death will mean nothing. My sacrifice will be in vain. Do you understand? You're humanity's protector now. You're the

future's only hope."

His strong hands had gripped my shoulders so hard they nearly broke. Then he hugged me for the last time and disappeared into the night.

The next time I saw him, he existed inside of an urn.

I denounced him that day. Poured gasoline over his ashes, lit a match, and watched him disappear with dry eyes. The hardest fucking charade of my very long life.

"That was delightful," Sebastian said, patting his stomach.

Juliet was only halfway through her plate and slowing down. I let her off the hook for tonight but decided a bigger breakfast would be in order tomorrow.

I finished my last bite and set down my fork, dreading what I had to offer next.

"They're calling it a harmonious future, saying it's the only way for lycan and vampire to live in peace—by enslaving humankind. But it's a classist system meant to benefit the royals and alpha packs. It's a game of power and blood and death. We are the superior race; of that I harbor no doubts. But that doesn't mean we must be cruel and torture our food."

Cam's vehement words scoured my soul, leaving a bitter taste in my mouth.

"Play the game, my son. Move all the pieces into place and strike from within. You know the chessboard better than anyone, including me. Use it. Embrace it. Own it."

I fought the urge to clench my fists. Cam gave up everything for this future. Decades of planning since and it was finally time to make my move. I couldn't afford to falter, not even for her. My darling Juliet.

I sipped my wine, collecting my thoughts and easing my insides. Then smiled indulgently. "Can I interest you in any dessert, Sebastian?"

Desire lit the Regent's features as he shifted his focus to Juliet. She pushed aside her plate, her throat working to swallow her last bite.

"Yes," he replied. "You most certainly can."

Chapter Twenty-One

JULIET

The chicken turned over in my stomach. I knew this was the plan, yet a deep pain echoed in my heart upon hearing Darius's words.

Can I interest you in any dessert, Sebastian?

My instincts rioted, hating the idea of letting yet another man bite me.

And yet, that's always been your purpose, my logical side reminded. *Why would that ever change?*

Because Darius asked me if I wanted to be shared.

And you never told him no.

I wanted to growl in frustration at that pliant voice, the one always spouting reason and reminding me to obey. Why now, of all times, I didn't know. Maybe it was exhaustion. Or perhaps I'd hit a limit of some kind. An impenetrable wall lined with foreign words detailing a past where humans had rights, where vampires didn't use my kind solely for food and sexual gratification.

Impossible.

Go away.

You're going to die. Do as you're told.

I'll die anyway.

A finger trailed down my neck to the chains of my dress, fondling the metal. "Do you have a preference, sweet girl?" Sebastian asked, his voice indulgent.

I'd like to drive a stake through your dead heart.

The foreign thought popped through my head so suddenly that I nearly gasped. To think about killing a vampire was tantamount to treason.

What is wrong with me?

Ice cubes danced along my spine.

Pull it together. Obey. Or die.

Would that be so bad?

Yes!

The sound of a chair scraping over the floor followed by Darius's familiar footsteps had me glancing up at him. His scowl told me that was the absolute wrong thing to do. He grabbed me by my hair, yanked my head back, and captured my gaze.

"Is something wrong, darling?" he asked, a growl in his voice. "Did you not hear the Regent?"

Had I missed something? "I..." I swallowed the oversized rock clawing at my throat. Or I tried to, anyway. "N-no, Sire."

His brow furrowed, his grip loosening slightly. "Are you feeling all right?"

Say no, Darius whispered through our connection, his voice clear in my mind. *Tell me you're unwell. Do it now.*

The command in his tone made me flinch. "I'm not feeling well, Sire. My apologies."

He tilted my head to the side, ran his finger over my pulse. "Hmm. Did I work you too hard earlier, darling? I noticed you barely touched your food."

I'd only eaten about half of it because of the rich quality. It upset my stomach to eat too much. "I'm sorry, Sire."

He shook his head in reproach, his irritation evident. "She's still new to this, doesn't realize that she needs to tell me when I've drained her too thoroughly." He tugged on my hair, making me flinch, and cast an apologetic look at Sebastian. "Clearly, I have some work to do with her."

I couldn't see the Regent, but I heard the smile in his voice as he replied, "Discipline is important."

"Indeed. I have half a mind to let you drain her dry right now for her impudence, but then I wouldn't be able to apply my own brand of punishment later." He sighed, long and hard. "What would you do, Sebastian?"

"Spank her ass raw, fuck her, and then drain her." The words sent a tremor through me. I'd seen that particular brand of discipline administered on my own matron more than once. It usually took her days to recover.

Darius chuckled. "A delightful idea, but it would take up much of our remaining time together before dawn. And we still have a discussion to finish." His thumb brushed my pulse while he spoke, applying a subtle pressure that felt more like a brand. Ownership. Possession. A way of marking me as his in the most basic of ways.

"Too true," Sebastian said, standing beside us. "I suspect there will be more dinners in our future. Perhaps I will indulge in your offer of dessert then."

"She'll be more experienced," Darius responded. "In all ways." The implication churned my stomach. He was offering more than my blood.

Experienced. In all ways.

He meant sexually.

As in, he would share my body in the future to make up for this transgression.

My mouth went dry, my heart hammering against my ribs. Darius intended to share me beyond drinking.

I no longer needed to fake feeling ill because now I truly did.

A foreign touch drifted up and down my arm, shooting ice through my veins. "I've always enjoyed a good game of delayed gratification," Sebastian murmured. "Gives me more to look forward to on my next visit."

"I promise she'll be better behaved as well," Darius replied, his grip tightening on my hair. It pulled so harshly my eyes started to water. Or maybe that was the deep sense of betrayal simmering beneath my skin.

I trusted you.

Because you're a stupid, naive little girl. Trusting a vampire. What were you thinking?

Another tug forced me to my feet.

"Go to my room, Juliet." His growl pierced the haze of my mind, settling across my shoulders. "Wait for me. Naked."

"Y-yes, Sire." It came out raspy, twined with fear.

He truly meant to punish me this time. I could feel it in the angry lines of his body, the way he shoved me away from him as if I were nothing but a piece of meat, and the dismissive way he turned his back on me.

Try not to disappoint me again.

I had failed miserably, yet I didn't understand what I'd done wrong. My heels clacked over the marble, dragging me toward his room with heavy steps of dread. At least he would be with the Regent for a while longer discussing their future plans. Politics. Cam.

The name sliced through the fog of my shame and terror, sending a jolt of confusion through my thoughts.

Everyone knew Cam—the treacherous royal who tried to assassinate the Goddess. *He* was Darius's maker? Regent Sebastian had referred to Darius as Cam's only heir, another term for progeny. That essentially made Darius royalty—the next in line.

Why does he live here? I took in the ornate fixtures on the walls, the oil paintings, fancy chandeliers, handwoven rugs.

They screamed wealth and privilege, as did everything else about Darius. His age, his control, his prestige.

I reached the door to his room and blew out a breath.

What awaited me in here? What would he do? Nothing good, not with the way he vibrated fury downstairs. I'd never felt him so furious. He always maintained an air of calm, his countenance patient to the extreme. Well, I'd apparently crossed a line. I just didn't understand how. I did everything he asked. I ran. I learned how to play with knives—not well, but I tried. He'd forced me to fire a gun just yesterday. I never complained, not once, even when I felt like running those laps would kill me.

Well, I did question him today. But he kissed me afterward. That meant I did well, right?

"I don't understand," I mumbled to the door. "None of this makes any bloody sense!" I slammed my fist against the wood and jumped at my own outburst. The sound bounced off the walls, no doubt reaching the vampires downstairs.

Oh no.

Oh no, no no.

I slid into the room, needing to hide. Maybe they would assume it was someone else, a servant accidentally dropping something. I flicked the chains of my dress from my shoulders, allowing the garment to pool on the ground and slipped beneath the comfort of Darius's sheets.

Protection, my soul sighed.

A lie, my mind replied. *You're not safe anywhere.*

I winced and cocooned myself even deeper within the blankets. My shiver had nothing to do with the temperature and everything to do with the immediate future.

My eyes refused to close even as my body relaxed into the comfort of the plush mattress. Darius could enter at any minute, enraged, and demanding penance.

For what?

My sins. My wrongdoings. My disrespect.

I shuddered, my vision blurring.

"I hate this," I whispered.

For over two decades, I simply accepted my fate, bowed to the will of the vampires around me, did as I was told to survive. And for what? To live in constant fear? To be bitten and drained to within an inch of my life over and over again? To be forced to sexually please whomever my master demanded?

That wasn't living. It was walking death.

I had it wrong this whole time. The rules, the decorum, the constant obeying. I followed them all to placate the superior beings and to keep them from killing me. What I should have been doing was rebelling to encourage them into ending my misery.

"I'm such a fool," I marveled. It was death I needed to court, not life. To put an end to it all.

Yes, a dark part of me whispered. *Tonight*...

I nodded, feeling suddenly relieved. No more pain, confusion, or turmoil. No more pleasing a master I couldn't understand. No more false promises of a changed future and poison nonsense.

No more anything.

My body relaxed, my eyes falling closed.

The future was blissful.

Quiet.

Death.

Chapter Twenty-Two

Darius

I closed the door after watching Sebastian depart.

"Thank. Fuck." I ran a hand over my face, blowing out a breath.

Our conversation had gone well, his support clear and true as he endorsed me for the position of sovereign. Another chess piece moved into place, shifting me into the perfect position for ascension.

I smoothed my hand down my tie and pulled out my phone. Ivan answered on the first ring.

"Good. You lived through the meeting."

I snorted. "You forget that Sebastian is half my age and of nonroyal blood." To kill him would have been as easy as flicking my wrist, and I had considered it more than once tonight.

"Ah, but he's the Regent. He carries the power of the law." His mocking tone made my lips twitch.

"Yes, which only means the paperwork and consequences would be mildly irritating. And, admittedly, keeping him alive also serves a more useful purpose."

A beat of silence as Ivan read between the lines. "He's agreed to back your candidacy."

"Better," I replied. "He's agreed to nominate me formally at the Parliament Gala in a few weeks."

"Well, shit. That went better than expected. What did you do, let him fuck Juliet?"

My amusement died on a growl. "No." I hadn't even been able to let him feed on her, let alone touch her. Fortunately, she seemed to have received my message to feign illness and did so spectacularly. I would be rewarding her once I joined her upstairs.

He chuckled. "I'm sure her blood was enough, then."

I didn't bother correcting him and started toward my room, eager to reconnect with Juliet. Focusing on Sebastian had required cutting off her thoughts, and, oddly, I rather missed having her in my head.

"I need you and Trevor to make the appropriate preparations for the gala," I said as I reached the top of the stairs. "Also, message our royal friend with an update. He'll approve of this outcome."

"Considering it removes him completely from the scheme, I agree. As for the gala, options A and B, correct?"

"Yes." Option A, my opponent balked and withdrew his interest in becoming the new sovereign. Option B, a lethal accident lurked in his future. I preferred the latter. Gaston was a sadistic ass who preferred his blood young, as in under the age of ten.

"On it. Anything else?"

"Not yet."

"Sweet. Go play with your fuck toy to celebrate."

I stood just outside my bedroom and couldn't fight the

smile his words evoked. "I intend to."

"Not jealous at all," he replied and hung up.

My lips twitched again. Ivan would be extremely jealous if he knew what I had planned for my sweet Juliet.

I twisted the handle and slipped inside the dimly lit room. *So quiet.* I closed the door softly, my footsteps silent against the carpeted floor.

Juliet's small form was curled into a ball in the center of my bed, her hair spilling seductively over my silk pillows. She didn't stir as I approached, her slender shoulders rising and falling in soft, peaceful breaths.

Gorgeous, I thought, loosening my tie. I should request she sleep here every night. Naked. Wrapped up in my sheets.

Warmth touched my chest. The only reason she slept elsewhere this week was to protect her from my harsher needs. She required rest. I required sex. The two did not mix, but I couldn't go without her any longer.

I slipped the knot from my neck and let the ends hang on either side. Juliet still had no idea I stood behind her, lost to her dreams.

I shrugged out of my jacket, laid it over the chair beside the bed, and unfastened my cuff links. They dropped to the nightstand with a clink that resonated through the room. My darling blood virgin, however, remained soft and unbothered, like an unknowing mouse resting in the middle of a viper's den. She didn't seem to hear me slip out of my shoes or unfasten my belt, her body peacefully still in slumber.

Hmm, how should I wake her? With a kiss? Lightly tracing her spine? I considered my options while moving around the foot of the bed, needing to see her face. My fingers busied themselves with unbuttoning my still-tucked-in shirt. Juliet would remove my pants for me. Preferably with her teeth.

Except as I reached her again, I frowned. Dark circles rimmed her eyes, her skin pink with exhaustion.

No, not exhaustion. Devastation.

I brushed my thumb across the damp stains on her cheeks. Her lashes fluttered open, two pinpoints of pain staring at me with abject fear lacing their depths. She jolted back, pulling the covers as she went, her body curling into the fetal position.

"Juliet," I murmured. "It's just me. Sebastian's gone."

Her pulse spiked, calling to my predatory instincts. *Terror.*

She smelled delicious, but I preferred my lovers aroused, not petrified. I left my shirt partially unbuttoned and sat on the bed beside her, my hand catching her shoulder as she tried to roll away.

My brow furrowed. "What's wrong, Juliet? Are you hurt?"

Her breath shuddered out of her on a harsh sound that suspiciously resembled a laugh. "No. Yes." The hoarse quality of her voice coupled with the wet stains of her abandoned pillow confirmed she'd been crying.

I lay down next to her on top of the comforter. "Look at me, Juliet."

"Why?" she mumbled sullenly.

"Because I told you to."

She tugged her lip between her teeth and tightly closed her eyes. A tremble worked its way through her limbs, beneath my palm, until she gasped for breath and finally met my gaze. The fire in her pupils shrouded in agony was an intoxicating combination.

"I hate you," she whispered. "I hate you more than breathing."

"That's quite a statement," I replied, surprised and a little turned on by her furious outburst. "May I ask why?"

"Why?" she repeated. "Why?" Louder now. "I have no choice. No freedom. No reason to live other than to survive, which means little when my life—however short it may be—is spent slaving away for you and your kind. Being used to the point of death, revived, and used again!

And it goes beyond just sharing my blood. You intend to require sex. My body isn't even my own. My mind sure as hell isn't my own. Nothing, Darius. Nothing belongs to me!"

She let out a cry and flung my hand from her as she rolled to her back, the heel of her palms digging into her eye sockets.

"Death would be easier. Kinder. If you possess any humanity inside you, you'll kill me. But I know you won't. I'm too expensive of an investment, and even now, I feel compelled to beg for your forgiveness for an outburst even an animal would proclaim in my position. And I'll accept my punishment because that's what a good blood virgin does."

Her hands curled into fists above her head, lifting and crashing downward. I caught her wrists before she could harm herself, my knees going on either side of her hips in the process. She growled beneath me, bucking like a wildcat, her gaze crazed with fury and fear.

"Juliet," I soothed, my voice calm as I restrained her as gently as I could.

"I hate you!" she yelled. "I want to die!"

Fuck.

She'd finally shattered. All the mind control indoctrinated into her through years of harsh conditioning had finally subsided to the reality of our situation.

"Kill me," she begged, her words slicing my heart. "I want to die. Please kill me." Fresh tears spilled from her eyes, the fight leaving her body on a whoosh of air that sounded so painful I felt it deep inside.

This was the moment I had most desired and dreaded. The moment where she broke so completely, so utterly, that emotionally she had nowhere to go but up.

I shifted off of her prone form, my back going to the headboard as I pulled her quivering body onto my lap. "Juliet," I murmured, my arms holding her close. "You're safe with me."

Another of those harsh laughs left her, fractured by a sob. "Safe," she mumbled. "You plan to share me with Sebastian, let him spank me and fuck me raw."

Her use of his earlier words simmered in my blood, but I swallowed back the fury. "Never, Juliet. He'll never touch you."

She shook her head sadly. "He will."

"No, Juliet. He will not." I pinched her chin, forcing her gaze upward. "You are mine, and I will not share you with him."

"You already said you would." It came out soft and defeated, and suddenly, I understood what had pushed her over the edge. I'd destroyed her faith in me with a few carefully worded phrases. It went beyond that, of course, her background having paved the way to this unavoidable end, but my statements tonight cracked what remained of her glass walls.

"Oh, darling." I sighed and kissed the top of her head. "I only *implied* a future experience to satisfy him tonight."

"Experienced. In all ways." She uttered the words on a shaky exhale and trembled violently, her disgust and revulsion written clearly across her rounded shoulders. It seemed my earlier proclamations had struck a nerve. Considering them from her point of view, I could see why.

"It's true that you will be more experienced—in every way—the next time we have him over for a meal." I lifted her chin again, catching her focus. "Because I don't plan to entertain him again until after I'm crowned sovereign." I let those words sink in, but only torment stared back at me. Her emotional haze was clouding her logic. She needed more information to understand. Specific words. Comfort. Trust.

"Juliet." I traced my thumb over her quivering bottom lip. "It is considered quite unbecoming for one in a lower position—such as a regent—to request anything of a sovereign. Especially, favors involving something as precious as an *Erosita*."

She blinked those big brown eyes up at me. "*Erosita?*"

I smiled. "Yes. The formal term for a human bonded in the ceremonies. It's a title of sorts that carries great respect among my kind." And a hell of a lot of envy. "You will be my *Erosita* once we complete the ritual."

"More blood," she mumbled.

"Yes, and the communion of our souls." *Mind, body, and soul.* We would share everything then—our blood, our passion, our thoughts. I nuzzled her hair, my chest tight.

"I'm sorry for earlier, darling." The apology escaped me without preamble. I wasn't even sure what I meant to ask forgiveness for, but the words felt right. They felt needed. None of this was fair to her. All her irate comments, her accusations and statements, were founded in truth. She never asked for any of this; none of her kind did.

"I want to understand," she whispered. "I *need* to understand."

My gaze fell to hers, the yearning swimming in her chocolate depths a palpable thing. "You need to see," I replied, agreeing. That had always been part of the plan, but not until she could truly appreciate what I had to show her. "You're right, Juliet. It's finally time." Tomorrow I would make the arrangements. Now that she had broken free from the shackles of her brainwashing, I could move to the next phase of her training.

A firm introduction to reality. Not the one painted in her books, texts, and presentations given by the Coventus. But the real world and what had become of it outside the confines of wealthy vampire society.

I kissed her hair, holding her tight.

This was just the beginning of her reeducation. Poor darling. If she thought tonight's truth hurt, she had a lot more pain coming.

Chapter Twenty-Three

JULIET

We're flying.

On a jet.

In the starry night.

Never in my wildest dreams had I imagined such an experience.

The nearly full moon painted the dark sky in shades of alluring colors. I took in every detail, memorizing the scene in case I never saw it again.

"Midnight," Darius said, his phone at his ear. He sat beside me in a pair of black trousers and a cream-colored pullover that offset his darker features. I wore jeans, a deep-red sweater, and boots. It was by far the most suffocating outfit of my existence. No part of me was on display except for the hint of my breasts at the V-neck collar.

"Main courses for six," he continued, pausing to listen. "No, room for one. The others will handle their own accommodations." He reached out to grab my hand, pulling it into his lap to rest against his thigh. "Yes, that would be acceptable."

My attention drifted to the stars again. Darius had dimmed all the lights, granting us an undisturbed view of the exquisite scenery.

Amazing...

"That is correct. Thank you." Darius ended the call and relaxed beside me, his thumb lightly brushing my hand. "We should be landing in about an hour."

I nodded mindlessly, unable to truly focus with the giant, distracting orb outside my window. The stars beyond it twinkled in the midnight sky, soothing my soul.

"I can feel your fascination burning through our connection, Juliet," he murmured. "It's such an unusual sensation. Very little intrigues me these days." He lifted my hand to his lips and nibbled my wrist, causing my belly to flutter.

"Where are you taking me?" I asked, my lips moving before I realized what I intended to say. My heart faltered for a beat at the bold inquiry, but my mouth refused to retract it or apologize.

I wanted to know.

No, I *deserved* to know.

"Chicago," Darius replied.

I blinked, surprised at his easy acquiescence. *Of course he replied. Why wouldn't he?* I shook my head.

If last night taught me anything, it was that I didn't understand Darius at all. I expected a beating—or worse— for my behavior, and instead he spoke to me in calming tones while holding me all night.

He promised never to share me. He didn't yell at me when I ranted incoherently. He let me cry. He even kissed away my tears.

And now he answered my question without hesitation.

"Chicago," I repeated. The name struck a familiar chord, but not from my studies at the Coventus. "That was a popular city in the former United States, right?" It came up numerous times in his history books. "Does it still exist?"

"Everything still exists. The question you mean to ask is, what has the city become?" He lowered our joined hands to his thigh and sighed. "You know it as Lilith City."

My gaze finally left the window, my heart in my stomach.

Lilith City? That was the heart of the vampire world. The Goddess herself lived inside those notorious walls, maintaining law and order among her kind. Blood virgins only visited for political functions or to undergo a trial and execution.

Did Darius intend to hand me over to the vampire court for punishment? To have me put to death for insubordination? To make a public example of me?

Goddess, I deserved it. Especially after last night. I'd broken every rule, allowed emotion to control my behavior, acted poorly in front of the Regent, and considered death a better alternative to fate. The list of my transgressions was endless.

Am I going to die?

Would that be so bad?

Darius leaned into my space, pressing his lips to mine. My thoughts melted into a warm puddle as his tongue slipped inside my mouth, binding me to the present.

Safe, my soul whispered. An instinctual trust that surpassed logic. He could be flying me to my death, or worse, and I couldn't stop myself from returning his kiss.

"Relax, Juliet," he said softly. "I have no desire to punish you. Not for doing exactly what I wanted." He kissed me again, this one slower, more intimate. His hand still held mine, his thumb drawing languid circles against my wrist.

"Darius," I whispered, finding my nerve.

"Yes, darling?"

"Tell me why we're going to Lilith City." It came out bolder than I expected, the request sounding more like a demand.

He smiled against my mouth. "Hmm, I knew you were the right one." His alluring eyes brimmed with approval as he held my gaze. "What did the Coventus teach you about Lilith City?"

"It's the revered home of the Goddess and the vampire governance board." The words sounded textbook to my ears, but accurate.

"Revered home of the Goddess," he repeated with a snort. "Let me guess; you were forced to pray to her, right?"

I nodded. "She is the supreme being."

"More like a supreme bitch." He shook his head. "I've known Lilith for over two thousand years. Goddess, she most definitely is not. Just a very old royal vampire with a penchant for power."

My mouth hung open in utter shock at his easy candor. He had just insulted the highest-ranking official in our world—the Goddess herself—while maintaining a sardonic tone.

"You could be killed for such a statement," I whispered, dismayed.

They're always listening, my matron had warned. *Never take Her name in vain.*

Darius chuckled. "Sheep scare so easily." He squeezed my hand. "Don't fret, darling. Lilith may desire to kill me, but it won't be for belittling her precious title. None of my brethren consider her a supreme being, merely a royal queen. Humans are the ones taught to worship her, mostly because she finds it amusing."

I frowned. That couldn't be right.

Except, well, maybe it was… Why would he lie?

The Coventus had held rituals where blood virgins read

passages from ancient Latin texts thanking the Goddess for gifting us all life. All the ceremonies were led by the matrons, not the vampires. They merely lurked along the sidelines, serving as guards to keep us all in line.

"The vampires never kneeled or paid homage to her during the rituals," I said, realizing the truth as I spoke the words. "Your kind doesn't worship her."

"No. However, there are many who respect her leadership." The way he said it suggested he was not among those who did.

"Whom do vampires revere?" I wondered out loud, curious now.

"Ourselves, mostly." He drew his thumb over my knuckles, his voice thoughtful. "The Coventus preaches propaganda to keep humans in line. Having a higher power to pray to gives you all a false sense of hope that is easily manipulated. It's actually quite brilliant in terms of a control mechanism, and also terribly sad."

Control mechanism—an accurate summation of my life. I never had a choice, not once, and until Darius came into my life, I never desired one.

"We are the predators; humans are the prey," he continued softly. "And my kind has always enjoyed playing with our food." His gaze dropped to my neck while he spoke, warming my blood.

Yes, please, my body whispered. *Bite me.*

"And you?" I asked breathily. "Do you enjoy playing with your food too?" *Do you enjoy playing with me?*

His lips curled. "Stand," he said, releasing my hand.

My breathing slowed, his demand heating me from the inside out. *Dare I refuse him?* More importantly, did I even want to?

The answer came as I rose, my legs sure. Even after my convictions last night, I still desired to please him. Not the vampire. Not society. But Darius himself.

Because I enjoy satisfying him.

"Straddle me, Juliet."

I slid onto his lap, my thighs parting intimately over his as my hands fell to his flat abdomen. "You still haven't told me why we're going to Lilith City."

"I know." He wrapped his palm around my nape, his other hand going to my hip. "It's a quick stop on the way to our true destination, one that allows me to reveal the truth of our world to you." His thumb stroked my pulse. "I want to show you what the Coventus has hidden."

"Why?"

"You'll see when we get there." His nose stroked my cheek as he slowly inhaled, his touch a featherlight caress. "You smell amazing," he murmured, his grip tightening around my nape. "My own version of heaven."

His lips skimmed my jaw, causing goose bumps to prickle my arms. I loved the feeling of his mouth on me, the way it whispered over my skin, leaving a smattering of heat in its wake.

"You asked if I enjoy playing with my food," he said softly against my ear. "Was that an invitation, darling?" He nuzzled my neck, his teeth skating over my sensitive skin. "Because it certainly sounded like one."

My throat went dry, my eyes falling closed.

Please...

Darius's fangs taunted the vulnerable place below my ear, sending a tremble down my spine. Not of fear, but of temptation. I craved his vampiric kiss, his possession, the feel of him absorbing my essence and *owning* every intimate piece of me.

Think, Juliet.

There was something I wanted to know.

Several somethings, actually.

But, *ohhh*, maybe they weren't that important. Not with Darius's mouth against my pulse, lightly nibbling.

"Answer me, Juliet," he demanded in a deceptively soothing tone. "Tell me if that's what you meant."

Was it? I couldn't remember. Not with the way his hand felt splayed against my hip, the other holding my nape, and the hint of his incisors teasing my sensitive skin.

"Bite me," I begged, my voice husky with yearning. "Please."

He chuckled. "Do you desire pleasure, sweetheart? Is that it?" He pulled me closer, up his thighs, placing my center against his unmistakable arousal. I arched into him on a moan, thirsting for more.

Who am I?

Who cares.

I pulled at my sweater, needing to remove it. So hot and restricting, and—

Darius grabbed the hem, holding it against my stomach. "Clothing remains on," he said, his voice low and commanding.

I groaned and met his heated gaze. "Why?"

"Because we're landing soon." He nipped my lip hard enough to draw blood. It hurt rather than pleased—a punishment for being too eager? "Because you're tempting enough as it is, and my control isn't infallible." His tongue lightly traced the wound, sending a shot of ecstasy to my core and chasing away the residual pain of seconds ago. "Because I intend to devour you properly later, once our work is done."

"Properly?" I repeated, my mind foggy from the delirious sensation of his mouth teasing mine. "Do you intend to finally deflower me?" A thrill went through me at the prospect, followed by a shadow of concern.

Would it hurt?

Would he still want me afterward?

Would I survive?

The last thought gave me pause, my pupils fully focusing on Darius's handsome face. His smoldering gaze ignited a flurry of butterflies in my lower belly. Oh, it would hurt—no question—but Darius never gave me pain without pleasure.

"Claiming your body is the final phase of the ceremony, Juliet." His hand slid beneath my sweater, his touch soft against my bare skin. "It will make you mine. Indefinitely."

"Isn't that the point?" I asked, breathless. "Or are you waiting until I've proven myself in some way?"

His thumb glided up my side, tracing my ribs. "You have nothing left to prove to me. I know you're perfect for my needs."

"Oh." I licked my lips, considering. "Then… tonight?"

Amusement touched his gaze. "So eager for me to fuck you, darling?"

"I… I just don't understand why you haven't yet." I cleared my throat. "My matron prepared me for the night of my purchase, but—"

"I hardly touched you," he finished, his palm slipping up to caress my breast. "No bra. Does this mean you are without panties as well?"

I pressed into his touch, desiring more. "You told me the 'no undergarment' rule still applied."

His lips twitched. "Indeed I did." He thumbed my nipple, exciting a tingling sensation between my thighs. "Not fucking you has been a challenge, but it serves two purposes. First, showing restraint is considered a strength among my kind, an important consideration when vying for a position of sovereign. Second, the ceremony only works when blood is exchanged at least three times prior to the claiming."

I frowned. "So if you had deflowered me before I drank from you…?"

"We could never be connected."

"And if someone else had deflowered me?"

"We could never be connected," he repeated. "Even now, if another vampire were to take you, it would destroy the process."

"Because I would be bound to a new master?"

"No, you would merely be ruined." He pinched my stiff peak, then massaged the hurt with his clever fingers. I fought back a moan while trying to process everything he just said, but it was difficult with his hand branding my tender skin.

"So." I cleared my throat, my attention shifting between arousal and information. "Um, does the ceremony only apply to blood virgins?"

"Not blood virgins, but virgins in general. And the human must remain untouched in all ways. Meaning, if you had drunk from another of my kind or been deflowered by anyone prior to me, we would not have been able to initiate the ceremony. Also, sharing your blood doesn't disrupt the ritual, nor do sexual acts without penetration, but anything tied to the bond—sex and vampire blood— can shatter everything we've built."

His hand dropped from my breast to lift my sweater, his gaze falling to my teased nipple. I didn't bother pointing out that he'd just demanded I keep my clothes on, not with the soothing air rushing across my skin. He bent to nibble my breast, his stubble chafing my stiff peak.

"From the moment you imbibed my essence, Juliet, you were forever bound to me and no one else."

"Unless someone else takes me before you," I breathed, referring to his previous comment about the potential for someone to interfere with our bonding process. That seemed to be a solid argument for him to take me sooner rather than later.

Darius captured my taut bud between his teeth and bit down. Hard. His name left my lips on a hiss as tears glistened behind my eyes. There was no pleasure in this vampiric kiss, just a harsh tugging of my essence into his mouth and a branding of my flesh. My nails curled into his shirt as I fought the scream building in my throat.

A wave of euphoria shocked my system, tightening my skin to a painful degree.

Oh, Goddess, what is he trying to do to me? My thighs clenched as another ripple of rapture pulsed through my bloodstream.

"Darius," I breathed, grasping his shoulders. The

weight of his erection against my tender core licked fire across my skin. I writhed wantonly in his lap, desiring more friction, more something. More *him*.

"No one else will take you, Juliet," he vowed darkly against my abused skin, his grip on my neck tightening. "Ever."

I panted against him, my heart pounding. "But you told the Regent—"

"Enough," he growled, raising his head to capture my gaze. "I insinuated to Sebastian that you would be more experienced, allowing him to assume I meant to share you more indulgently in the future. That was his mistake because I have no desire to ever allow another to touch you, let alone feed from you. Anyone who tries without my consent will die. Do you understand?"

The vehemence in his tone sent a jolt to my chest, derailing the rhythm. "Y-yes, Sire. I understand."

He sighed and pulled me closer, his lips meeting my forehead as he wrapped his arms around me. "Juliet, the ceremony binds us until either I die or another being claims your body." He paused, letting the information settle between us.

"Meaning only you can take me to bed," I said slowly, translating his words. "Now and forever, or the connection breaks."

"Yes, which would render you mortal again, causing you to age normally." He pressed his mouth to my hair, sighing. "This is why *Erositas* are so coveted among my kind. They are quite literally forbidden fruit. It only takes one intimate touch to shatter the eternal bond. Why would I jeopardize something so sacred for the likes of Sebastian?"

I stilled against him. "But, but you told me sharing is a requirement for my position at your side. That was the point of the training with Master Ivan and Master Trevor."

"Yes, *Erositas*—especially ones with your precious blood type—are expected to offer sustenance to guests under our current political structure. It's a way to belittle the relationship, to remind humans who is in charge, and also serves as a punishment to vampires who choose the ceremony."

"A punishment?" He loosened his hold, allowing me to shift backward. "Why?"

"The world we live in is all about power and control, Juliet. Forcing a vampire to share his mate is the ultimate form of dominance." He drew his thumb over the wound on my breast and brought the blood to his lips, licking it slowly while holding my gaze.

"Is that what I am? Your mate?" I couldn't help the note of wonder in my voice. All this time, I thought the ceremony was merely a way of binding me permanently to his side as a blood slave whom he shared and enjoyed for eternity. It granted me protection without freedom. Not that I had minded, as my purpose was to please.

Until Darius introduced me to the notion of choice...

His pupils dilated as he sliced open a wound of his own and lowered his healing essence to my nipple. My skin hummed with electricity, mending beneath his touch.

"Yes, you will be mine in all ways," he confirmed softly.

"And you will be mine?" The words were out before I could stop them, and they seemed to amuse him.

"Are you demanding exclusivity, darling?"

"I—I don't know," I answered honestly. "You said I can't be intimate or it fractures our connection. What happens if you take another to bed?"

"The ceremony binds you to me, not the other way around. I could take several blood virgins, if I wanted, without harming our connection."

I frowned. Darius could take other lovers, while I had to remain faithful. It meant I only had to sleep with him— a positive—but I disliked the notion of him pleasuring another. A knot formed in my stomach as I realized that Darius might have already taken other lovers while performing the ceremony with me.

He hadn't drunk my blood in several days, other than the medial sip. Hadn't shared my bed for two nights in a row either. Had he been indulging in another? Or several others? Was that how Darius refrained from deflowering me, by obtaining gratification elsewhere?

"This is unfair," I blurted out, my heart hammering painfully in my chest. I didn't want to share Darius. Nor did I want him to share me. It felt wrong. Cruel. Unjust.

He's mine.

"It's nature, darling." He slipped my sweater back into place, his hands falling to my hips with a gentle squeeze. "Now, I need you to buckle up. We're about to land."

Chapter Twenty–Four

JULIET

Darius escorted me down the stairs of the private jet to the black car waiting for us. He exchanged a few short words with the driver, shook his hand, and helped me into the back, where he settled beside me.

Lights unlike any I'd ever witnessed paved the way, leading to a horde of skyscrapers in the distance. So very different from Darius's isolated estate and the bare walls of the Coventus.

He reached over for my hand as the car left the airport behind, driving us toward what appeared to be a barricade of sorts in the middle of the otherwise vacant road. I peered through the windows, studying the odd formation.

No, not a barricade. A line of soldiers dressed in black, holding guns. *Just like the Coventus.*

I froze. *They are here for me, to take me back, to—*

"It's border patrol," Darius murmured, squeezing my hand and pulling me closer. "Their job is to keep everyone inside the city limits."

We slowed to a crawl, then stopped as the uniformed men surrounded the car. Darius rolled down his window, his expression bored. "Evening, gentlemen."

"Sire," a deep voice replied.

He's human, I realized with a start. *How?*

His deep-blue eyes met mine briefly before he glanced down at the clipboard in his hands. "How long are you visiting?" he asked.

"As long as I want," Darius replied, his voice underlined with authority. "I own several properties here."

The male flipped through his documents, nodding. "Right. Yes. Of course." He raised a hand, waving to someone. The soldiers surrounding the car immediately stepped back. "Have a good evening, Sire. Apologies for the intrusion."

Darius didn't reply, merely rolled up the window and relaxed as the car began to move.

"Human guards," I whispered, glancing over my shoulder at them. There were at least fifty, likely more.

"Yes, it's a coveted position among your kind because of the benefits."

"Benefits?" I repeated, shifting forward again.

"Yes. Sex, decent food, reasonable living conditions. The Vigils—as they are called—are given these luxuries in return for their service at the borders, where their primary job is to catch anyone trying to escape." His green irises flared as he met my gaze. "You will see them all over the city. They maintain law and order and are allowed to administer punishments within reason."

"Humans," I said, astounded. "Working for the vampires?" I thought most were enslaved or in various camps. Those soldiers were wandering free. With guns.

"The Vigils serve the lycans too. As I said, it's a desired

placement. Not many are selected, making it rather competitive." He brought my hand to his lips, kissing my wrist. "Force the masses to contend for a coveted position in society so they don't band together and rebel. It's a textbook control mechanism, and flawlessly executed. Essentially, humans regulate themselves without the higher beings having to put in any effort."

I opened my mouth, closed it, then opened it again. But I had nothing. No words. Not even a question.

He smiled sadly and brushed his lips against mine, lingering. "The Coventus taught you all about vampire political affairs, but nothing about Blood Day or the factions. And, likely, very little about lycans." Another kiss, this one longer, his tongue dipping in to taste mine. "Mmm, that's going to change, darling. I want you aware and knowledgeable, not sheltered and docile."

His mouth captured mine, silencing any sort of response I might have desired to voice. Not that I had one. My mind was still reeling from trying to comprehend the Vigils. *Humans policing humans. Vying for positions. Regulating ourselves.*

Darius grabbed my hips and pulled me onto his lap, forcing me to straddle him like I had on the jet. A whirring sounded behind me—a privacy screen being deployed?— as my sweater disappeared over my head, dropping to the seat beside us.

"I need to feed," Darius murmured, his lips dropping to my neck. "I wanted to on the plane, but now is more appropriate." He nuzzled my collarbone, breathing deeply. "Touch me."

My palms went to his shoulders, obeying him instantly.

"Lower, Juliet."

"Yes, Sire." I trailed my fingers down his sweater to the bulge growing beneath his trousers.

He gathered my hair into one of his hands at the back of my neck, exposing my throat. "Unfasten my pants," he whispered, his lips at my pulse. "Pull out my cock." His incisors pierced my skin on the last word. Hard. Sharp. Fast.

My eyes threatened to close even as I loosened his belt, popped the button, and slid the zipper down. His arousal—all hot, silky male—met my palm on an eager pulse. I ran my grip over him the way I knew he desired, and he rewarded me by palming my breast.

"Darius," I moaned, the ecstasy of his bite spiraling downward to the sensitive spot between my legs. He shifted my weight on his lap, moving me off-center until my core met his strong thigh. My head fell forward on a sigh, but he used his grasp on my hair to tug me back up, keeping my throat exposed to his voracious mouth.

I increased my rhythm, moving my hand over his shaft in the way my lower body craved. If the pants didn't exist, I would have been tempted to press my damp center against his erection.

Oh, Goddess, yes...

I wanted him inside me.

To seal the bond. Make me his in every way. Claim him as mine.

Except he wouldn't be. Not really.

A lie, my soul whispered. *He's mine.*

Electricity hummed across my skin, his essence mingling with mine as he drank his fill. I gave myself to him completely. Trusted him to know when to stop. Luxuriated in the ecstasy his mouth evoked. Slid my hand up and down and imagined him repeating the same motions inside me.

I wantonly pressed my aching core against his leg, requiring friction. Needing more. Needing *him*.

The hand on my hip slipped lower, his thumb unerringly finding that special place through the fabric of my jeans. A single expert press sent me flying over the edge, my scream unencumbered as his name rolled off my tongue in waves.

It was always like this—explosive.

Intense.

Overwhelming.

Insanity.

My body shook, my limbs refusing to function, my hand grasping him far too tightly. He groaned against my neck, his fangs leaving my skin. Another shock wave slammed into me, sending me spiraling even deeper. A second orgasm? A continuation? Oh, I didn't know, didn't care, just lost myself to the sensations. Hot and cold, light and dark, sound and silence.

I hardly registered Darius pushing me to my knees, his cock finding my mouth and lodging deep. Swallowing was my only option. Every salty, warm drop went straight down my throat. My own euphoria still trembling through me as my lungs burned with the need to breathe.

"Fucking perfection," Darius praised, his fingers combing through my hair. I met his gaze through the black spots dancing in my vision. "Hmm, you look gorgeous like this, Juliet—waiting so patiently for me to allow you to breathe again." He brushed his knuckles over my cheek, collecting the tears I'd unknowingly shed, and brought them to his lips. He licked them slowly, prolonging the moment while my vision clouded into a haze of black.

My eyes opened and closed several times, clearing my foggy vision to reveal a city skyline filled with twinkling lights. I blinked again. And again. But the floor-to-ceiling windows remained showcasing a night filled with activity.

"Darius?" I whispered.

No response.

I rolled onto my back—the mattress beneath me molding to my body—and took in the high ceilings. A fan rotated overhead, doing little to cool my clammy skin. The sweater and jeans were not helping.

Why had Darius redressed me? No, better still, why did he leave me here?

I stretched my arms and legs and slid off the fluffy white comforter. The silver and black adornments of the room were very masculine and clean, but the air lacked the familiar scent I craved.

A walk-in bathroom with marble furnishings and an oversized shower stood off to the left with a closed door beside it. I twisted the handle slowly and found a hallway bathed in light.

Voices floated to my ears—a female. Followed by a deep laugh that made my stomach flip.

Darius.

With another woman?

I started walking before I could stop myself and found him in the middle of an oversized living area with his arm spread along the back of a couch. A gorgeous blonde sat in the chair beside him, her legs crossed and angled toward Darius and her lips creased into a charming smile. Her bright-blue eyes found mine and widened for a moment, as though shocked to see me.

The feeling was mutual. Even more so considering I'd just pleasured Darius before arriving here. He had no need for another, and I was not sharing. If he required more blood, he could have mine. And my body. And my mouth.

He glanced up as I approached, the ankle resting on his knee shifting to the ground just in time for me to plant myself on his lap.

Mine.

I made sure my expression conveyed that while meeting the blonde's gaze. Her response was another one of those tinkling laughs.

Darius's arms came around my waist, tightening slightly. "What happened to bowing for our guests?" he asked softly.

My spine went rigid. *Bowing. Guests. Formalities.* We were in the middle of Lilith City, and I had just forgotten the most fundamental of rules. Clearly, the death wish from last night still remained because I was going to get myself killed for behaving this way.

I needed to apologize. To grovel. To… to… oh, Goddess, I had no idea what to do to fix it. Formalities weren't required with Darius, but everything changed with guests.

I tried to move, to fall to the ground, but he held me against him, his arms thick bands of solid muscle. Tears flooded my vision. "Sire, I—I—"

"Oh, stop torturing the poor girl, Darius," the blonde said, her tone chastising. "You know I hate all this submissive shit."

He chuckled, his lips caressing my neck. "Juliet, this is Mira." He nipped my pulse. "She's an old friend."

My nostrils flared. An old friend, as in a former lover? Or someone he still enjoyed intimately?

Another of those too-happy giggles from the blonde. "She reminds me of Izzy." Her eyes twinkled as she met my gaze. "So possessive."

I dug my nails into Darius's arms, not at all amused by this female and her joviality. But the man beneath me seemed quite entertained as he chuckled again. "It's a rather new development, Mira. I kind of like it."

"Liar. We both know you love it," she replied, smiling indulgently before fixating on me again. "You can put your claws away, sweetheart. I'm not interested in your future mate. I already have one of my own."

I gaped at her. "You're an *Erosita*?"

She laughed so hard that tears leaked from her eyes. Apparently, everything in this world was humorous to this woman.

Maybe she's not quite right in the head?

"Mira is a lycan," Darius said, his lips grazing my ear. "She's mated to the alpha of her pack."

"A lycan." I blinked. "Oh." I'd never met one before, had always expected them to be more animalistic than human. But in her cream-colored dress, tousled curls, and perfect manicure, she appeared quite human. "Nice to meet you," I added awkwardly.

"The pleasure is all mine," she replied, her focus shifting to Darius. "Now that she's up, you should get ready."

"Indeed." Darius slid his palms to my hips and squeezed. "I just need Juliet to let me up first."

"I believe she's claimed you," Mira murmured, eyes twinkling again.

"It would appear that way," he replied, his hands gently guiding me off his lap.

I slid to my feet and turned as he stood, my lips parting without sound. *What did I want to say?*

He wrapped his palm around the back of my neck and tugged me into a kiss that ruined my train of thought. Not that I had one anyway. I hardly recognized myself anymore.

She's claimed you.

Yes. Yes, I had. Which was wrong. Humans had no rights of possession, and yet, I wanted Darius to be mine. I showed him that with my mouth, dueled with his tongue for balance and demand, and felt him grin against my lips.

"You make me so proud, Juliet," he whispered, his thumb stroking my pulse. "But I need you to be on your best behavior for dinner. My presence always attracts attention, and being rumored as a sovereign candidate in the Jace Region is only adding to the excitement of my presence here tonight. It is imperative that I be seen as accepting of our current affairs, which may include saying or doing things you won't like."

Mira snorted. "Don't forget about the live-meal entertainment and tastefully decorated waitstaff."

He ignored her and focused on me. "I need you to play the part of submissive blood virgin, or questions will be raised, and those dining with us tonight are not beings you want to intrigue. Do you understand?"

He continued to trace patterns against my throat, distracting me only slightly from his request. "Another dinner."

Darius smiled. "Yes."

"And you wish for me to maintain formalities as taught by my matron."

"Yes," he repeated.

"Such as bowing."

"Unfortunately, yes."

To adhere to my training and the codes set forth by my matron. Why did that suddenly feel like an impossible task?

Because you know better now. But surely I could maintain decorum for a dinner. Unless… "Will there be sharing?"

"No." An emphatic response. "You will be silent unless spoken to, eyes downcast, the picture of subservience, and you will refer to me as your Sire, not Darius. But absolutely no sharing." His grip tightened, his mouth brushing mine. "The only tasting allowed will be my lips on your skin, Juliet. If I request a drink, you obey. If anyone else asks, I shall handle it. Understood?"

I swallowed. *No sharing.* I could accept that. Submission came naturally. Not having to talk would be a blessing. I would observe and nothing more. "Will this be our future?" I asked softly. "Events that require my silence and subservience?"

"Once I am named sovereign, yes. This will become a common outing when inside Lilith City for political affairs." He tucked my hair behind my ear and palmed my cheek. "We're dining tonight with several influential vampires. They are powerful, they are mean, and they believe me to be on their side."

"With one exception, which—"

"Isn't relevant," he interjected, silencing Mira. "Juliet, the rumors of my purchasing you have spread, and it is vital that we be seen as a proper master-and-blood-virgin couple. If anyone suspects otherwise, there will be punishments, such as the one I mentioned earlier."

"Sharing," I whispered.

He nodded. "I don't want to share you, but I need

them to think I wouldn't care. It lessens the amusement." He kissed my forehead and sighed. "Consider this an introduction to the roles we will play. I need you to be the perfect submissive, just as the Coventus taught you. All right, sweetheart? Can you do that for me?"

A request, not a demand. Although, we both knew I had no choice. I couldn't refuse him, not when this was my entire purpose for being.

It would be far easier for him to compel me into subservience, but Darius desired my compliance. Just as I craved the opportunity to please him. My chest warmed at the prospect of making him happy, to hear him praise me again as he had moments ago.

You make me so proud, Juliet.

Energy sizzled across my skin, his words repeating in my thoughts. I needed him to say those words once more, hopefully later tonight.

"Okay," I agreed, my heart smiling. "I will be who I am meant to be at your side. In public."

He kissed me tenderly. "Sweet Juliet, my perfect poison." Another kiss, this one longer and punctuated by his tongue. I chased the euphoria his mouth offered and fought the urge to growl when Mira cleared her throat.

Darius sighed. "There's a dress waiting for you in the closet beside my suit." He nibbled my lower lip. "I'll help you change."

"Worried she might hate you later?" Mira asked with a sardonic twist of her mouth.

"We both know she will," he replied. The words he added next were in a language I didn't speak, but they sparked a hint of sadness in his eyes. "Just remember this is all a charade, Juliet. Please."

Chapter Twenty-Five

JULIET

Death stared at me from across the dining table in the form of two glassy eyes. She seemed almost at peace with her blue lips curled at the edges, as if she'd been in on a secret the rest of the world knew nothing about.

The other naked female wasn't dead, yet. Her quiet whimpers taunted my ears while I forced myself to swallow another bite of my pasta. A smattering of tomato sauce hid the splatters of blood that had landed in my dinner from the gluttonous vampire to my left, but its concealed color didn't stop me from tasting the rusty essence.

"A little tangy for a B positive," the vampire opposite me said as he lifted his dark head from between the dying brunette's thighs. "But not horrible."

Darius shrugged. "My tastes of late are too rich for comparison." His palm rested against the back of my neck, his thumb stroking my pulse possessively.

I took another bite, ignoring the bile rolling in my stomach.

A charade, Darius had called it.

Looks pretty real to me, I thought as the woman took her last breath. It stuttered through the air with a finality, followed by a sigh from a redheaded female vampire. *Veronica*, Darius had called her.

Their names weren't ones I recognized, but I gathered from their statures that they were old and powerful. Darius, however, was the highest-ranking member at the table. It showed in his easy candor and the way he handled the waitstaff while the others observed.

He lifted the hand not caressing my neck, signaling something to the restaurant waitstaff. Probably his way of indicating that their dinner was dead.

I suppressed a shudder. They killed so easily and without a hint of remorse. Even Darius had sipped from the woman as if she meant nothing.

A trio of humans adorned in nothing but various metal piercings appeared to handle the corpses. They moved silently while the vampires eyed them with a predatory gleam.

I coerced another forkful of pasta down my throat. It tasted bitter and wrong, but I had no choice or I would end up like the women on the table. There were several others in this room, all being devoured in a similar manner, most of them silent. I refused to be the next one.

Pick. Up. The. Fork.

The vampire beside me—Brent—started fondling the chains hanging from one of the staff member's breasts.

Ignore him. Swallow the food.

"So pretty," he mused, tugging sharply. The metal ripped from her skin, causing her to flinch without yelping. Blood poured from the wound, some of it landing on my plate.

I almost dropped the fork, but Darius's grip tightened beneath my hair, his hand grounding me in the present.

Don't vomit, I told myself, breathing deeply through my nose and out through my mouth. *It'll only make matters worse.*

The female yelped as Brent yanked her into his lap, his mouth fastening over the wound. No one jumped in to stop him, not even the other waitstaff. They continued cleaning up the table as if nothing were out of the ordinary.

Because this happened every day.

Everywhere.

Act normal. Darius's voice in my head heated my blood. Whether it was him or my imagination, I didn't know. Didn't care. I latched onto our link, drowned in his power, and listened for further instruction. *Set your fork down.*

I did.

Good, darling.

The woman whimpered as Brent moved her to the table, her body replacing the two already removed by the other waitstaff.

Juliet, pretend to be finished with your meal. Wipe your mouth with the napkin. Say nothing.

A chill threatened to sweep down my spine, yet somehow I complied. Dabbing my lips, folding the fabric primly over my plate, eyes still averted while the human's breathing shallowed.

They were all feeding from her except Darius. His focus was on me, his thumb gently stroking the column of my throat.

"Darius," a deep voice said from directly behind me.

The hand at my neck disappeared as Darius stood. "Well, this is a surprise."

"I've said the same phrase about you several times lately," the newcomer replied, a note of amusement underlining his tone. "When Sebastian mentioned your interest in becoming my new sovereign, I thought surely he had misunderstood. Yet, here you are with your delicious new blood virgin. Fascinating."

Icy droplets froze my veins, sending a spasm to my heart.

My new sovereign.

A royal was behind me. *Jace*, my memory supplied based on my knowledge of the seventeen territories. Sebastian resided in his area, meaning the sovereign position Darius sought also existed under Jace.

"Mind if I join you?" the royal vampire asked.

"Please," Darius replied, his demeanor unfazed. The rest of the table had gone still upon Jace's arrival, leaving the human on the table barely breathing, but alive.

Fingers trailed down my arm. "Stand." The command didn't come from my master but from the royal vampire.

I couldn't say no to any of them, and especially not him. I did as he requested and fell into a bow, my head touching the ground in a severe sign of respect.

His resulting chuckle was alluringly masculine, warming my skin. "She's lovely, Darius, if a little too eager to please."

"I consider that a benefit," my master replied. "But do what you wish."

My breath caught on an inhale, my heart stuttering to a halt.

Sharing.

He promised that wouldn't happen. Yet, his words implied otherwise. An act to show nonchalance? To take away the fun of a potential punishment? Because this was the one vampire in the room Darius couldn't refuse? The royals were gods, the oldest of their kind, and revered by all. Only the Goddess stood alone at the top.

Jace slid into my vacated seat. "Come, young one. You may sit on my lap."

I hesitated, unsure if he meant me or another.

Who else could he be talking to?

Right.

I rose onto my stilettos, head lowered, and accepted the hand he held in my direction. His thighs were solid muscle, reminding me of Darius.

"Now, let's have a proper look at what all this fuss is about," he murmured while collecting my hair at the base of my scalp with one hand. With a sharp yank, my head came up, my gaze landing on his striking silver-blue eyes. They narrowed before trailing over my features, as though inspecting a new purchase. "Lovely shape and bone structure."

"Fuckable mouth," one of the others supplied helpfully.

He ignored the comment, his focus shifting to the cut of my maroon dress. The finger of his free hand traced my collarbone to the center and down to where the fabric met my belly button. My nipples pebbled beneath his touch—a sign of arousal derived from fear. His pupils dilated at the sight, his touch drifting up to reveal my reaction to the table.

"Beautiful breasts," he murmured, fondling my flesh and pinching my stiff peak. "Responds wonderfully as well."

If Darius minded, he didn't voice it. "You see why I've decided to keep her, then."

"I do," Jace replied, still stroking my skin. "She's going to be quite popular at future functions." His striking eyes met mine again. "Perhaps you and I can discuss that future—in private—while I acquaint myself with your new asset."

A sharp, invisible spear pricked my side, leaving a mark inside my heart.

Darius couldn't say no. I knew this, understood why, and still hated it when he said, "Absolutely. Just let me know when."

"Now would be lovely." Jace pressed his nose to my neck, inhaling deeply. "I'm quite famished, and nothing else on the menu has whet my appetite."

"That's why I ordered a few desserts for later." Darius sounded bored. "Actually, they should be about ready in the room."

"Excellent." Jace lifted his head and smiled. "Tell me your name, beautiful."

I swallowed and somehow managed to say, "Juliet."

"Lovely." He kissed me on the cheek. "Stand again and escort me to your room."

"Of course, Your Highness." I slipped from his lap, his hand in mine.

Jace chuckled. "She's well educated."

"Indeed." Darius pushed away from the table, saying a polite goodbye to his friends. They must have understood that he had no choice but to leave, not with a royal requesting his attention. He added a comment to the waitstaff on our way out, saying to add whatever other "items" they ordered to his bill.

How many humans would they devour in one sitting?

Don't think about it, I told myself. *You're in far bigger trouble.*

The hand holding mine squeezed as I selected the button to our floor. Darius joined my other side, his posture aloof. I kept my gaze averted and focused on not screaming. Or running. Or crying. Or demanding they add me to the menu downstairs so maybe I could join that smiling woman on the table.

Maybe I'll die from the voracious royal instead.

But I don't really want to die, do I?

Conflict warred in my heart and mind, an innate part of me wanting something more from this life. An option, a choice, *something*.

It's all just a charade, I reminded myself. *Right?*

Darius had warned me tonight would be hard, that he would do and say things to maintain his status. Was this one of those things?

No, surely not. He hadn't expected Jace—a royal—to crash our dinner party. This wasn't part of Darius's plan at all.

The bell dinged, indicating our level. I led the way as requested, my steps far steadier than my heart.

Darius promised not to share, but he had no choice. He couldn't refuse a royal.

If Jace wanted me, he would have me. The ceremony would shatter. I wouldn't be bound any longer, nor would I ever be bound again. Wasn't that what Darius had said? That once taken, I was forever soiled? A human destined for the breeding camps, or worse, the dining hall downstairs.

My knees shook as Darius slipped his key into the lock. The doors slid open to reveal three naked women, all kneeling with their heads bowed.

"Your dessert specials?" Jace asked.

"As you said, the menu downstairs was distasteful."

Jace chuckled, his chest warming my back. "One might think you knew to expect me, Darius."

"Perhaps I did," he replied stepping inside and shrugging out of his jacket. "Come on in and join the fun. I'll even give you first dibs."

"How generous." Jace's hands fell to my hips as he pushed me through the threshold. "I choose Juliet."

Darius smirked. "Excellent choice. Would you like her in here or the bedroom?"

"The bedroom," he replied, the door closing behind us, sealing off my only chance for escape.

Trapped.

The word rattled around in my head, shooting energy to my limbs. I couldn't do this. I refused. I didn't want anyone else. Only Darius. And maybe not even him.

This world… this life… I refused.

It wasn't right.

I needed to escape. To run. To *scream*.

My mouth opened, my lungs ready, but a hand covered my lips before I had a chance to voice a sound. An arm—solid as steel—clamped around my abdomen and yanked my back into a hard chest.

Jace.

The royal knew my intentions and had stopped me before I even thought to act.

He tsked in my ear. "Oh, darling." He nipped my neck, and it felt so wrong to feel his mouth there that I couldn't help the cringe ricocheting up my spine. "Are you trying to deny me?"

I squirmed against him, tears popping into my eyes. *No!* I wouldn't do this. Not without trying to at least fight.

No more rules.

No more decorum.

No more formalities.

Death was a better fate.

Jace chuckled darkly, his mouth at my ear. "I'm going to enjoy this far more than I care to admit, Juliet." He lifted me and I kicked back at him, but my resistance only earned more amusement from his chest.

"Don't hurt her too badly." The nonchalance in Darius's tone hurt.

He didn't care. Perhaps he never did. Was everything a lie? Had he already gotten what he needed from me?

Did I mean nothing to him?

No. I refused to believe that. Darius confided in me. Told me his plans, introduced me to this new world. Why would he disgrace me now? This had to be a ruse, just like with Sebastian.

I sought Darius's gaze and his mind, my eyes brimming with tears. He merely stared back, unfazed, and kept his thoughts locked up tight. No communication. No advice. Nothing but silence.

This couldn't be happening. It had to be an act. He couldn't just leave me to this fate, not after everything—

"It'll only hurt for a second," Jace murmured, his incisors grazing my neck.

Darius, I pleaded, my heart shattering beneath his indifferent gaze. *Please don't do this to me.*

No reply. Not even a grimace.

I could see it then, the monster lurking beneath the veneer. I was a means to an end. He never needed me to win a position of power, just the favor of a royal. The one at my back.

Hatred poured out of me. Betrayal. Fury unlike any I'd ever known.

I *trusted* him. Cherished him. Wanted to be everything for him. And he threw me away like a piece of trash at the first sign of victory.

My chest fractured as pain unlike anything I'd ever experienced scored my soul. Tears leaked from my eyes, falling to the floor, my pupils locking on my executioner.

He did this to me. Chose me for this deranged project. Tricked me into believing in another version of this world, with possibilities and choices.

I'll never forgive you, I told him with my eyes. Not that he seemed remotely bothered. Pure indifference. He never cared. It was all a lie. The only charade that existed here was between us.

My determination and strength vanished. There wasn't any point. This had always been my fate, just more prolonged than I had anticipated. I was never meant to live.

More tears fell, dampening my skin, my spirit, my heart.

Hope and desire died inside me, leaving a shell of a woman crafted by vampire kind. *Take me. Use me. I no longer care.*

Jace's mouth sealed around my pulse, his teeth puncturing deep. I didn't fight him. Didn't whimper. Didn't even move. Just held Darius's gaze, allowing him to see the woman he had broken.

Congratulations, I thought bitterly. *You'll make an excellent sovereign.*

Chapter Twenty-Six

DARIUS

Enough.

I sent a blast through the connection to Juliet, forcing her to lose consciousness. Jace caught her without preamble and flashed me an irritated glance at being cut off in the middle of his scene.

If you hadn't gone off script, that wouldn't have been necessary, I told him with a glower. *Asshole.*

He glanced pointedly at the indents in her neck. *That could have been a hell of a lot worse*, he seemed to be saying. Likely because his fangs had been lodged inside her skin when I knocked her out.

You weren't supposed to bite her, I returned. Not that he could actually hear me, but my glare conveyed my feelings well enough.

He rolled his eyes. "Hold her while I decide which of your desserts I want to enjoy with your Juliet." His voice lacked the annoyance clearly written in his features.

"Of course," I replied, sounding just as nonchalant despite wanting to introduce my fist to his face.

Jace handed Juliet to me with great care before moving to the humans on the other side of the room. I sliced my tongue and dabbed it against the two shallow puncture wounds on her neck. It wasn't really necessary from a healing perspective. I just didn't appreciate Jace leaving marks on her.

My Juliet. I nuzzled her warm cheek and withheld a sigh. The hatred in her expression had nearly broken my composure. I expected it, but I wasn't prepared to *feel* it.

Jace touched the humans, describing their physical attributes as he guided each of them to the floor into a deep slumber. When the blonde hit the ground, he asked if I had a preference.

Mira appeared from the bedroom, her steps silent over the ground while I engaged in the script we had decided upon earlier.

We commented on their blood types and personal preferences while Mira skimmed each of the humans with her fancy scanner. Her technology overrode the listening devices buried in their arms. They doubled as trackers in case the mortal somehow escaped. Juliet had come equipped with a similar one that I removed after knocking her out in the limo on our first night. I'd left it somewhere in the formally called country of Italy—where the Coventus also happened to be located.

"Perhaps we should see who screams the loudest?" Jace suggested upon Mira lifting her fingers into the five-second countdown.

"Sounds delightful," I replied on cue.

Mira's hand closed. "Clear."

"Thank fuck," Jace said, sweeping his hand down his face. "I thought Darius might actually try to kill me."

"You weren't supposed to bite her," I growled, finally able to say the words out loud. The script had called for scaring her, not tasting her.

"If it makes you feel any better, mate, I didn't swallow."

I took a step toward him—ready to show my oldest friend how much that didn't improve matters—when Mira moved between us.

"You two can hit each other later. We need to move if you want to reach Majestic Clan by sunrise." Mira nailed me with her icy blue eyes, the alpha inside her lying just under the surface. "Wake her up and dress her for the drive. You have ten minutes."

I didn't bother arguing, my feet already moving to the bedroom. If the look Juliet had given me before passing out was anything to go by, she'd wake up fighting.

"Juliet," I murmured softly while laying her on the soft white comforter. "Open your eyes, darling."

Her lids fluttered, her cheeks a soft pink. So beautiful and innocent. Stirring her from slumber was a luxury I could enjoy for a lifetime.

"Darius?" she breathed, her pupils narrowing as her brain caught up with the moment. "You!" Her palm sliced through the air, and I caught it before it could connect with my face. She tried again with her other hand, and I pinned both of her wrists above her head.

"Juliet." I kept my voice low and calm. "I need you to listen to me."

"I hate you!" she shouted, squirming beneath me and trying futilely to escape my hold. More words of disdain fell from her mouth, some of it surprising me. Either she truly craved death or she felt comfortable enough around me to say these things. Because no human yelled like this at a vampire.

"Settle. Down." Threat and command underlined my tone, requiring her submission. If anyone overheard her, there would be hell to pay, and I wanted to be the only one to ever make her bleed.

I collected her wrists with one hand and used my other to cover her mouth while stretching out on top of her. My cock lengthened, excited by the prospect of more, despite my brain's focus on the long night of travel ahead. Her fighting me had been such a turn-on, one I wanted to both punish and please her for—a sexy contradiction. One to take up later.

"I'm sorry Jace bit you," I said in as soft a voice as I could muster with my arousal heating my blood. "It wasn't part of the plan."

Her eyes narrowed, an indication that she still desired a piece of my flesh. Or worse.

I sighed. "Juliet, I told you this was a short stop on the way to our true destination. We're leaving in a few minutes and I need you prepared. You can hate me later, but right now, I need you to trust me and do as I say."

Her expression didn't falter.

"Consider everything I've told you, darling. I warned you tonight would be a charade, and yes, I promised no sharing. I'm sorry—"

"It wasn't his fault," Jace said, interrupting my explanation. I glared over my shoulder at the pompous ass leaning against the doorway. "Don't look at me like that. You're the one taking forever in here."

"Because you scared the life out of her." *And pissed her the fuck off in the process.* Not that I could entirely complain about that last part. I had wanted her to grow a backbone and leave the subservient bullshit behind. It seemed my wish had finally been granted in the form of a seething female.

"I had to make it look believable, Darius. I have a reputation to uphold and all that."

I shook my head, annoyed, and met Juliet's confused gaze. "He's an old friend—my oldest, actually—and a prick."

"Yeah, well, this 'prick' saved you from having to dine

with those imbeciles downstairs for another hour. You're welcome for that, by the way. Remind me *not* to help next time, if this is the thanks I'll get."

"You're both children," Mira growled. "Why isn't she dressed yet?"

"Because Jace interrupted," I replied, again glaring over my shoulder. "Both of you—out. Give me five minutes and she'll be ready."

"She better be," Mira replied, completely unfazed by my tone. "You"—she pointed to Jace and then the door—"out."

"I love when you go all alpha on me, baby. It's adorable."

"Yeah?" She batted her long eyelashes at him. "I'll be sure to mention it to Luka."

Jace chuckled as he left. "I'm not afraid of your alpha mate, Mira, darling."

"What about my claws?" she asked, following him.

Fucking flirt. Royal vampire or not, Jace was going to get himself killed one of these days for pissing off the wrong lycan.

I concentrated on the task at hand and found a much calmer version of Juliet beneath me. "I'm going to let you speak now."

She blinked in response.

My palm slid to her throat, circling it possessively. Her pupils flared, her tongue darting out to lick her lips. Now wasn't the time, but I wanted her. No, I *needed* her.

Before she could move or voice her denial, my mouth claimed hers. I unleashed all my pent-up frustration from the evening with my tongue, brutally coercing her to accept my apology and comply.

She didn't move at first, didn't react, but slowly she yielded to my kiss and returned it with a moan I felt deep within.

Mine.

I hated that Jace had touched her. Had put his mouth

on her. I needed to erase him and everyone else, remind myself that she belonged to me. I kissed her jaw, her neck, the spot where Jace had dared to mark her, and sank my teeth into her throat. She arched into me on a cry of pleasure, her body shaking beneath mine. This wasn't about blood or needing to feed, but about reaffirming her place at my side.

"No one else," I whispered, more to myself than to her. "I'll kill anyone who touches you." I released her hands, my fingers trailing down her arms to her dress. I ripped it off of her in one pull, leaving her exposed. "Fuck, I need to claim you, Juliet. I need you to be only mine."

She threaded her fingers in my hair, yanking my head upward. "I won't share you."

I smiled at her proprietorial tone. The ceremony was so rare, so few vampires choosing to take a mate, but I knew of one similar to this where the female felt just as covetous as the male.

Ismerelda.

The name was the splash of cold water I needed to break the moment, a severe reminder of our mission.

I kissed Juliet soundly, promising her with my lips that we would revisit this discussion soon. "We need to get ready," I said, pulling away from her. "I'm taking you somewhere very special to me, Juliet. But it's very, very dangerous. You'll need to do exactly as I say."

"It's not another dinner, is it?" she asked warily.

I chuckled and helped her up from the bed. "No, only a few minutes have passed since the last one."

"Oh." She glanced at her ruined dress on the bed. "I didn't pass out from blood loss?"

"No, I compelled you to sleep." I brushed my knuckles down her cheek. "You were only out for the few minutes it took to organize the humans in the other room."

"Organize?" she repeated.

"Yes." I found her clothes from earlier—jeans and a sweater—and handed them to her. "Mira has a way to alter the devices implanted in their arms. Anyone listening in is hearing a lot of screaming and male grunts right now. It'll calm during the daytime hours and pick up again in the evening."

She pulled on the pants first. "Why?"

I helped with her sweater, combing my fingers through her thick hair as it fell over her back. "It provides an explanation for my absence, as well as Jace's." We did this every time we visited Lilith City together. It helped us maintain our reputations while granting us the freedom to visit our obligations up north. "Mira has a friend who keeps the humans sedated and healthy in our absence. But we only have roughly seventy-two hours at our disposal, which is why we're in a rush."

Her brow crumpled. "Why would you need to pretend to be here?"

There were too many answers to that question. I cupped her cheek and gave her the most straightforward response I could. "We're going somewhere vampires typically avoid."

"Will you tell me where we're really going?"

I smiled at her boldness and pressed my lips to her ear. "Majestic Clan headquarters, where Mira is from."

She gasped. "Lycan territory?"

"Yes, darling." I nuzzled her neck, licking the mark I left there. "You'll understand when we arrive. But can you trust me and follow my lead?"

Juliet met my gaze, her expression concerned. "Is Jace going to bite me again?"

I snorted. "Not if he values his life."

Her pupils widened. "But he's a royal, right? Don't you have to obey him?"

"Yes, Darius. Perhaps you should bow more? Kiss my hand? Pray to me?"

My eyes lifted to the ceiling. *Prick.* "Have you forgotten how to knock?"

"I heard my name from your sweet human's mouth

and hoped she desired more teasing." He sauntered to my side, his silver eyes gleaming with mirth as he extended a hand. "Sorry for the theatrics earlier, Juliet. I'm Jace and delighted to officially meet you."

She grabbed my arm, her nails digging into my shirt. The fighter I awoke only moments ago had lost herself again behind a sea of doubt.

I pulled Juliet close, kissing her forehead. "You don't need to fear him. He's a royal jackass, but also a friend."

"Love you too, mate." Jace clapped me on the back with the hand she rejected. "And it's Mira we should fear because she's pacing in the other room. If we don't start moving, she might go wolfish on us."

My lips twitched despite the severity of the moment. "One of these days she's going to kill you."

Jace shrugged, unconcerned. "She's welcome to try. Now, shall we? I'm eager to get this show started."

That made two of us. "Juliet?" I asked, rubbing a hand down her back. "Can you trust me?"

She didn't move, her gorgeous eyes transfixed on Jace, her body rigid.

His expression softened. "I'm sorry for the fright, darling. I barely had my fangs in you before Darius knocked you out." His pupils narrowed up at me. "And it's a bloody good thing I caught her, by the way, or I could have ripped her throat out by accident."

"Don't blame me. You're the one who bit her without permission."

"And you're never going to let me live it down, are you?"

"Not anytime soon," I admitted. "Now apologize to Juliet again."

Her eyes widened at my demand, her lips parting on soundless words.

Jace merely gave her his most charming smile. "I'm so very sorry, sweetheart. Will you please forgive me so Darius can stop acting like an ass?"

Her jaw completely unhinged, all signs of composure gone as she remained frozen at my side.

"I've done as you requested, but she doesn't seem keen on accepting." Jace frowned. "Is it because I'm a royal that she expects such horrid things of me?"

"The Coventus definitely enjoys its propaganda," I muttered.

"Clearly." Jace smoothed his hand down his tie. His jacket had disappeared in the living area somewhere. "Shall we go, then? Perhaps I can make amends in another fashion."

"Juliet?" I prompted softly, rubbing her back. "I need to know you'll follow my lead outside this room. Please?"

She blinked those gorgeous eyes up at me. "I have a choice?" It came out hoarse, but it was better than her remaining silent.

Best to admit the truth, not lie. "Not really, no."

She didn't appear at all fazed by that blunt reply. Her gaze—now curious instead of petrified—flickered to Jace and then back to me. "You trust him?"

"With my life," I replied, meaning it. "He's my oldest friend."

Jace smirked. "For what it's worth, I trust him too."

She glanced between us again. "All right. Then we should go."

I pressed my lips to hers. "You'll understand everything soon. I promise."

And then I'll claim you as mine. Completely. In every way. Forever.

226

Chapter Twenty-Seven

JULIET

Darius's hand firmly gripped mine while we descended the stairs, Mira in the front, Jace at the back. They didn't move quickly, just casually, as though they didn't have a care in the world.

A royal is working with Darius. Does he dislike the alliance as well?

I resisted the urge to check my neck, to feel for Jace's marks.

He never drank from me.

My certainty of that fact increased with every step. My body felt refreshed, not weakened, and I couldn't actually recall him sucking on my neck. I vaguely remembered the prick of his fangs as he had initiated his bite, then everything went black.

I glanced over my shoulder at him now, and he met my gaze with a smile in his silver-blue eyes. He didn't resemble the terrifying royal from dinner at all now, just a regular male with an incredibly attractive face. No mistaking his vampire roots, not with a bone structure like that.

Darius pulled my attention back to the stairs as we rounded yet another corner. The tennis shoes he'd given me felt foreign on my feet. They were so flat I almost felt unstable. Somehow I managed to move alongside him without stumbling, but I missed my heels.

Mira held some sort of device that seemed to be directing us. When we reached the bottom, she paused, hit a few buttons, and led us through a door into a dull corridor. No one spoke, but I sensed Darius's alertness.

Majestic Clan. Lycan territory. What reason could he possibly have to go there? Vampires and lycans worked together as the supreme world leaders but notoriously stayed within their own domains. That didn't mean they couldn't cross borders; they just preferred not to. And yet, this visit was of a clandestine nature. Why?

We stopped at a steel entryway, Mira playing with the item in her hand again. The metal hissed open after a moment to reveal a garage full of cars.

She moved with purpose toward a large black vehicle and smiled as another female slipped into view. They embraced with a hug and kiss on each cheek but didn't say anything. Jace followed suit, while Darius merely nodded.

The back doors opened to reveal two males waiting inside dressed in jeans and T-shirts. They signaled for us to move. Darius lifted me into their waiting hands and hopped up on his own to join us. They gestured to a boxlike compartment swathed in black. Darius lay down inside it first, then held out his arms for me to join him.

A very different way to travel, but all right.

I pressed myself lengthwise against him and jolted when something warm and hard met my back. A glance over my shoulder displayed a smirking Jace, his hand falling to my hip.

A drum kick-started in my chest, sending goose bumps down my limbs.

Why is this happening?

Darius's finger found my lips, silencing my ability to ask for an explanation. His gaze burned with warning.

Shh, he hushed through my mind. *There are listening devices everywhere.*

Would have been nice to know that before we started, I thought back at him. His twitching lips suggested he either heard me or understood my look.

A swathe of dark fabric covered our bodies, followed by a case clicking into place over our heads. I shivered despite the two warm males pressed up against me.

It's so dark…

I know, darling. Darius's murmur sent a shiver of delight down my spine. His mental presence felt so intimate, as though he belonged there. *It's only until we breach the city limits undetected,* he added.

That part I still didn't quite understand. They were going through a lot of effort to conceal this visit, just to avoid some questions. *Are you not allowed to visit the lycans?*

Oh, we're allowed, but it's uncommon and raises questions. Questions, Juliet, that we cannot afford. So I need you to remain calm and quiet for me, okay?

The vehicle started to move, our bodies knocking into each other in the confined space. Jace inhaled deeply, reminding me of his presence. Not that I had forgotten with his hips pressed against my backside and his nose in my hair.

Calm. Yeah, that wouldn't be an issue at all.

Hmm, I have an idea for how to pass the time. Darius tilted my chin up and captured my mouth. His tongue slid inside to slowly caress mine, shooting my heart rate up a notch.

Jace nuzzled the back of my neck, his palm a brand against my hip.

Oh, Goddess, what are you doing to me? I was trapped in a

confined space between two vampires—one I adored and the other a stranger.

Darius's palm slid beneath my sweater, traveling up to cup my breast. I arched into him, my blood heating at the sensation of his erection meeting my lower belly. He pushed back, forcing me into the aroused male behind me.

Jace remained still, apart from his thumb gently tracing the top of my jeans.

This is wrong. He shouldn't be here.

Embrace it, Darius replied, massaging my nipple. *Jace won't hurt you.*

Whatever I could have said back to that was swept up in another soul-binding kiss that left me breathless against him. Jace's lips were in my hair, his breath hot against my nape.

Darius, I—

He tugged my lower lip into his mouth, biting down gently. *Stop thinking, Juliet.*

I did. My brain shutting down and allowing him full control as he devoured me from the inside out, possessing my every breath.

Jace remained a solid warmth at my back, shielding me from the world. I should have been afraid, terrified even, but I felt oddly protected between them. Maybe because, despite their clear desires, they didn't push me. Jace never strayed from my hip, his mouth staying in my hair and not touching my skin, while Darius kissed me soundly, his caress gentle against my breast.

When the car rolled to a sudden stop, their grips tightened, but their embrace didn't end. If anything, it intensified with Darius's mouth moving more urgently against mine and Jace's palm sliding up and down my thigh.

I fought the urge to moan, some sane part of me knowing I had to be quiet. It just felt so good, so *hot*, that I could hardly contain my need for more.

Pleasure me, I begged. *Please, Darius.*

The vehicle lurched forward, knocking me against him and back into Jace and fracturing my mind from the lust-induced fog surrounding me. I shuddered, my body begging for more while logic threatened to pull me into the present.

Darius's tongue continued to coax mine, his touch searing my skin. I fell into his embrace again, my heart beating in time with his, my core aching with need. It overwhelmed my senses, making me oblivious to our surroundings.

Until we halted again.

Jace chuckled behind me, the first sound to grace the air in longer than I could remember. "That's one way to keep her quiet, Darius."

The mouth against mine curled. "I thought you might approve of that."

"I'd approve more if you let me properly indulge in her."

"Not a chance in hell," Darius replied, his nose skimming the flame dancing along my cheek.

"In the nearly three thousand years we've known one another, you've never turned down the opportunity to share." Jace kissed the back of my head. "You chose well, mate."

"I know." Darius's hand slid out of my shirt and up to cup my face. "Stay calm for me."

I didn't get a chance to reply before a pale light slithered into our black cavern. Jace disappeared, exposing me to the chilly night air. Darius nudged me onto my back and rolled over me, then extended a hand to help me out of our former safe haven.

"There we are," he murmured as my feet touched the paved ground.

A few masculine chuckles had me jumping to his side. Over a dozen pairs of yellow eyes glowed in the night, the moon overhead our only illumination. Darius stroked his palm down my spine as a white wolf approached and sniffed my hand. My pulse beat erratically in response, but I forced myself to stay still.

He—I assumed the wolf was male because of his size and stature—growled low in his throat and took a few steps back.

Um...

"You should know that fear is an aphrodisiac to a predator," a feminine voice warned from the darkness. A woman stepped through the trees alongside the road with a pair of white wolves on either side of her. The moon highlighted her pale skin and ash-blonde hair, giving her an almost ethereal appeal as she walked over the pavement. "Although, I'm sure Darius doesn't mind."

"Ismerelda," he murmured, a fond note in his voice. "You shouldn't be this close to the border."

She tsked. "When Luka told me you'd initiated emergency protocols for an unexpected visit, I knew there had to be an important reason. Now I see why." She walked up to him and kissed both his cheeks, her intimate knowledge of him clear in the way she hugged him. "I've missed you, sweetheart."

"I've missed you too," he replied softly, holding her for too long of a second.

The hairs along my arms rose in retaliation, displeased with this development. How dare he bring me here to meet with a former lover? I made to step away, when his arm came around my waist, keeping me beside him.

"Juliet, I'd like you to meet a very old friend of mine, Ismerelda."

She smiled warmly. "That's a name I only ever hear when you pay a visit, Darius. Everyone else calls me Izzy now, even Jace."

"It's shorter," Jace replied, as though that explained everything.

Izzy laughed, her gorgeous face lighting up beneath the moon. Her light-green eyes met mine and crinkled at the side. "Welcome to Majestic Clan."

Darius squeezed my side. "This is who I wanted you to meet, Juliet," he murmured. "Not only is Ismerelda human, she's also an *Erosita*."

My lips parted. *An* Erosita*? In the woods? Surrounded by wolves?*

Someone who understood my fate? Could tell me the truth about what awaited me at Darius's side?

It was almost too good to be true. A trick of some kind. *If she's an* Erosita, *where's her Sire?*

"It's true. Cam is my mate." Her smile was sad. "You may know him as Darius's maker, or perhaps as Jace's cousin."

I knew him as both, but wait... *Is? Present tense?* My brow furrowed. Cam's betrayal and subsequent death was well known. The Coventus had described him as a corrupt vampire who unsuccessfully tried to take over the alliance and was killed for his attempt.

But if she's his Erosita, then she should be dead too, right?

Darius's words from the plane slipped through my mind. *"Juliet, the ceremony binds us until either I die, or another being claims your body."*

If Izzy was Cam's mate, then his death would have broken their bond and returned her to a human status several decades ago. Yet, she didn't appear a day over thirty, suggesting her immortality was firmly in place.

"He's still alive," Darius confirmed softly. "But no one knows where."

"We've all been led to believe that Cam's dead, but Izzy's existence proves he's not," Jace added. "And one day, we will free him."

Izzy smiled, but it didn't quite reach her eyes. "Well, now that introductions are finished, perhaps I can accompany Juliet back to the compound while you two ride in the back? It'll be dawn before we reach our destination at this point."

Darius kissed my temple, his voice low as he asked, "Are you comfortable with riding up front next to

Ismerelda?" *It is your choice, Juliet,* he whispered through my thoughts. *She won't be offended if you refuse.*

I didn't need to think about it, my decision made the moment I realized who and what she was. "Yes. I would like to talk to her."

Darius hugged my side. "I thought you might." Another brush of his lips. "I'll be right behind you if you need me, at least until sunrise."

"What happens then?" I asked, suddenly concerned. Sunlight couldn't kill a vampire, but it severely weakened them. Hence the reason they preferred to roam at night.

"I'll go back in the trunk coffin with Jace where it's safe." His lips curled. "You're welcome to join us again."

A wolf howled in the distance, causing everyone to lift their heads and stare in the direction of the sound. When a second howl graced the night air, the lycans began to move.

"We need to go," Darius said, propelling me toward the front of the car and Izzy. She grabbed my hand and guided me to the middle seat between her and the driver while Jace and Darius settled behind us. The rest of the lycans disappeared in wolf form or on motorcycles.

"Nothing to worry about," Izzy murmured. "Just a warning of human scouts on the horizon. They sometimes like to prowl along the border, usually because they're bored. But they won't venture too far into the territory, not without repercussions from our own patrol."

"You mean the Vigils?" I asked, recalling the formal term Darius had used.

"Yes, the human vigilantes who prey on their own kind to earn favors from vampires and lycans." She scoffed. "Walking scum, if you ask me."

"Opportunists," the driver beside me said, his voice rough and low. Definitely a lycan.

"Sure." She snorted. "Anyway, you must be very overwhelmed."

I considered her statement while Jace and Darius spoke

softly to one another behind us. Their words were too quiet for me to hear, but I knew they would have no trouble understanding me even if I whispered. "Am I allowed to speak freely?" I asked, more to the beings in the back seat than those in the front.

"You may say whatever you want, Juliet," Darius replied, confirming my suspicion that he was listening. "In fact, I encourage you to."

"How nice of you," Izzy deadpanned.

"She comes from a different world than you, Ismerelda. She asks permission because the requirement has been instilled into her through years of torment." He sounded irritated, reminding me of the time he told me to stop bowing.

"Fucking vampires," she grumbled.

"Lycans are not any better, sweetheart," Jace said. "No offense, Hunter."

The lycan beside me grunted. "None taken."

"Ignore all of them and talk to me," Izzy encouraged. "How do you feel?"

How do I feel? I suddenly had the urge to giggle. The last ten, twelve, twenty-four, however many hours, had been an emotional whirlwind . Had dinner with Sebastian only been the night before? Now I sat beside an *Erosita* and a lycan, with a royal vampire and Darius behind me.

Dear Goddess, I was losing my ever-loving mind.

I had gone from wanting to die to not knowing up from down.

One kiss from Darius confused my entire world, a touch from Jace had me wanting to scream one minute and moan the next, and to top it all off, we snuck out of a city of vampires to visit a lycan clan.

My lips curled despite my mind rattling with thoughts, and the giggle threatening my throat exploded through my mouth on a laugh. It was either that or cry. No, wait, tears were leaking from my eyes too.

And I couldn't stop, the burst of energy filling the quiet

car with a sound I rarely ever heard, let alone made.

"She's losing it, mate." Jace's voice barely pierced my thoughts because I didn't care. It felt too good to just let the emotion fly free.

I could laugh here. Cry. Scream. Whatever I wanted. With no punishment.

Safe, I realized. Darius had brought me somewhere *safe*. I met his concerned gaze in the mirror. This was what he wanted me to see—life outside the confines of vampire society. And I had no idea what to do next.

Chapter Twenty-Eight

DARIUS

Juliet's laugh went straight to my heart. It was so laden in emotion, so broken, all I wanted to do was drag her into my arms. But a sharp look from Ismerelda kept me in my seat.

"Tell me what happened to Viktor," Jace said, helping me shift focus back to our primary objective.

"He tried to touch my blood virgin, so I killed him."

Jace smiled. "That's what Sebastian reported, but what really happened?"

I shrugged. "I may have discreetly indicated that he had permission to fondle my property while no one else was looking."

He chuckled. "Brilliant. And how do you plan to handle Gaston?"

I loosened my tie, slipping the knot from my neck. Formal wear grew tiresome after a while. "My hope is this impromptu rendezvous with you in Lilith City reaches his ears and he backs down when Sebastian nominates me at the Parliament Gala. If he doesn't, then he may experience a fatal demise. Purely coincidental, of course."

"Like my former sovereign, Adrian?" he asked, amused.

"Pity those rogue lycans got ahold of him." A snort from the driver's seat followed my words, bringing a smile to my lips. Hunter was an excellent marksman, one I valued having on my side.

"Pity," Jace agreed, sounding the least bit saddened by it. Which, of course, he wasn't since the whole bloody plan had been his brilliant idea. Jace was the first pawn put in place as a royal with inherited standing.

When he took over the former Northwestern United States, I chose to live at my estate in Washington under his rule, waiting for the next step. Over a century later, he orchestrated the plan of bringing me on as one of his two sovereigns, granting me power and authority over his land and vampires.

There were other pieces in play elsewhere, all strategically lining up to eventually overthrow the alliance. My ascension was only the beginning—a sign to the others that the game had begun.

And all the while, we searched for Cam's whereabouts. He was the rightful king among our kind. Not Lilith, the queen bitch who stole his crown.

"A thousand years ago?" Juliet gasped from the front, her laughter long gone thanks to Ismerelda's storytelling. She was deep in to the history of how she met Cam, her voice hinting at a much happier time in her life. I couldn't begin to imagine what it must be like for her to know her love existed in a place she couldn't find.

Their mental bond had fractured—an indication that he had cut her off—likely to hide her from whatever torment our kind was inflicting upon him. Not to mention, it protected her existence.

The royals thought Cam had killed his *Erosita* before the supernatural uprising, a scene he had strategically orchestrated to protect her from the inevitable future of human enslavement. He hid her among the Majestic Clan, some of our only lycan allies, knowing the vampires would never think to look for her there.

And then he had been caught and tried for treason. Not because of the treason Lilith claimed he had committed, but because of his potential threat to her power.

A note of awe entered Juliet's voice as she asked Ismerelda about her relationship with Cam. She wanted to know about possessiveness and if vampires typically took more than one mate.

"I think she wants your fidelity," Jace murmured, listening.

"It would seem that way." I smiled. "She's grown quite proprietorial, but I don't think she understands why."

"The bond."

I nodded. "She's channeling my emotions for her." I had to keep all my instincts locked away out of fear someone might test them, and it seemed by doing so, I'd shoved some of them into her through our connection.

"I think there might be more to it." He cocked his head to the side, listening as Juliet quietly spoke about our relationship progression. "She likes you."

"Because she has no alternative."

He lifted a shoulder. "I provided one in the coffin and she barely knew I was there, something we both know never happens to me."

With his dark hair, silver eyes, and striking face, no one ever denied him. Hell, some of the humans we ordered for sharing had actually appeared relieved to be chosen by him. Not to mention, the majority of those sent to the royal sex-training camps desired his harem above all others.

"She's afraid of you," I pointed out. "The Coventus taught her to fear all royals and influential vampires."

"Yet, she doesn't fear you," he mused. "Fascinating considering you are one of the most powerful of our kind. You have Cam's essence flowing through your veins, marking you as a true prince."

"Something she doesn't understand."

"Oh, I beg to differ. She senses it plenty, but trusts you despite her instincts because her emotions are telling her you're safe."

I considered her in the mirror, her flushed cheeks and thoughtful eyes. She was deep in conversation with Ismerelda, completely unaware of us discussing her in the back seat. They were going over the benefits of being mated, the immortality, the mental connection we'd only begun to explore, and the pleasures shared between vampire and *Erosita*. Juliet blushed at that, her voice dropping to a whisper as she asked if Cam had waited a long time before deflowering Ismerelda.

I smiled, sensing Juliet's frustration at my delay in culminating our own bond. Now that she knew everything, I would be able to provide her with a proper choice, something I hadn't considered in the beginning but now desired. Having her at my side would prove beneficial so long as she actually wanted to be there. If she didn't, then she could live the rest of her days here among the lycans and other humans they kept safe.

There was a whole clan of mortals living mostly as they once did with freedom and families, hidden among the trees by the lycans who controlled this territory. No one thought to scout the forests for stray humans, assuming them all rounded up or dead. Besides, what lycan would allow fresh meat to roam free? That's what the others thought, thereby marking this as the safest territory for mortals. And my Juliet, should she choose to stay.

"How are Ivan and Trevor?" Jace asked, refocusing me

on the present.

I provided him a brief update, including Ivan's thoughts on current political affairs and who we might want to consider for our side. Jace listened to every word, nodding in agreement and adding his own ideas to the mix. We rarely had an opportunity to chat freely about our plans and used the time to our advantage. Jace caught me up on the royals and their antics, even mentioned Kylan killing his entire harem out of boredom.

"Is he falling into an immortal insanity?" I wondered out loud, curious. Some of the oldest of our kind lost touch completely with life and started dabbling in death to pass the time. It seemed Kylan might be heading in that direction.

"His motives remain unclear, but something isn't quite right. He's secluded himself for the time being, stating he requires time to mourn."

"Sebastian said he tried to move up the Blood Day ritual to replenish his harem."

Jace scratched his chin. "He did, but it lacked heart. I'm still trying to figure out what's happened. Regardless, he's lost the plot and clearly doesn't mind killing for sport."

"A summary of most of our kind."

"True." He glanced out the window, taking in the last vestiges of the night. "Sometimes I wonder if we'll ever be able to right all these wrongs."

"We won't," I replied quietly. "But we can try to improve the future." *By returning Cam to his rightful throne and treating humans better than cattle.*

Vampires and lycans would always rule, our preternatural nature placing us at the top of the food chain for a reason, but that didn't mean we had to relegate humans to camps. They were our source of life. We needed them more than they needed us, something the alliance had forgotten when nearly wiping humans out of existence.

"Yes," Jace agreed. "We can try."

The horizon began to lighten, indicating the coming day. "Time for a nap," I drawled. Not that we needed to at our age, but old habits and all that. Besides, I wanted to be rested and alert when Juliet joined me later. There was an important discussion in our near future, and I needed to be prepared for whatever she had to say.

Chapter Twenty-Nine

JULIET

"This is where Darius usually stays," Izzy said, flipping on the lights to a bedroom decorated in shades of brown.

We had spent the entire drive here talking about her life, Cam, what it was like being a vampire's mate, and her view on the current affairs. My mind spun with thousands of additional questions, but my body required rest after all the traveling and stress.

"This is lovely," I told her, touching the wooden door frame. "May I sleep here?"

She smiled. "I don't imagine Darius would like you sleeping anywhere else."

"You always were an intelligent woman." Darius's voice came from down the hall, his saunter sure and confident as he strode toward us. I'd never seen him up and about during daylight hours. He didn't appear any different, not even as he kissed Izzy on the cheek. "Thank you, love. I can take it from here."

"Now you be nice to her, Darius." She gave him a stern look. "I like her."

He smiled, his green eyes meeting mine. "Don't worry, Ismerelda. I like her too."

My heart fluttered at the sincerity of his tone, my cheeks heating. He never spoke about me in that manner to anyone, not even Trevor and Ivan.

"Good," Ismerelda replied, satisfied. "Cam would approve too." The last was spoken a little wistfully as she patted Darius on the arm and walked away, leaving us standing alone in the threshold.

"Are you all right?" he asked softly, his expression softening. "I imagine this is all a bit overwhelming."

A bit overwhelming? I wanted to laugh, or perhaps cry.

There were free humans outside. Wandering. Laughing. *Living.* We had passed them on our way to this oversized log cabin. They'd all watched us curiously; some had even waved.

And beyond them had been lycans, some in clothing, others in wolf form.

"Welcome to the heart of Majestic Clan," Ismerelda had said.

After everything she'd told me on our way here, I shouldn't have been surprised. But seeing her reality was far different than hearing about it.

"I want to explore later," I said. "Please." My brow furrowed. I didn't know how to behave here, around him. Did decorum still apply? "Am I allowed to explore?"

Darius tucked a strand of hair behind my ear and cupped my cheek. "You can do whatever you want here, Juliet. No permission required."

I leaned into his touch, seeking his intimacy and warmth. His other arm came around me, pulling me into the hug I didn't realize I needed. He held me for a long moment, one foot inside the bedroom, the other in the hallway, and said nothing.

"I'm not sure how to act," I admitted in a whisper. "We went from a dinner horror show to, well, this, and I don't know what you expect from me." Moisture welled in my eyes with the words. "Tell me what to do. Please." I needed his guidance, his understanding, his words.

I needed *him*.

"Shh, it's all right." He ushered me into the bedroom and closed the door, then took me in his arms again, holding me tightly. His strength enveloped me, lending a sense of security and familiarity that I craved.

"It's all so much to take in. I never even dreamed… never thought to consider… Darius, there are humans outside. Living with lycans. Is it this way with all the clans? Can I stay here?" The words were clumsy and rushed, tears streaming down my cheeks.

I hadn't realized just how exhausted and overwhelmed I felt until now. My legs threatened to give out, my heart hammering in my ribs. Everything crashed over me at once—Sebastian, the lethal dinner in Lilith City, Izzy, this log cabin filled with fresh air and happiness…

"Darius." I clung to him for support, and he lifted me off the floor.

"I have you," he murmured, carrying me to the bed and holding me on his lap.

I curled into him and stopped fighting the onslaught of sensation desecrating my being.

Too much. It was all too much.

The conversation with Izzy had been enlightening and terrifying, and so, so *sad*. She chose this life. She chose Cam. I never had that, had never even *hoped* for it. And then to see her life here—even a glimpse of it—the freedom, happiness, humans *smiling*, while I lived in a world controlled by vampires… I shuddered. Darius had shown me such an existence what felt like years ago, by having me read all those books and walk through the history of human nature.

It had felt like fiction at the time, but now, *now*, I understood it. Had witnessed the differences in a few short hours, seeing Izzy laugh and tease supernaturals—as a human.

I would never have that. This was a visit, not my life. And even if it was, I didn't belong here. How would I ever fit into a world with choice? I couldn't even ask to wander without permission, and worse, I didn't *want* to explore without Darius's blessing. Because a part of me lived to serve him.

Even as I asked if I could stay here, I knew I didn't really want to. My mind rioted at the insanity of it all, smearing my vision and sending violent spasms down my spine.

Crying was a weakness. Forbidden. Not tolerated by vampires. And yet, *my* vampire held me through it all. He whispered foreign words in my ear, in a lyrical and sweet language. They soothed my aching heart, distracting me from the commotion in my mind.

"What are you saying?" I asked against his chest, his dress shirt ruined by my tears.

"I'm reciting an old poem." He drew his fingers through my hair and down my back. Again and again. "It's about forgiveness and compassion, but has no true translation. The language is too old."

I sniffled, my eyelashes still damp. "Why are you so different from the others?"

"You mean my brethren, like Sebastian and Brent?"

"Yes. You can be so cold—like them—yet, also warm. Why?"

He shifted, his legs stretching out to cross at the ankles as he repositioned me on his lap. I pressed my cheek to his shoulder, my gaze on the dark-wood wall.

"The coldness is natural, a product of age. However, unlike most of my kind, I haven't lost my sense of humanity. Vampires and lycans are the superior races, but humans are the source of our life force. Without your blood, vampires would die. Without your ability to procreate, lycans would also die." He rubbed my back while he spoke, his touch peaceful and right, lulling me into a state of comfort I'd experienced with no one else.

"There has to be a way for us all to live in harmony without relegating your kind to camps and torture," he continued. "We managed it for several thousand years, which, of course, changed after humans discovered our existence. Still, the solution put in place—today's society—wasn't the only option. That's Cam's belief, and there are many among us who agree with him. Including me."

"And Jace."

"Yes. Trevor and Ivan as well, and several others you've not met yet. We've been positioning ourselves appropriately throughout the world for the last several decades in hopes of staging a coup d'état. My becoming a sovereign beneath Jace is the signal to the others that we're ready to begin shuffling the pieces on the board."

"Why now?" I wondered. "Did something happen to prompt the change?"

He shook his head. "Not exactly. We had hoped to have a better idea of Cam's location before we began, but it's become increasingly clear that we need more positions in power to find him. The changes we seek won't happen overnight, or even within the next few decades. This is a long game we are playing, one that started a century ago and continues today."

I blinked, my vision blurry. "So humans will continue to suffer."

"Unfortunately, yes." He hugged me to him. "But it's not only humans, Juliet. The nomad lands are terrifying and desperate and far worse than even the lowest of supernatural classes. Our society today is based on aristocracy and power, and it's grossly inadequate for all parties involved. Only the most powerful and ancient of our kind—the royals, for example—benefit. The rest are left to their own devices, or to starve."

I hadn't seen that aspect of our world. The Coventus's teachings centered around the influential lifestyle because that was always my future—to be the slave of a wealthy vampire. Like Darius.

My focus slid to the man holding me, to his handsome face, alluring gaze, and full mouth. "Why did you pick me?"

His palm slid up to my neck, beneath my hair, to grasp my nape. "When one in my position is interested in procuring a blood virgin, we are sent portfolios of all the candidates. I requested my first set two years ago and received a monthly dossier, but none of them piqued my interest. I had almost given up on the idea, as we were running out of time, but then your profile crossed my desk." His thumb stroked the side of my throat, skimming my pulse.

"Your intellectual aptitude and affinity for languages were the first marks in your favor. But it was your eyes"—his irises sizzled with green fire—"that sealed your fate. I knew you would be able to bring my enemies to their knees with a glance, and become my own perfect, intelligent, gorgeous weapon."

I licked my suddenly dry lips. "The Coventus taught me to do whatever my master desires, meaning I would try to help you with anything you asked of me regardless of the ceremony. So why bother with the ritual? Is it because you need me to be immortal like Izzy?"

"The ceremony affords us a deeper connection and a way to communicate should we need to. And yes, your immortality carried an important purpose. I needed you less breakable for the situations I had originally intended for you, which is also why I started training you about weapons and self-defense." The hand not on my neck fell to my thigh, his fingers splaying possessively across my jeans. "But those plans have proven impossible."

I swallowed. "What do you mean?"

"I can't put you in a situation again like I did with

Viktor. Hell, I can't even share you." Those last five words were spoken with a hint of frustration. "I've tried, even managed to a little with Ivan and Trevor, but when Sebastian visited, I couldn't do it. That's why I sent you upstairs."

I frowned. "But I thought I displeased you. I went to your room expecting your punishment."

"Oh, darling, no." He pressed his lips to my forehead, his arms folding around me. "Any frustration you felt was directed at Sebastian, not you. My words were all part of the charade we must play to survive. I had intended to pleasure you until you couldn't walk, but instead found you devastated." He pulled back, his gaze again meeting mine. "Was that because you thought I intended to harm you?"

"I—I, yes. You said I disappointed you earlier in the night, and I thought I had again with Sebastian." My throat worked over the words, my emotions surfacing again. "I expected pain."

He sighed, his forehead falling to my shoulder. "I've never desired to hurt you, darling. Not cruelly, anyway." He kissed my neck, my ear. "I much prefer sexual games to punishing ones."

"I don't understand how to act anymore," I admitted. "You asked if I wanted to be shared with Sebastian, and I didn't, but I'm trained to do as you wish. Then with our last dinner, you promised not to share me, but Jace bit me. I'm so confused, Darius. I don't know how to please you or what you want from me. I keep making mistakes, but I promise to do—"

His lips sealed over mine, silencing my despair. He kissed me softly, his mouth gently gliding against my own. I slid my fingers into his hair, holding on to him, desperate for him, breathing him like air.

I need you, I told him. *Please, Darius.*

He responded by shifting my legs until I straddled him, his hands seizing my hips as he deepened our embrace. My tongue parted his lips, demanding more. He didn't smile or react, but let me take what I desired, exploring his mouth as he always did my own. And I tasted every inch of him, claiming him as he did me and marking him as mine.

I won't share you, I warned him. *Izzy was Cam's only mate, so don't tell me it's not possible. I won't believe you.*

He broke the kiss, green flames dancing in his gaze. "You're demanding my fidelity." Not a question, but a statement.

I didn't hesitate, my heart and soul refusing to back down from this. "Yes. You said vampires can take more than one *Erosita*, but that's not acceptable to me. If I am to remain loyal to you, then I expect the same."

"And now you're giving me an ultimatum." He rolled me off of him and onto my back, his body caging me against the mattress. "Have you forgotten who is the master here, Juliet?"

I shivered beneath him, his position and tone reasserting his dominance. Not that I ever denied it.

"If you take another, I'll kill her." I realized as I said it how true that statement was. Darius had taught me enough self-defense with weapons that, paired with my proprietorial emotions, I could kill. "I won't share you," I repeated, this time out loud. "I refuse."

He chuckled, his lips falling to my neck. "Fuck, Juliet." He pressed his erection into my hip, his body all brute strength above me. "I don't know if you're just saying these things because of my possessiveness influencing you through our bond, but it's arousing as hell." He slid between my legs and settled his hardness at the apex between my thighs. "You're mine too, Juliet. But society will force me to share you. It's why I brought you here— not just to learn, but to offer you an escape."

I stilled beneath him despite the fire scalding my veins. "What?"

"You can stay here if you want. Humans, even blood virgins, go missing every day. No one would suspect anything after my taking you up to the suite with Jace. If anything, they'll be shocked you survived." His lips met my neck, his kisses filled with reverence. "You've already done what I needed by assisting me with my reemergence into society. I've acquired the requisite results, which means you've upheld your side of our arrangement."

His breath shuddered across my skin, trailing goose bumps across my flesh.

"What are you saying?" I asked, my breath catching in my lungs.

"I'm saying that you could have a real life here, Juliet. No one would be surprised by our short-lived bond; they would just assume I grew tired of you as my kind is wont to do."

My eyes narrowed at his words. "Short-lived?" I grabbed his shoulders and shoved, needing to see his face. "You're suggesting our ceremony be *short-lived?*" Hadn't he promised me immortality in exchange for my agreement to help him destroy his competition? Or had he only meant to provide me temporary immortality through the election process, and not beyond it? "Are we not completing the bond?"

He stared down at me. "You no longer desire the ceremony?"

That was not at all what I'd just said. I shook my head, confused and conflicted. What was the point in initiating the bond only to leave me here? I thought Darius wanted eternity, to train me to be his perfect poison always, not *temporarily.* I pushed him again, this time intending to shove him off of me, but the hard vampire didn't move.

"Juliet, are you rejecting my bond?"

My eyebrows jumped up. "Rejecting the bond?" Was he joking? "I just told you I don't ever want to share you, and you replied by informing me that my purpose in your life is essentially done!" I couldn't help raising my voice. All of this was complete and utter madness. "You required my acceptance of our deal, stating I would gain immortality, then you tell me vampires can have more than one *Erosita*, and now, you intend to leave me here. Alone. In a world I don't understand because you no longer need me and our bond can be short-lived."

I officially hated that term. I officially hated him. I officially hated everything. This life. This world. This situation. I wanted to scream—an act forbidden by vampires. But why did I care? What purpose did it serve to always be in perfect order? *To please my master.* I almost laughed, but instead another sound parted my lips.

A screech filled with all the emotions and hatred I felt for everything and everyone. My world shattering beneath a veil of hurt and torment.

No more.

Darius wanted to leave me here? Fine. But not without him realizing just how much he'd broken me first.

Chapter Thirty

JULIET

"Fuck!" Darius's palm covered my mouth, the complete opposite of what I desired. I squirmed beneath him, fighting with everything I had to dislodge his much bigger body, to no avail. "Stop!" he demanded.

"No!" My shout came out muffled behind his hand. Tears burned my eyes as I glowered up at him. He could silence my mouth, but not my mind.

I hate you! Why even bother with the ceremony if you didn't intend to see it through? To just leave me here? Alone? Without you? I tried futilely to throw him off me again and screamed internally in frustration when he didn't even budge.

You should have just compelled me to help you without all the extra requirements! That would have been a better fate than forcing this temporary bond between us just to shatter it once I completed my purpose. Or is that how you play with your food, vampire? Promise her eternity just to steal it away and leave her in a place with complete strangers while you go off and find a new mate?

He held me down, his gaze smoldering with unveiled fury as I trembled angrily beneath him. *Let. Me. Go!*

Both of my hands were locked over my head in one of his while his thighs pinned mine to the bed, his other palm still covering my mouth. "You have completely misunderstood my intentions," he growled.

I snorted. *I've misunderstood everything all along because you prefer to talk in riddles than to actually explain yourself.*

His eyebrows rose. "You want a full explanation, Juliet? Then I'll give you one." His hand slid from my lips only to be replaced by his mouth. I bit his tongue in response, eliciting a deep snarl from him. But he didn't stop despite the blood pouring from the wound, his lips devouring mine in a punishing kiss that stole my breath.

Walls crashed down around us, an influx of sounds and voices piercing my ears.

The assault left me dizzy and floating in a consciousness that didn't belong to me.

Darius.

His mind surrounded me, encasing me in his memories, his thoughts, his feelings and intentions. I gasped, my lungs enflamed with the need to inhale, but all I absorbed were more words and emotions.

Tenderness, fear, possession, hurt.

Taking her here is the right thing to do, even if it kills me to leave her.

I can't keep her. Not in this world.

I'm losing focus.

Fuck, she's amazing. So broken, so beautiful, so mine.

Breaking her is going to be the most fulfilling and devastating act I've ever committed.

This world is too dangerous for her.

I'll kill anyone who touches her, even though I shouldn't.

Cam is counting on me. But all I can think about is her.

She'll be safe with the Majestic Clan, even more so than with me, but I'll rarely see her. A sacrifice I have to make—for her.

I'll be miserable without her, but how can I be so selfish?

What if she remained at my side? It would hurt her even more, society would make so many demands... I can't do that to her.

What about the original plan? Have I forgotten everything?

This could never be short-lived, not between us.

Oxygen burned my insides as he released me, his mouth a hairsbreadth away from mine as I panted from the onslaught of his invasion. Two orbs of liquid emeralds seethed down at me, his cheeks pink from the exertion of allowing me into his mind.

"Darius," I breathed. I had nothing else to say, only my lips on his mattered now.

I closed the gap between us, kissing him with a fervor that was amplified by his thoughts. He had left the door to his mind wide open, showing me everything. His unhinged desire, the restraint it took for him not to claim my body, the anger he felt at society, his possessive instincts, his heart...

I arched into him, needing more. His hand slid to my hip and then up beneath my sweater to palm my breast. I moaned in encouragement. My exhaustion no longer mattered, nor did all my tortured emotions. *Only him.*

"Take me," I whispered. "Complete us."

He groaned against my mouth, his grip on my wrists tightening. "It'll hurt, Juliet. Especially like this."

"It'll hurt more if you don't." I rubbed against his arousal, my thighs straining beneath his. "Claim me, Darius. *Please.*"

His mouth dominated mine with a brutality I felt to my very soul. I fell into his kiss headfirst, my brain no longer functioning, my heart no longer beating, my lungs pumping mindlessly.

Darius was everywhere. *Everything.* My obsession, my reason for being, my life.

He sat up, pulling me with him, and yanked my sweater

over my head while I tore through the buttons of his shirt, leaving our chests bare against each other, as our mouths continued to destroy one another. My jeans were next, my shoes vanishing along the way, and then he lowered me to the bed, naked for his perusal.

"I will never tire of seeing you like this." His voice held a note of awe, his eyes simmering with unrestrained yearning as he discarded the remains of his shirt. My pulse spiked in response, begging for his bite. I wanted everything he had to offer. All of it. Always. He slid his belt through the buckle slowly, tauntingly, then let the leather fall to his side. "I should make you unbutton my pants with your teeth."

I shifted onto my elbows, eager to try, but he'd already popped them loose, the zipper inching down to reveal his engorged cock. Moisture beaded at the top, so deliciously alluring. I loved tasting him, was addicted to his flavor and pleasure.

His pupils dilated. "You're eyeing me as though you want to devour me, sweetheart."

"I do," I moaned, my nipples tightening to painful points.

He grinned. "Soon." He slid his pants down his strong thighs, then kicked them off onto the floor along with the rest of our clothes.

I fell from my elbows to my back and met his ravenous gaze. A shiver of longing cascaded goose bumps down my arms. *Darius is finally going to claim me.* A maelstrom of fire and ice swirled in my lower belly at the thought. I wanted this, craved it, and feared it all at the same time.

"Are you wet for me, Juliet?" he asked, his body hovering above mine on his hands and knees, trapping me against the bed.

"Yes," I whispered.

He sat back onto his heels between my splayed thighs. "Show me."

I parted my legs wider for him, displaying my intimate

flesh.

"Use your fingers." A quiet command, not a request. "Dip them into your sweet cunt and bring the moisture to my lips."

A hot flush swept over me at the wanton directive, even as my hand dipped down to touch my shaved mound and lower. I arched into my palm, desperate for the friction. It felt so good, yet not nearly good enough. I whimpered at the contradiction, my lip caught between my teeth. Tension curled in my limbs. *So close…*

I slid two fingers inside my tight channel, hoping for sweet relief, but all it did was worsen the ache pulsing between my thighs.

"Go deep for me," he urged, his eyes on my hand.

"Yes, Sire." My touch did little to alleviate the need clawing at my insides. If anything, it only magnified the torment, sending a fresh surge of warmth to my already weeping core.

"That looks delicious, darling." His thumbs skimmed my inner thighs so close to where I desired him most, eliciting a guttural sound from my throat. He bent to press a kiss to my working hand. "Give me a taste, love."

I shuddered and lifted my fingers to his waiting lips. He groaned as he took them into his mouth with strong, luxurious strokes of his tongue. I wanted him to do that to my clit, to drive me to that place he'd introduced me to, the one where I let go of all my thoughts and only *felt*.

"Darius, please…"

He grinned. "Mmm, I do love when you beg." He lowered my palm to the bed and pressed a kiss to my aching center. "Is this what you need?"

"Yes," I hissed, my lungs forgetting how to function.

"Do not come," he warned, sending a flush of heat up my abdomen to my breasts. My nipples hardened to excruciating points, his mouth hovering against the heart of my desire, breathing me in.

"I…" No words followed. I was strung so tight with

anticipation I couldn't tell if I wanted to yell or to cry. No longer knew how to beg. No longer understood words...

And then his tongue parted my folds.

I fisted the comforter on either side of my hips, his name renting the air on a scream. One stroke against my sensitive nub had me teetering on the edge of an explosion. But his tongue went in the wrong direction, drawing a path up my body to my breasts, where he nibbled my tender peaks.

"Darius," I panted, my body demanding release. All of the emotional upheaval, the teasing in the car, the insight into his mind... "I feel like I'm on fire..."

"Good," he murmured against my nipple. "That's exactly where I need you."

I opened my mouth to ask what he meant, when the head of his arousal nudged my entrance. His hands went to my hips, holding me down, his mouth still on my breast.

"You have permission to scream, Juliet." His fangs pierced my areola, blasting ecstasy through my bloodstream, centering in the ache between my thighs. I cried out—confused and *hot*—and he thrust forward.

I forgot how to breathe, my body too shocked and pained by the invasion to function. Tears glistened in my vision, my body frozen in time.

This was the act I feared for so many years—the act of being ripped in half for a vampire. And I'd craved this from Darius.

His palms traced my sides, his lower body still as my walls shuddered around his harsh intrusion. I barely registered my stinging nipple or the way his tongue traced the rivulets of blood trickling down my breast.

"Deep breaths," he instructed softly, his hips flexing subtly.

I winced, not ready. His hands gripped my waist, his fingers bruising my skin, as though he had to fight to stop himself from seeking more friction. His mouth moved to my neck, his lengthened incisors skimming my pulse.

"I need to move," he whispered, his voice agonized. "I need to fuck you, Juliet."

My throat worked over the words I needed to say, but no sound escaped my lips. I wanted to ask for another minute, to beg him to go easy on me.

"Fuck," he groaned, his teeth sinking into my flesh.

I flinched, startled.

It hurt, but, oh, that felt rather interesting.

I tilted my hips again, his hardness rubbing some place deep inside that shot adrenaline through my veins. "Darius," I breathed.

He slid out of me and back in—hard—and I moaned in appreciation. He repeated the action, his own groan adding to mine. Heat spiraled from where our bodies joined, rekindling a flush of excitement. His mouth remained on my throat, his fangs teasing my blood.

I tilted my head, granting him full access, inviting him to drink his fill. "I'm ready, Darius. Make me yours."

"Oh, darling," he whispered. "Don't you realize? You've been mine from the start." His incisors pierced my skin again as his lower body began to truly move. He'd been teasing before, testing my boundaries. Now he no longer cared, his body taking mine the way he needed.

His hands were on my breasts, my hips, and my breasts again, his sanity a loose thread in his thoughts.

Mine.

Finally.

So fucking tight.

So good.

More…

I screamed as he powered into me, his hungry thoughts and the sensations his body created, spiraling me over the edge into oblivion.

My nails dug into his back, holding on as he owned me in the way only Darius could. His hips driving violently into mine, his mouth dragging the life essence from my body into his, and his hands possessing every inch of my skin.

I cried out beneath him, the brutality of his assault exactly what I anticipated and yet so much better. He took me with a ferocity renowned for his kind, but hot emotions overshadowed the cloud of hunger. His mind remained opened to mine, his thoughts and feelings heightening our union.

Gripping my cock so tightly, I barely fit... Fuck, I can't stop. I'll never stop.

He picked me up, my legs going around his waist. I rode him, forcing him even deeper, as his thighs drove each thrust.

"Darius," I moaned, my body fracturing beneath the onslaught of pleasure and pain. He'd already pushed me through one climax and another was already building.

"Drink from me," he demanded, lifting his wrist. He sliced his fangs across his flesh, blood welling from the wound. "Finish the ceremony."

A choice. If I chose not to imbibe, the connection would falter. I only understood because he showed me with his mind how the process worked. His body claiming mine with a savage need to finish this, to complete the bond, but not without my final consent.

I was never going to refuse.

I accepted his wrist, my mouth latching onto the laceration and sucking deep. His sweet blood pooled into my mouth, his resulting growl filling my ears.

Mine, I heard him shout. Whether out loud or not, I couldn't tell, too lost in the feeling of our bodies, minds, and spirits marrying one another in an eternal promise.

His pace quickened, my hips bruising from his punishing grip and harsh assault, but pleasure mounted deep inside with each upward stroke. I released his wrist, my mouth finding his while his arm wrapped around my back. His other hand dropped to my waist, his grip firm as he propelled himself into my body.

Fucking me. Loving me. Annihilating me.

I returned the pressure in kind, meeting him move for move, needing to stake my claim too, and I felt him smile against my mouth.

"The perfect mate," he said, capturing my tongue with a bold strike of his own. "You feel fucking amazing."

"More," I begged. "Give me more."

He flattened me on the bed, his cock lodged deep inside me. "Hold on to me."

I wrapped my arms around his neck, holding on for dear life as he took me to a new level of existence. My heart raced, sweat trickling down my brow, the pain almost too much to bear.

But it also felt so, so good. Better than I ever imagined.

My body shook, the fire in my veins reaching a melting point. And still, I needed more. Of what, I didn't know. I was lost to his movements, his speed. He rotated his hips in a way that stroked my clit, but it wasn't enough.

So hot.

No, too *hot.*

Oh, Darius.

He owned me. My entire being existed for this joining of souls and flesh. It burned, searing every nerve, singeing my heart. I couldn't breathe, my body trapped in the throes of an impending spasm that refused me.

It hurts...

"Come for me, Juliet," Darius demanded harshly against my lips. "*Now.*"

I pulled my mouth away from his on a savage exhale, his name the only one gracing my tongue as I shattered beneath his command.

His resulting growl rumbled through my chest, clawing its way to my heart and soul. It wrecked me from the inside out, solidifying his claim and my own while my body shook violently in the blissful agony of our addictive passion.

"*Mine.*" Darius's fierce proclamation rattled the walls as he followed me into delicious oblivion, his rapture scorching through our connection and stirring another explosion from within.

Black and white lights danced behind my eyes, my world flipping upside down in an instant. I lost consciousness, too absorbed in the bliss of my soul lifting to a new plane of existence to remain among the living.

This is what it feels like to fly...

I floated higher, happier than I'd ever been, and found myself staring up into Darius's grinning green eyes. His thick cock pulsed inside me, hot and very hard. "Are you ready to continue?" he asked softly. "Or do you need another minute?"

"There's more?" I asked, dazed.

"Oh, Juliet." His lips curled into a dazzling smile. "That was just the beginning."

Chapter Thirty-One

Darius

Juliet slept so peacefully that I hated to wake her. We were well into the evening hours after having spent much of the day fucking. She was an excellent student, taking my direction without hesitation and relying on her instincts.

I smiled, thinking about how she'd knelt for me, her hands on the headboard while I drove into her from behind. My cock throbbed for more against her firm ass.

Not yet.

She needed to recover from earlier before we ventured into that territory. Her immortality was firmly established, her life force thriving inside me, but she still required sustenance to stay healthy.

I nibbled her neck gently, my tongue gliding over her pulse. She groaned, her backside pressing into my eager groin as she stretched and yawned. "Darius?" she murmured, her voice groggy with sleep.

"Juliet." I kissed her bare shoulder. "It's after midnight."

"Mmm." Another stretch that had me growling low in my throat.

"Keep doing that, and we won't be leaving this room today."

She stilled, then repeated the action.

Little rebel. I flipped her onto her back and knelt between her spread thighs. "Juliet, do I come off as the joking type to you?" I had meant my threat. She could go a day without food, especially with my blood running through her veins.

"Erm, no." She licked her lips, her brown gaze falling to the arousal between my legs. Her cheeks flushed, her pupils dilating with hunger.

"Don't look at me like that unless you plan to do something about it." I grasped my cock and gave it a firm stroke, my muscles clenching with need.

She shivered visibly, lifting to her elbows. "I, uh…" Her stomach growled on cue, causing my lips to twitch.

"Yes?" I cocked my head. "Are you desiring an appetizer, darling?"

She groaned and fell back onto the bed, covering her head with a pillow. Her hardening nipples and glistening pussy told me exactly how she felt about my offer. I placed a kiss at the apex between her thighs. "You can't hide from me, Juliet."

Goose bumps pebbled along her flesh, her lust thickening the air. I gave her a long, deep lick before crawling over her and caging her with my arms. She jolted as my erection prodded her slick entrance.

"Are you sore?" I asked softly.

Her mumble was unintelligible behind the pillow. I removed the barrier with a flick of my wrist and gazed down at her flushed face. So beautiful and turned on, but another gentle stroke against her folds confirmed my suspicions.

"I should fuck you to prove a point." I nipped her lower lip. "You need to tell me when I push you too far."

She swallowed. "H-how?"

"Just open up your mind," I murmured. "I'll listen."

Her brow rose, her doubt filtering through the bond.

My lips curled, amused. "I didn't say I'd stop, but I'll listen."

I slid into her slowly, her sweet heat enveloping my cock in a sheath of damp arousal. Her cheeks reddened to a deep, luscious shade. I ran my nose along her soft skin, inhaling the sweet aroma while setting a luxurious pace. Her eyes rolled into the back of her head on a moan, all earlier hesitation gone.

I kissed her neck, her jaw, the sensitive spot below her ear. "It doesn't always have to be hard, love." Another kiss to her temple. "I can be tender, too."

Her palms slid up my arms, her fingers gripping my shoulders. "I think I prefer rough."

"I know you do." I lifted to my elbows again to find her gaze. "But you need more energy before I take you like that again. I want a partner in the bedroom, not an unconscious doll."

Her hips rose to meet mine, driving me deeper. "I'm coming back with you." She spoke the words on a groan, her pupils engulfing her alluring brown irises.

"Are you?" My soft question didn't match the hard thrust of my hips as I tested her pain tolerance.

She bit her lip, her back arching. "I am," she gasped out. "You're not leaving me here."

"You'll be safe." An important factor considering my political agenda. "And if you chose to remain faithful, we could be together in the future."

Her nails dug into my skin. Hard. "You're mine."

I smiled at her ferocity. "I know, darling. But you have a choice."

She lifted into me again, guiding my erection to the place she desired inside. "No, Darius. I'm going with you." Her eyes fluttered closed, her expression the perfect picture of agonized pleasure.

"It hurts, doesn't it?" I asked, keeping myself sheathed inside her.

"Yes," she whispered. "But I want more."

"Harder?"

"Yes," she repeated. "And tell me I can come with you. Stay with you." Her gaze pierced mine on those last three words. "Say it, Darius. Please."

I released the answer in a kiss, allowing her to *feel* my emotions and punctuating them with my increased momentum. Her heart beat rapidly against my chest, her breathing erratic. It wouldn't take long for her to come, and the thought of that alone brought me one step closer to climax. Feeling her walls grip my shaft was one of the most amazing experiences of my very long life. I would never tire of it, would never tire of *her*.

"Oh, Juliet," I whispered against her swollen lips. "Don't you understand what it means to be my mate?" My weight fell to one elbow while I used my other hand to angle her hips for a more intense connection.

A guttural sound parted her lips, her approval evident in the way her back bowed off the bed.

"It would hurt like hell to leave you here," I continued, my voice darkening from my mounting need. "But I would do whatever you asked, whatever you wanted." My tongue found hers, yearning to prove my point, to claim what I owned and to reciprocate in kind. She shook beneath me, her pleasure cresting at its peak, awaiting my approval and final touch.

"Fuck, your body is perfect," I said, awed. "*You* are perfect."

"Darius," she breathed, a hint of urgency in her voice. "*Please...*"

I drew out the moment, plunging into her with a

frenzy, enjoying the freezing of her limbs as she fought to hold on to her sanity. A light sheen of sweat decorated her skin, her eyes closed so tightly she had to be seeing stars.

Gorgeous.

"I'll take you wherever you want to go, Juliet," I vowed. "So long as you take me with you." I kissed her deep, her limbs violently trembling around me. "Come for me, sweetheart. Embrace me."

Her scream pierced the night, my heart, and my soul, and I followed her over the cliff with a mind-blowing orgasm that put all the others to shame.

Fuck.

I growled her name, my seed filling her so deep, staking my claim. My arms shook from the effort to remain hovering above her, my legs actually weak from the force with which I took her body. Her pleasure contracted around me, squeezing every last drop into her greedy little cunt.

My forehead fell to her neck, my eyes glistening with tears at the impact. I would never desire another, not after Juliet. All those years of doubting the *Erosita* bond, wondering why Cam would ever choose to engage in it, and I finally understood.

Juliet's the other half of my soul. It could be the bond talking, some magical twist of fate, but I doubted it. Not with the way my body and mind reacted to her presence. She did everything I wanted, fought me when I needed it, submitted when I required it, and still wanted to remain at my side.

"I'll never leave you anywhere you don't want to be," I murmured. "And if being by my side proves too much, I will find a way to return you here. To safety."

She cupped my cheek, lifting me from her neck to gaze dazedly into my eyes. "Your world terrifies me, but I can survive it with you."

I shifted to kiss her palm and rested my face against her hand. "It won't be easy. Lilith City was just the beginning."

"I know, and that would have been more bearable had you told me what was happening."

"I needed your reactions to be genuine."

"Then trust me to know how to act, Darius." Her eyes burned into mine. "I spent twenty-two years learning about vampire politics and decorum. You want me to be your weapon, right? Use me, but communicate. I can do this if you believe in me."

So fiercely intelligent, my Juliet. "I don't deserve you." Not in this life, but perhaps an older one. "But I'm keeping you anyway."

Her eyes glimmered with a happiness that touched my heart. Then her stomach rumbled, reminding me of her needs.

I smiled. "I did promise you an appetizer, hmm?" I pulled out of her slowly and knelt between her thighs. "Your pussy looks so good with my cum dripping out of it," I told her, dragging my finger through her tender folds. "Open."

She parted her lips, accepting my sex-drenched finger. Her pupils flared as she sucked my skin clean.

"I want you to do that to my cock," I said, awed.

"Yes, Sire," she replied, voice husky. Her legs bent as she repositioned herself onto her knees and grasped my hips.

I groaned as she bent to take me into her mouth, her head a tangle of dark curls mussed from our lovemaking.

"Fuck," I growled, tangling my fingers in her hair to force her lips to the base. Her tongue worked me over thoroughly, licking up every drop. My dick practically shone when she finished, her mouth puffy from my forceful attentions.

I tightened my grip on her dark strands, giving it a sharp yank to tilt her head back for my rewarding kiss. She deserved so much more, but first, she required proper sustenance. As much as I would love for her to live on my cum alone, that seemed improbable and a bit cruel.

Her breaths came in pants as I pulled back, her pupils large and overwhelmed. "I'm definitely going to fuck you again," I promised. "After we eat."

Something akin to disappointment flashed in her eyes. "Another dinner."

I laughed, my chest light with humor. Of course she would dread everything to do with food after the last week. "It won't be anything like the others, love." I slipped from the bed and gathered her into my arms. "Shower first." The hot water would be good for her muscles, as would some explicit care to her more sensitive regions.

She didn't argue, her body caving to my will while I bathed and clothed her. Only her eyes told me she didn't much care for her outfit. "It feels hot," she muttered.

"That's the purpose of a sweater." I tugged on the hem. Ismerelda had arranged for some clothes to be delivered during daylight hours, the sizes perfect for Juliet. My clothes were already in the room, where I kept them indefinitely. We would have to add a wardrobe for Juliet for the rare occasions we were able to visit.

I pulled a navy long-sleeved shirt over my head and paired it with jeans that matched Juliet's ensemble. Her eyes ran over me with interest, and I cocked a brow. "Yes?"

"Nothing, it's just, well, I like this look on you."

I wrapped my palm around the back of her neck, beneath her damp hair. "Mmm, the feeling is mutual, Juliet." I kissed her for a second longer than was necessary. "Let's go find food so I can strip you again later."

Her expression softened. "So, that's the point of the clothes."

I chuckled. "No, but we can pretend it is if that makes you feel better." No woman I'd ever met preferred to wander around naked. I wanted to fault the Coventus for that, I really did, but my heart just wasn't in it. My mate wandering around nude for a lifetime would not upset me. Not in the least.

269

My fingers linked with hers as I guided her down the hall toward the kitchen. Jace stood just inside, his head bent over a blonde lycan's shoulder, his lips at her ear. Whatever he said painted her cheeks a deep red, her arousal and excitement more than evident.

Spying us in the doorway, she giggled and darted out of the room, leaving Jace smirking after her. "That'll be fun to chase later."

I shook my head. "You seriously have a death wish."

He pressed a palm to his chest. "What? She's not a mated lycan and definitely of age to make her own decisions."

"She's the alpha's daughter," I reminded, opening a cabinet to pull out two bowls while Juliet rested against the counter. "Surely he has some political arrangement in place for her."

Jace waved a dismissive hand. "Not for another few years. It's fine."

"Lycans prefer virgin mates."

"There are things I can do to her that maintain her virginity," he drawled. "Surely you discovered a few of them with Juliet?"

She cleared her throat beside me, her face flushing a delectable shade of crimson. I brushed my knuckles over her cheek before opening the fridge. "How do you feel about soup?" I asked, spying a vat of chicken noodle on the top shelf. *Comfort food.*

"Okay," she said, her eyes still on Jace.

He had a curious gleam in his eyes as he glanced between us. Then his lips curled. "You two had a good day. Sleep much?"

"Stop embarrassing her," I chided, pouring the liquid into the bowls. "I want to keep her, not scare her."

"Does that mean she'll be coming back with us?" he asked, fully aware of my thoughts about leaving her here.

"Yes," Juliet replied before I could. "I can play my role as required."

My lips twitched at the certainty in her tone as I glanced at Jace. "She's requested I communicate more."

"Fancy that." Jace smiled. "Well, then on that subject, I have an idea to run by you both."

I put the bowls in the microwave and turned around. "Regarding?"

"Gaston," he replied. "I think I know a way to make him step down and to ensure your victory without further bloodshed. It will also solve your sharing problem."

My eyebrows rose. "All right, you have my attention. What's your idea?"

Chapter Thirty-Two

DARIUS

A Few Weeks Later…

This was a horrible plan. Killing Gaston would have been so much easier, and far more pleasurable.

"Relax," Ivan murmured beside me. "Or you're going to shatter that glass."

"I'm going to shatter something," I muttered. *Such as Jace's face if he kisses Juliet one more time.*

I'm fine, Darius, she replied, her voice soothing. She sat across the room in Jace's lap wearing a black gown cut to her belly button. His arm was around her shoulders, his opposite hand tucked beneath the slit of her dress to rest on her bare thigh.

I agreed to do this, she reminded. *It's the best way and also my purpose as your mate. Trust me to play my role.*

My grip loosened, her calm tone relaxing my bonded-male instincts. Jace had suggested this scene as a way to demonstrate to society my lack of affection and care toward my blood virgin.

"Removing the forbidden allure will take away all of their fun," he had said. "And it also serves as a way for you to show me favor, something the masses will more than appreciate in this political game. Gaston won't stand a chance because he has nothing of interest to offer me, and he knows it."

I finished my drink and set it on a nearby tray. Word of my nomination had already spread, Sebastian making a point to tell everyone in the room that he was the one to thank for my newfound political aspiration. I would enjoy killing him some day, once his usefulness no longer applied.

"Looks like Gaston has just received the news," Ivan informed, his chin nodding at the vampire in question. His bald head glistened in the chandelier lights as he spoke to Sebastian, his face paling.

"He looks thrilled," Trevor said, handing me a replacement flute. "Don't break this."

I snorted. "I'm in control."

"Sure." He grinned. "Keep telling yourself that."

"She's had you by the balls since you brought her home." Ivan sounded far too amused. "It's been entertaining as hell to watch."

I sighed, secretly thankful for their distraction. "Why am I always surrounded by children?"

"Because you're so fucking old?" Trevor suggested. "Just a thought."

Ivan chuckled. "And true." His lips twitched. "You're being summoned, Darius."

I glanced at Jace's table, noting his raised brow. "Hmm. This should be fun. If you'll excuse me." *I'm going to kiss you, Juliet*, I told her as I approached. *Prepare yourself for it.*

Why does that sound like a threat?

Because you know me well. I took another sip of my champagne before passing it off to a human servant without a word.

"Your Highness," I greeted formally, my fingers knotting in Juliet's long strands. "One moment." I tugged her back and kissed her as I promised, my teeth scraping possessively over her tongue. Her sweet essence filled my mouth. "Mmm, that's better," I murmured, releasing her as suddenly as I had grabbed her.

Jace chuckled, his fingers combing through her now tangled strands. "Was that an invitation to taste her again, Darius?" A brilliant reference to our time in Lilith City for the benefit of the room. Some days I suspected Jace knew how to play this game better than me, perhaps because of his experience on the royal court.

I lifted a shoulder, feigning nonchalance. "You're welcome to do whatever you'd like to her." Cold words that I could only utter because I trusted him. Maybe this was a good plan after all.

His silver gaze glimmered. "I may just take you up on that offer later."

I brushed my knuckles down Juliet's exposed arm, eliciting goose bumps in my wake. "She would be happy to oblige in whatever you have in mind."

Jace kissed her throbbing pulse and then her cheek. "I look forward to it." He sighed, relaxing into his chair. "Join us, Darius." He gestured to the chair beside him. "Gloria can share with Lisa."

Gloria's expression remained stoic as she stood and moved to the chair on his other side, silently sitting on Lisa's lap. Both humans were members of Jace's royal harem. They were alluringly dressed in navy lingerie, but their collective beauty was nothing compared to my Juliet.

"Thank you," I murmured, sitting beside him.

The symbolism was not lost on the room. Inviting me to sit at his side indicated his favoritism in my accepting the position as his new sovereign. I met Gaston's fuming gaze across the room. *Message definitely received.* Sebastian stood beside him, his lips curled in triumph. The power-hungry vampire assumed I would benefit him somehow. He would be sorely disappointed.

"I was just telling Benedict how thrilled I am by your interest in finally joining my political council," Jace said conversationally. "Adrian left a rather large gap in my team, and it will be nice to have someone competent at my side to replace him."

"Hopefully, I can live up to your expectations." A scripted response that he knew was intended to be sarcastic despite my respectful tone.

"Oh, I believe you already have." Another stroke through Juliet's hair trailing all the way down to her waist. "I've never understood the allure of procuring a blood virgin—perhaps because I have my own harem—but I haven't been able to stop thinking about your Juliet's blood for weeks."

I allowed myself a smile. "She is quite addictive."

"Which I imagine is why you chose her as an *Erosita,*" Jace added thoughtfully. "Another aspect I've never comprehended, but can definitely respect where she is concerned." He smirked at the other aristocrats seated around us. "She screams beautifully."

Their lust-driven expressions said they desired a taste themselves, but no way in hell was that happening.

"Your Highness," a familiar voice said from behind us. "May I have a brief word?"

Jace waited a beat before turning. "Gaston. Of course." He trailed a finger down Juliet's throat. "Go back to your master like a good pet."

"Yes, Your Highness," she murmured dutifully, sliding from his lap to mine. I wrapped an arm around her exposed lower back and splayed my hand along her side. Her hair fell to one side as she taunted me with the column of her neck.

Desiring a bite, darling?

Only from you, she replied.

I kissed her pulse and nibbled the tender skin. *I'll take your femoral artery later.*

She shivered. *Yes, please.*

"How can I help you, Gaston?" Jace asked, his body angled toward the older vampire. Fury flashed through my opponent's eyes at the blatant disrespect of his position. Most of our brethren would stand in his presence, but a royal could get away with remaining seated. And Jace took full advantage of that right while also delivering a very clear message. *I don't support you.*

Gaston cleared his throat. "As you may know, I've put my name forward for the position of your sovereign."

"Yes, I'm aware." Jace kept his voice politely curious, his charade flawless.

"In light of recent events, I believe it best that I withdraw my candidacy." It sounded like those words hurt Gaston to say, but he delivered them appropriately. "Darius is far more suitable for the position." He couldn't conceal his grimace as he spoke the words. I hid my grin against Juliet's hair.

"On that, Gaston, we agree," Jace replied. "I accept your withdrawal. Is that all you needed?" The quick dismissal had a few heads turning our way, their gazes curious. Royals were commonly rude to their constituents, but to be rude to one as old as Gaston would certainly reach the gossip circuit.

"Yes, Your Highness. That's all I have to say."

"Excellent. Nice speaking with you, Gaston." Jace turned around before the male could reply. "Now, where were we? Oh yes, discussions of later and the things I want to do to your Juliet..."

I slid into the limo beside Juliet and captured her hand in mine. She said nothing as Jace joined us, his expression impassive for those watching our departure. The two members of his harem were riding with his driver and following us back to my estate.

"Well, that went as predicted," Jace said as soon as the door closed. "But we'll need to keep an eye on him."

"Yes, your blatant rejection definitely wounded his ego a bit."

Jase shrugged. "Anyone who preys on children deserves to be taken down a peg or two."

I couldn't agree more with that statement. Juliet relaxed into my side as the limo lurched forward, her arm wrapping around my abdomen. A very different reaction from all those months ago when I procured her from the auction.

"Tired, darling?" I asked softly, fondling her hair.

She nodded.

"That's too bad," I murmured. "I have plans for you later."

Arousal slithered through our bond, heating my blood and hers. Clearly, she wasn't *that* tired.

"While I've always enjoyed voyeurism, we need to discuss your ascension."

I sighed. "And so my life in politics begins."

It didn't matter that the coronation wouldn't take place for another three months. Those who mattered had been in attendance tonight at the Parliament Gala, and they were all in favor of my placement as Jace's new sovereign. There would be no contest to my accepting the position.

The dinner invitations had already started, as well as the high society events. My schedule had quickly gone from quiet to busy in a matter of hours.

I'll be with you, Juliet whispered, my thoughts completely open to her.

I squeezed her hand. *I know.*

Jace started discussing the future, his ideas, how we could work together, and also commented on the ongoing charade with Juliet. So long as our brethren thought I openly shared her with him, no one would bother asking for a taste. She was used goods, thus making her not nearly as exciting. More like a pretty ornament that smelled delectable.

Is he staying at the estate tonight? she wondered.

Yes, with his harem, and possibly for a few days.

To solidify his support of you as the new sovereign?

That, and to hide for a few days. There were very few others Jace could be himself around. It helped that my home was also listening-device-free, allowing him to say and do whatever the fuck he wanted.

That will be nice, she admitted, her mental voice soft.

My lips curled. *You like him, don't you?*

I sensed her mental shrug. *He's growing on me.*

So long as you're not inviting him into our bed later, I'm okay with that.

Never. Only you, Darius.

For eternity, I reminded her.

For eternity.

I closed my eyes while Jace droned on about the Blood Alliance, listing names of those he thought we could sway to our side and why. Soon others would begin to join the ranks, their identities only known by a few.

My ascension served as the signal that the fun was about to begin.

For the king had stepped onto the chessboard accompanied by his queen.

It's time to play.

Epilogue

JULIET

Blood Day

Darius's hand tightened around mine, his body rigid as the rituals began.

Chants and prayers from the humans lined up in rows across the field littered the air, the Goddess herself sitting high on the platform. We sat behind her, beside Jace, and all the other royals, sovereigns, and regents. Vampire high society, a group we were officially members of after Darius's formal acceptance of the sovereign position last week.

Lycan clan leaders—including Mira and Luka—filled up the other platform, their expressions bored as they watched the proceedings.

Latin words echoed around us, the humans pledging their undying devotion to Lilith. I'd never seen her in person, but she was just as gorgeous as I imagined. Long, flowing, ash-blonde hair, pale skin, sharp green eyes.

She didn't sit with any others, her throne situated highest on the stage. "My children," she murmured, a smile in her voice. "Today marks our one hundred and seventeenth Blood Day. As with those before you, twelve lucky souls have been chosen to compete for immortal blood status. Of these twelve, two will be chosen for immortality."

Silence fell over the crowd, the eagerness to know those names clear in their anticipatory stances and expressions.

This was what Darius explained, the art of pitting humans against one another. By forcing them to compete, they failed to work together. And it showed in the way they all appeared separated from one another, not a single human attempting to comfort another.

"The rest of you will be sent to your respective factions," she continued, her voice far too kind for a vampire. "Now, may the ceremony officially begin. Magistrate?"

A dark-haired lycan cloaked in royal-blue robes stood, a large book in his hand.

The human classifications, Darius explained. *He's going to call them up one at a time to inform them of their fate. Prepare yourself, Juliet. This is going to become ugly quickly.*

I swallowed. *Yes, Sire.*

A nervous hush fell over the crowd as he positioned himself behind a podium, opening his book to begin.

I glanced over all their downturned faces and the army of Vigils surrounding them with guns, a chill creeping down my spine.

For twenty-two years, I understood my fate. I knew my future before it ever began, was trained to be the perfect blood virgin, and had feared my turn on the auction block.

While observing these humans awaiting their own futures, I realized how much better I had it. At least I knew what to expect. These poor beings had no idea where they were going, and worse, no choice. It was all dictated by a book, a magistrate, and a fake goddess.

We'll seek justice for them all, Darius vowed, sensing the direction of my thoughts.

Yes, I agreed as the first name was called.

Heels clicked up the stone stairs as the first lamb approached her impending slaughter. Her nightmare was about to begin. I'd survived mine. If only she could be so lucky. But I knew she wouldn't. None of these humans would.

I yearned to cry for them, but instead I held my position—a servant at Darius's side. One day I would be allowed to fight, and when that day came, I would be ready.

To the future, Darius murmured.

To the future, I echoed.

The Story Continues with Royally Bitten...

BLOOD ALLIANCE SERIES

Dear Reader,

Thank you for reading! This series is my secret indulgence, the one where I give my dark side free rein.

I've always wondered what would happen if supernaturals really existed. There are so many stories about them hiding in reality (I write two series myself), but why would such powerful beings lurk in the shadows when they could rule? I ran with that idea and the Blood Alliance was born.

I have a lot more planned for y'all. It's going to be dark, wicked, and a hell of a lot of fun. Unless you're human, in which case, life really sucks. Pun intended.

Royally Bitten is on deck. It's not about Jace, but Kylan. I know, the harem-slaying royal is probably not who you expected, but trust me, he's going to shock you. I loved playing in his head.

Thank you again for reading!

Cheers xx

Lexi

Acknowledgments

First and foremost, thank you, Julie Nicholls, for creating such inspiring cover art. Without your designs, the Blood Alliance series would have remained a short story, but you just had to go make those beautiful white wolves and inspire the lycan side of my story. Now I have this giant world to write and it's all your fault. Thank you! <3

Second, to my husband for your unerring patience, support, and love. I thank you in every book because you are my heart and the reason I have time to write every day. I love you always.

Allison: You are the most amazing alpha reader EVER. Except for when you point out all of my errors and repetitive words and force me to write hotter sex scenes. Oh, but that's your job and also why I adore you. Thank you for everything!

Delphine: I happen to think "proclivity" is an amazing word that should be used in every other sentence. I suppose that's why I need you to rip apart my books ;) Thank you for everything. Your eye for detail is top-notch and greatly appreciated, always!

Pam: Thank you, thank you, thank you! I'm pretty sure you want to kill me right now for constantly moving my deadlines. *Hides* Thank you for being so amazing, fixing my mistakes, and keeping me in check.

Louise & Melissa: My two favorite "Minions," you complete me. I'd be lost without you both, and I appreciate you ladies more than words can express. <3

Amy, Barb, Joy, Louise, Sarah & Tracey: Thank you all for beta-reading *Chastely Bitten* and helping me strengthen the relationship between Darius and Juliet. First books in a series are always the hardest, and I appreciate you all so much for your time, input, and guidance in this process.

Famous Owls: Thank you for being such an important part of my team and for always making me smile. You all rock!

None of this could be possible without my ARC team and Foss's Night Owls. Thank you, thank you, thank you!

And to the readers: Thank you for reading Darius and Juliet's story. I hope you enjoyed them, as I'm sure they will be back in future books. This world is huge. I am excited to go play!

About The Author

Lexi C. Foss is a writer lost in the IT world. She lives in Atlanta, Georgia, with her husband and their furry children. When not writing, she's busy crossing items off her travel bucket list. Many of the places she's visited can be seen in her writing, including the mythical world of Hydria, which is based on Hydra in the Greek islands. She's quirky, consumes way too much coffee, and loves to swim. Cheers!

Also By Lexi C. Foss

Blood Alliance Series
Chastely Bitten

Dark Provenance Series
Daughter of Death
Divinity of Acheron

Immortal Curse Series
Blood Laws
Forbidden Bonds
Blood Heart
Elder Bonds
Blood Bonds
Angel Bonds
Blood Seeker
Assassin Bonds
Blood King
Wicked Bonds
Blood Edict

Mershano Empire Series
The Prince's Game
The Charmer's Gambit
The Rebel's Redemption
The Devil's Denial

CPSIA information can be obtained
at www.ICGtesting.com
Printed in the USA
BVHW050418301122
653097BV00021B/57

9 781950 694235